Death has a Price

By Dr. Jessie Hummel

ISBN

Hardcover: 978-1-969844-09-6

Paperback: 978-1-969844-08-9

Acknowledgment

To my wife, Adele, who never lost her patience as I spent so many hours on the computer and away from her. She inspired me to finish it even as she missed my company.

About the Author

I joined the writers' community several years ago. Being technically trained as a Civil Engineer and Land Surveyor, I didn't think I could write beyond the scribbles I made in field books.

To date, 9-1-2025, I have written 2 books.

I have sold several of my books over the years since I started, so I now call myself a published author. I am retired from my technical training jobs and now have a new endeavor to keep me going. If I don't spend time writing every day, I now feel I'm cheating myself.

'Death Has A Price' is a book about a horrible crime that has been committed, and the lengths someone will go to for revenge so they can move on with their life and punish the person who inflicted this upon them. You, the reader, will go on this journey of revenge. Enjoy the twists and turns along the way.

Table of Contents

Prologue

This all started when times were simpler, in his mind anyway. He learned to respect and honor life. His parents weren't fancy, but they believed people made the world go around. This was good when he was a child; he became a man. He tried to respect and love everyone he would meet along his way to the present reality. What he found was that his early understandings were less than truthful.

He woke up this morning and quietly gave thanks for waking up again. This would become the first day, not only in the rest of his life but also in his new life. This was the 366th day of his widower existence and a new beginning. He had been married for 35 years and always believed he would go first, but this did not happen.

Roscoe swung his feet out of the warm confines of his comfortable bed and couldn't help but think back over the last year. Roscoe woke up that day, which became the most terrible one in his existence, much like he did today, with one huge difference. His mate for 35 years was lying and breathing next to him. On that day, there was no indication at that early hour that it would be their last together. He's had this last year to think about that. At no moment during that year did he feel the joy of being with her or talking to her or all the other ways they gave each other the pleasure of life.

That day began as part of their typical routine of daily activities. He got himself ready for work and made coffee, set up for me the previous night— just one little item she did that he'd missed so much. He returned to the bedroom and kissed her goodbye, wishing her good health and hoping she would have a great day, all the while holding his tie so as not to disturb her. He drove to work, a trip of 12 miles, arriving approximately 30 minutes early, as is his habit.

Her call came at 9:37 a.m., a moment in time Roscoe won't allow to be removed from his memory. She said she didn't feel well and was having trouble getting a complete breath. He left the office and raced home without speaking to anyone except the receptionist. He got her into the car and went immediately to the emergency room. He signed all the forms allowing her entry to the horror house from which she would never leave alive. He has replayed those moments over and over for the last year.

This past year, he's had time to consider where the rest of his life will take him and what paths might emerge that he should pursue. One idea kept him company for many evenings over the last six months. The first six months were spent in a state of shock, with numerous details to attend to.

He has never been back to the home they shared. He asked the realtor who sold them the house to sell it again. Take everything in it, place it in storage, and send copies of the inventory to their son and daughter. They are wonderful, successful people. She is an editor at one of the major publishing houses in New York. He owns a medium-sized building construction company on the West Coast. They were both invaluable and somewhat understanding during the saddest time. They stayed in the house and argued with him over several things, such as not allowing the playing of 'Short People' at the service, and why they should not stay at home with them.

She was 5 feet 2 inches; it depended on her mood when asked. She said her only dislike of being short was not being able to reach into the top kitchen cabinets. Should she go first, her only request was for me to play the song 'Short People' at her service. Neither of the children was born yet when that request was made.

He knew that if he stayed in the house, he would tear all his clothes, turn all the pictures, and either cover or break all the mirrors. They said that wouldn't matter, but he knew it would have for many reasons they didn't want to think about at that time.

And so it was that Roscoe's current living quarters became leased. Nothing elaborate, but comfortable. He's always believed in large, comfy beds and a good night's sleep, a carryover from military life, the sleep part anyway. It's ironic that he only sleeps on one side of a great big king-size bed, and it gets turned and flopped and all those things. Occasionally, he wakes up all over the place, turning that off into a bad dream.

The bed is something he will miss in the months to come.

The leasing agent had been informed that he wished to go on a month-to-month basis, which they agreed to. He'll probably need to leave on short notice when his new endeavor begins, and doesn't want to be burdened with breaking a long lease. He's a law-abiding guy who never tried to get something for nothing. I frown on folks who always try to "beat the system," as they so fondly say it. One friend of his wife's used to brag that she'd attended a nice party and "used" a party dress from the department store, bringing it back the day after, with tags and all, saying she'd changed her mind. He never liked her and certainly didn't respect her.

He still works at the same place, and his fellow workers have all been as lovely as usual. After all these months, no one has invited him to dinner; that's the kind of teamwork they try to convince everybody in the workplace. Most upper managers appear to lack a clear understanding of people management. When he leaves, it will be cordial, and there will be no burned bridges. Roscoe's last name is Find, and he's a computer geek.

He's had the knack of keeping them humming almost all the time. He also had a sheepskin in bean counting, and during the late '70s, he realized the world, as most people knew it, would change. He went back and got a degree in MIS. The company he works for is a vast accounting service with offices worldwide, some of which are larger than others. His section is Computer Central, located in the Tampa Bay area. His salary, bonuses, and benefits have kept him in the middle to upper six-digit bracket for quite a while. Roscoe is not poor.

He stopped at one of the nicer local gin mills for an after-work libation. He's been a square bottle man all his life. For the same reason, he probably hasn't been back into his house, but he's found different places during the last year. While sitting in a booth in the lounge is pretty dim, a piano player softly plays and sings lounge-type songs, jazz, and light contemporary. This is only about the third time he's been out this year when he thinks about it. The ladies at the bar look at all the guys in the place, smiling at Roscoe as their eyes sweep the room. He hasn't had the least notion of the opposite sex for a long time. His second brown liquid slides down when the crooner starts singing, "What will you do for the rest of your life?" That makes him stop and think about that very thought.

What he's decided to do is simple: Roscoe will make all the folks who had a hand in his wife's agony personally aware of it. That's like all the doctors who were less than caring or indifferent. The pharmacists who liked to play God, and the drug stores that would steal. The lawmakers who influenced the pharmacists' attitudes. The insurance companies considered themselves God, and even hotel executives, airplane companies, taxi companies, and maybe even an unloving, mean mother-in-law. He's always wanted to dance on her grave; perhaps the chance will come.

As much as they loved each other, she was put through many harrowing experiences during her life. Before they met, she had been a victim of rheumatic fever and a lousy goiter incident. The fever gave her rheumatoid arthritis at a young age. These conditions compounded the two childbirths. A C-section took our daughter. Never one to give up, she remained as active as possible throughout her life. She tore up her left knee, which resulted in three surgeries and no real relief; all three surgeons are on my list. She couldn't get any peace taking the drugs, and they weren't strong enough. Who has ever given other human beings—the same ones who get up every day just as he does—the power to decide that one person must endure more pain than another? Statistics tell us women have a pain threshold 10 times higher than the other half of the species. He knows several Neanderthals who vehemently argue that, having never experienced childbirth, he doesn't venture into those stupidities. She put her pain on a scale of 1-10 and placed childbirth at 5, pain from the knee, back, or hip at various times at 9 to 10. It was at times like these that druggists would remind them that not enough time had elapsed, as determined by the insurance company.

Chapter 1

Roscoe knows who's first on the list. Much work and planning must be done before the trump card is played against this most deserving low-life scum. Roscoe has absolutely no respect for these less-than-caring humans. He has now decided to devote the rest of his life to avenging his wife's pain. The fundamental truth is that no one will be deprived of life, but very much of their liberty and any happiness they might have wished for. That being decided, it's time to set an outline for the basic plan of action. They'll be called targets. Several of the targets live in the Tampa Bay area, which will make two items easy: travel and work. He has no plans to quit his job just yet. He has about 3 months of vacation and 6 months of sick leave. The firm pays dollar for dollar for unused vacation, but only half that for sick leave. I suppose there will be a lot of sick leave in the future.

Roscoe doesn't look as dynamic as he is. He is Mr. Everyman in looks. You can look right at him and won't remember what you saw. That's always been considered a plus. His once-flowing black hair is now flowing graying hair that will change to all black again; gray hair is too easy to remember. His eyes are gray, which is why no one remembers them. He stands 5'9 12" from the floor barefoot and about 6 feet clothed. He dresses conservatively; it's the influence of being a bean counter. He blends into the crowd, a powerful asset for what's coming.

Much of the grief he plans to dispense will have to do with computer hacking, something he's spent his professional life fighting. It will now be one of his greatest assets. Gaining access to so-called safe databases will be the easy part. Many of the databases he will need are publicly accessible, like motor vehicles, license plates, etc. Getting into the medical and credit ones will take more skill, but he will manage. He will take extra care in some places; good security has been installed on many of these systems. The Internet will be instrumental. Remember the flick 'The Net'? That was such child's play.

Delivering grief in the mail, at the doorstep, where they work, and where they play will be fair play for Roscoe. Everything that has happened to Roscoe during his lifetime hasn't prepared him for what he is preparing himself to do. He misses his wife every minute of every hour of every day. One of his favorite challenges to friends, when the subject of politics arises, is that the U.S. is a police state. They all look aghast; some of these are also the earlier Neanderthals. He says, "You're at home relaxing, a knock at the door; you answer and open the door; how stupid to do that, and there are two guys in dark blue suits, white shirts, and black ties, and they announce they're from the IRS, what's your first reaction?" Everybody has said "FEAR." Case closed! His targets will have strange people knock on their doors, bringing the bogeyman.

He will need some accessories. A new vehicle. A new wardrobe. A new camera outfit. A new computer that's portable and powerful. A new satellite uplink and Internet access. Some of these are easy to obtain, others not so easy. The satellite stuff is supposed to be government, but there are ways around that; he's not worked where he does without gaining a wealth of knowledge about every kind of hardware and software. The vehicle will be the most difficult, in his opinion. It must be big and comfortable; he's been driving Town Cars for many years. It will have to have extra space for the computer office and possibly sleeping arrangements when necessary. It will have to blend into the surroundings, which eliminates motor homes. The vehicle situation must be investigated thoroughly.

For several days and weeks, he's been paying attention to what he sees on the streets and roads that fit his criteria. Blazers, Explorers, Mountaineers, Expeditions, Navigators, and seemingly countless others that all seem to look alike. These listed have adventurous names anyway. The vehicle must also have much power, maybe even enhanced after the sale, but not so that anyone might notice; he must always keep a low profile. He test-drove them all and liked them all as far as criteria went, some bigger than others, some smaller, depending on how you look at it. It's now apparent the Town Car ride will be gone; these vehicles are trucks, and there's no other way to slice it. The Expedition and Navigators are too big; they might look conspicuous. He'd better look some more. Can this be done by Town Car? Sitting there is too conspicuous, but driving is so comfortable and pleasant.

After several more weeks of paying attention to the roads and streets, he realizes several things: drivers are idiots, including himself, he's sure. He's a lane driver, gets into the lane needed to turn from, and stays there, whether it's fast or slow; it doesn't matter what's happening in a Town Car. When he gets where he's going, he turns, and it starts over. During these last several weeks, paying attention to what surrounds him has been an education.

Lane changing, as if half of the car length matters, is unbelievable. He's noted other vehicles that need to race and finds himself in front of them as often as not when getting to his turn, just giving intervals and staying in his lane. Maybe he will copy some of these license plates and let the bogeyman visit them, especially those who steal the front interval, causing the brakes to be applied. That'll start tomorrow.

His quest to find the invisible vehicle has succeeded. It's the minivan. They come in all shapes and colors, with doors sliding in front, sides, and maybe even the back. He stopped at the grocery on the way home when a guy was getting out of a Villager. He asked him how he liked it. He was delighted, saying he had had it for five years and would buy another one. That did it; the vehicle will be a Villager. Now, all that's left is to decide on the color.

It won't be a Villager; it's not made in the USA but is a cousin of the Nissan Quest. Once, a while ago, taking delivery of a Town Car, he got a new one every year; when the door was opened, he noticed it was assembled in Canada; while he has absolutely nothing against Canadians, he wants his cars made in the USA. He wouldn't take the Town Car, and they got him another one made in the USA. With his list of gadgets and things, mostly made in China and Korea, he hoped the vehicle could be made in the USA. Once with his wife, they wrote a letter to the President complaining about the flag's disappearance at Post Office buildings. They received a staff letter back that said nothing about what they wrote.

After searching for weeks, going from dealer to dealer, the vehicle will be the Silhouette minivan, the one John Travolta called the Cadillac of minivans in the movie Get Shorty. Dark blue seems to be the most used color, which makes it invisible. He will have to find a good mechanic; the Silhouette will require a lot of work to meet his new standards.

He let his fingers do the walking and got winded with no success in finding a good mechanic. Then he remembers years ago, he had a blowout, and the tow guy told him about a network of mechanics who feed off the tows, especially ones coming from the Interstates. It took some time, but the tow guy was found; luckily, he was still in the towing trade. The tow fella gave him the name of a local mechanic. It took a while to get in touch with him. He said he only worked on foreign cars, but knew a guy in Orlando who worked on minivans. Roscoe took a ride to Orlando and located the minivan mechanic. He told him what he wanted, said he could do it himself, and gave Roscoe a ballpark price. The Silhouette will cost more than Town Cars when everything is done to his specifications.

Window tinting was next. The mechanic says he'll put one tint above the current Florida legal limit, stating he's been doing it for folks ever since the new tinting law went into effect, and no one's been pinched. He says other states haven't bothered anybody if the vehicle is registered in a state that allows tinting. That's something else to think about: license plates, and he doesn't want to travel all over the country bragging that he's a Floridian. On the other hand, he doesn't want to get busted for illegal tinting. The mechanic mentions that most tire-wheel cover places can help in this department for a fee; he stresses the tire type over just the wheel cover place. Not wanting to draw the least bit of undue attention to his travels, Roscoe suggests the legal stuff and the next grade up to determine for himself if unnecessary risk is warranted under these circumstances.

Since the vehicle of choice has glass around it, he decided to have one side legal and the other illegal, once he got the van. He explains he wants a tripod mounted to the van floor with a flat head and a quarter-twenty-thread screw mount to support the servo drive digital tracking camera, which will be mounted on the tripod, which he didn't tell the mechanic. Let him think whatever he wants; he isn't a partner. Next, they discuss the worktable and chair; both must be portable, easily assembled, and sturdy enough to withstand daily use. Of course, the chair must be comfortable, with none of this aromatic junk. Extra power will be needed to supply the electronic toys. The mechanic says he can install as many batteries as needed. Roscoe tells him to count on at least two; if it changes, Roscoe will let him know. Now comes the bed; he knows he will miss the big bed once he hits the road. He tells the mechanic to make it as compact and comfortable as possible.

He's envisioning long hours of fixed surveillance, so a bracket to hold a TV and DVD player will be needed. If this gets into football season, he will rig a dish and an NFL Sunday Ticket to the TV. He remembers that's one thing his dearly departed wife tolerated with a massive grain of salt: his infatuation with professional football.

The mechanic asks, "Will the passenger area and seat be necessary?"

Roscoe hadn't thought of that, but it makes sense with all the toys to be installed.

The mechanic mentions, "How about welding the right-side doors shut?" That would render them unusable for ingress and egress; it's okay with Roscoe.

Roscoe asks, "Can the driver's seat be upgraded and swiveled?"

"Better is easy; swivel is illegal," he says, "but I'll do it if you want it."

That will take a little more thought. With all these suggested modifications, the word "mini" is starting to make itself felt. He assured us we could complete it and make it usable and comfortable. As for how long all this will take after he has the vehicle, he says to plan on four to six weeks, half of the estimate paid up front, the rest on delivery.

When Roscoe got home, he made a ham sandwich, got some chips, a pickle, and a cold beer, sat down with his small feast to review the events with the mechanic, and realized there was no napkin. Forgetting them was his standard, but she never forgot. He realized he still misses her and always will. It's these little things—they matter so much.

As the last beer goes down a welcome throat, he realizes he has never talked about the power train, engine, drive shaft, differential, and all that stuff with the mechanic. He thinks his cell phone is excellent equipment since it went digital. He had never owned one before; imagine the FBI trying to keep the digital phone out of the USA because they couldn't tap it so quickly. The first cell phones in Europe were digital and became available ten years before those in the USA. The mechanic gave him a "special" number to reach him at, probably his cell phone.

When he picks up, Roscoe asks, "What about the power train?"

"First, with all the interior work, I forgot to mention it, and second, there's no train; the Silhouette is front-wheel drive," the mechanic says.

He proposes a fully electronic integrated 5.0-liter V8 bored to 6.0-liter equivalents muffled to sound like the 3.4 V6 with which it comes out of the box. Increased suspension is proposed to carry the extra loads.

Roscoe tells him, "The temperature range of—20 to 100 F is a must."

"That will cost a little more."

"How much?"

"Just for the temperature stuff, the engine retro is standard for a Silhouette," he says.

"You're the first one who's ever talked about the interior first. Every other one that's come through was mainly for the retro engine, so it's part of the standard cost. Temperature ranges are not," he continues.

After a minute or two, he figures out the new cost, which is less than 2% above the current estimate.

"Count on 6 to 8 weeks because of the temperature," he says.

Chapter 2

It's obvious now that it's time to talk to the Oldsmobile dealer; directory assistance is invaluable. He'll do this over the phone. It will be a cash sale; they give Roscoe the keys that work, and Roscoe gives them cash; he hates car dealers. It's a gal on the phone, and she tells him there is one in the back lot that fits Roscoe's description. Since there were no plans to buy a vehicle today and no trips to the bank have been made, Roscoe asks her if she'll accept a check; she's very eager and says yes. Next, it's a call for a taxi.

The taxi driver takes him to the Olds dealership. It's almost closing, the receptionist broadcasts Roscoe's name, and the sales gal comes running. She tells him the Silhouette will be prepped while they do the paperwork. He asks to see it first; he doesn't like buying a pig in a poke, sure, she says, leading him through a corridor and down some steps and pointing to a dark blue minivan that looks new. He walks around it and finds the name Silhouette on it. He opens the driver's door and looks at his new home for the first time; it hits him that everything up to this moment has been supposition. After this lady gets his check, the revenge for pain will have begun for real. He makes a mental note to make the tires broader and better. He looks at her and says, "Let's do it."

"One thing 1'm substantial about is that the registration, which will produce the license plate, must say Sunshine State and not the local county."

She assures him it will.

When the new Silhouette and Roscoe arrive at the parking lot at the flat, he checks out the remote features. The mechanic will change all these, but playing with them is fun. Later, the local bus company was contacted, and a ride from Orlando to Tampa was booked for tomorrow afternoon. He calls the mechanic and tells him the vehicle and one-half the cash will be delivered tomorrow afternoon.

When the bank opens, he steps up to a teller window and withdraws the sum needed for the mechanic. He stops at his favorite breakfast place, any Waffle House, and has his favorite breakfast, pork chops and eggs. On to Orlando, he has always enjoyed the memorials along 1-4 between Tampa and Orlando; there's a flag raising at Iwo Jima by some unknown farmer, and an airplane that looks like it just dove into the ground advertising the local air museum. He gets there at about 12:30 p.m., and the mechanic is waiting. The mechanic calls the engine guy and gets that started. He thanked Roscoe and told him to call once every week starting today to check on the progress; he would never call Roscoe. Suddenly, it dawns on him: he's just given this man an expensive vehicle and a large wad of cash, and he's just going to walk away. This is a new world he's in; last night, he didn't want to buy a "pig in a poke," but today, he did, just like that. He can only trust from now on. Roscoe wishes him good progress, thinking in the back of his mind of the guy telling Tom Hanks for two weeks in the movie 'The Money Pit.' He calls the local taxi company to get to the bus station.

When he gets back to his flat, it's almost 6 p.m. Taxis and buses are what they are; neither of them is speedy. He called out for a pizza tonight. When it arrives, he pops up a cold one and relaxes. Even the pizza company remembers the napkins.

He's been out sick for three days and decides he'd better show his face at the paycheck factory. Before giving too much thought, he grabs the Yellow Pages and calls a local storage place. Looking for one that can be accessed 24/7, 365 days a year. There are many of them, but not all say yes very convincingly to the hour's thing. Since it's late, he decides to cruise the storage places to see which ones are within his driving range, a 20-mile radius from the flat, and are open and operating. There are five within this range. Two are open, and three claim to be but aren't. That was a worthwhile trip. At about 1 or 2 a.m., he will recheck the two open. So tomorrow will probably be another sick day.

He showed up at the office anyway; everybody wanted to know if I was all right; one even had the Forrest Gump to say he looked sick. The only storage place still open on his second cruise is within two miles of the office, so he'll sign up at lunch break. He doesn't see any need to have the storage this month since the Silhouette won't be ready for 8 weeks. He gives the clerk at the storage facility, ironically called 'Your Self Storage,' 6 months to begin in one month from today, and gets a receipt.

He made the first call to the mechanic today. The mechanic briefly told him the interior removal was almost done, and he had begun beefing up the suspension and installing engine mounts to prepare for the new engine and interior equipment.

Today, he began looking for the satellite upload. He found that it offered less than 15% more download capabilities, which were also included. NFL Sunday Ticket will be a snap now. He downloaded the tech specs from the Internet and faxed them to the mechanic.

It is hard to remember how business got done without the Internet or email, and when the FAX was the greatest thing since peanut butter. Tomorrow, it's the computer.

He ended up with a suitcase model with the AMD equivalent of the Pentium 6 doubled, 1024 MB RAM, and a pair of those 1000 gig drives. That should take care of all the computing power needed, and I got one of the HP 8 'n one color things with a video hookup that will take care of all the paper needs. I'm looking at a 100x zoom video camera with a download feature, so I can view it on my PC in real-time and feed it frame by frame directly to the HP, and it's no larger than the palm of my hand. These new toys are just great. I placed all the toys in the storage bin, which became usable yesterday.

He talked to the mechanic this morning; it was the fifth call. The mechanic asked, "Have the TV and DVD been purchased yet?"

He said, "I was looking but hadn't decided yet."

"Let me take care of it, and I'll add the cost to the remainder. I have a chance at a good deal and don't want to pass it up," he says.

Roscoe was not concerned about whether the warranty could be mailed.

"Don't worry, the driver's seat has arrived, and you will be pleased. You want comfort and all." He continues, "The engine with waterproofing and temperature rating of 20 to 100°F will be delivered by the week's end."

"What about the waterproofing?"

"With the temp range, it is standard and part of the cost."

Roscoe hopes the chance to find out never comes.

Today, Roscoe went to the phone store and picked up six little cell phones with six different numbers. The guy and the counter got nosy and asked about the intended use of the six phones. He canceled the order and walked out. That would have been his first real Forrest Gump. He realizes he must stay sharper than that. The jerk clerk would easily remember that sale. It's bad enough that if anyone were to ask him in several months, he'd still remember the wise guy who was buying 6, but he never got anything from Roscoe, but a nasty look behind his back. He got the six anyway; it just took a lot more legwork, six stores, and six names taken from the phone book.

He took all the gear from the storage bin today. He's testing all of it tonight and downloading all the database access codes needed from the PC at work and several others. He has collected three license plate numbers over the last several weeks. It isn't as easy as it sounds, at least for him. He found he had to wait until he stopped to jot them down. There were over a dozen promising candidates, but he wasn't approving of his memory except for these three. He doesn't intend to bring the bogeyman down on anybody who doesn't truly deserve it. The state's license plate database is easily accessible, and these three are now well-known. He will pick up the new Silhouette tomorrow. The reservations are made with the bus company, and guess what? That damn virus is back, so the bean counter will be sick again tomorrow.

This is strange; he's only called cabs to pick him up when traveling on business or vacation. Today, he's taking the bus to the station. So, what is the workstation if the bus station is where the bus stops and the train station is where the train stops?

Anyway, the cab and bus ride is very time-consuming. There are no stops for anything except the trip to the bank when it opens, and it's mid-afternoon by the time he gets to the mechanics.

It looks just like it did that night at the Olds dealership. Brand new and shining. The mechanic comes out to greet Roscoe; his name is Cecil. He says, "I hope you don't mind. I took a couple of liberties with your design, and they won't cost you a thing if you let me photograph it from head to toe."

"As long as I'm not in any, nor is it a license plate."

Cecil says, "No problem, and thank you. I took the photos this morning, and I'll give you a set." He motions for Roscoe to come to the driver's door, but before it can be opened, Cecil says, "If you're not as pleased as I believe you'll be, keep your money."

With that buildup, Roscoe can't wait to open the door.

Cecil asks Roscoe to stand just behind the door; he opens it, slams it hard, and looks at Roscoe, who can hardly hear it. Cecil looks at Roscoe and says, "That's just one of them."

Cecil motions for Roscoe to take over and open the door. As Roscoe reaches for the handle, Cecil slips the keys and steps back. Roscoe is prepared to see the finished product but doesn't expect this fanfare.

He opens the door and can't believe what he's looking at. The driver's chair is a dark blue Corinthian leather with armrests on both sides, which are as luxurious as the Town Car's. He climbs up into the seat, and it's as comfortable as the Town Car, but he can hardly believe it. Cecil reaches in and unfolds the top of an armrest towards the door; all the controls are in a panel, easy to get to; he tells Roscoe to open the other one. These are entirely different, with swivel and back release controls; they are amazing and will take some getting used to. Cecil says the seat was an absolute steal; it was originally designed as a captain's chair for a yacht that was never built.

He released the swivel, and Cecil's modifications to this project were noticed for the first time. The computer table is where the passenger seat was, with room for the printer. The dish will fit into a clip arrangement at the passenger window, entirely controlled by a remote from the right-side armrest of the chair. Swiveling around more, the tripod can be seen with the servo connection with a cable trailing to the computer table; all that's needed is to add the hardware. The bed is positioned behind the driver's chair at a suitable height for a futon bed; Roscoe hopes there will be no backaches. The TV is mounted in the back corner and is enormous, visible from the swivel chair or lying on the bed. Roscoe was always concerned about how cramped this would be; he couldn't get over how masterfully Cecil had done this work. All the desk material is rolled black stainless steel, as are the base of the bed and all the brackets and braces.

"That's all the fluff," Cecil says. "Start the engine, and let's take it for a spin."

Cecil sits on the empty computer desk. In goes the key, and the engine jumps to life. Roscoe can hardly hear or feel it. Off they go, the power can be felt, where it can't be felt in a Town Car, it's just there. It's very smooth, and the chair is excellent. Vision is superb on all sides. Roscoe takes it out on 1-4, and Cecil says, "Let's take it to Tampa. Please get a complete feel for it before signing off. Press it," he continues.

Roscoe eases it up to 85 and can hardly feel a thing; up to 100 and not a rattle, ease back so the cops don't get too nosy. Tampa's horizon arrives in no time flat; Cecil motions to a gin mill where we can stop for a libation and settle. The vehicle is more than ever planned for or thought it would be. Cecil said it was a challenge; once he knew it was more than an engine retrofit, he wanted to do his best to showcase it. Roscoe agreed with him ultimately. Even though Cecil tried to protest, he was prepared to add up to 20% and was glad to do so. Roscoe shook his hand, telling him that if ever another minivan remodeling was needed, he hoped he could be found. Cecil smiled and didn't say a word.

Roscoe left Cecil in the gin mill; he said he had friends in Tampa and had warned some of them he might be showing up tonight. Cecil wasn't Roscoe's concern; he fulfilled his end of the deal and was handsomely paid. All that's left to do is decide on the tinting, which he assures will only take about an hour. He drives straight to the storage bin and doesn't want neighbors to see it. That first day was late in and early out; he didn't recall seeing anybody who knew him. Tomorrow, all the toys will be hooked up. Right now, a taxi is needed to get home.

Several years ago, the office experienced some sabotage. He found a security firm that specializes in surveillance equipment; they installed some gear and, within three nights, caught the night watchman watching too much. Up till that night, he was moonlighting at his moonlighting job. He called his contact at the security firm and told him some state-of-the-art listening and tracking equipment was needed. One of the nice things about a security person is that they don't ask questions of the people paying them. He didn't even ask anything when it was charged to his plastic. He had to ship it to him at a Post Office Box that was secured a few weeks ago.

Right after the bell tolled five, he joined the hordes of departing people, exited the building, went straight home, picked up the toys, and headed for the van. Because of Cecil's excellent job, installing the computer, printer, and dish was easy. The electrical system has been beefed up even more than the engine power plant. The van's air conditioning, computer, accessories, and TV operate without draining the batteries, and when the engine is running, it's charging all the batteries. He swivels around a little more and clicks on the TV. The reception is a little poor inside the storage bin; that's to be expected.

Except for the surveillance gear, this adventure is ready to go. He starts the engine, pulls it out, and puts the Town Car inside. It's dark outside, so he grabs a bite at a local chock and puke shop and heads to the first name on the license plate list. Once the house is found, a good observation spot is located. Without attracting too much attention, the van is parked, and watching begins. This will become his new future. To get an appreciation for what a stakeout is about, two and a half hours creep by before he heads back to get the Town Car.

It's a big day today; the listening and tracking devices were at the Post Office. He turned in his notice at work, gave them the customary two weeks, and negotiated an extra two weeks if they couldn't find a suitable replacement to double the dollars if they called during that second set of weeks. Later at home, he emailed lovely, long letters to each of the children, explaining retirement and the country's touring without mentioning the true purpose; they both would have put him away if they knew. Almost immediately, he gets a return from the daughter, who congratulates him and announces that she has a bow.

"When will the tour get to the Big Apple?"

He responded that he wasn't sure because no plans had been formulated unless she had a good reason to be there sooner. There was no flip, so he didn't read.

Nothing too urgent. During the next several weeks, he must formalize a plan for at least six months to a year.

He gets the van out, checks the list of Evel Knievels, and gets a couple of hours of surveillance work; this time, he takes a tracking device along. After one hour, all the lights are out, and he makes his first venture into the unknown and the dark. He is wearing one of his new outfits, a basic black turtleneck, Dockers, socks, and shoes, which are real James Bond-like. He places a tracking device under and inside the rear bumper of Target's Ford Taurus. He returns to the van unnoticed, believing that's a good feeling.

All of the devices have peel-off backing with a strong adhesive, which is good because most cars are now made of plastic. He makes a mental note to remember never to leave the wrapping at the site.

It's been a productive two weeks for his new endeavors, not for his company; they just asked him to say another week. He'd figured they'd after no replacement showed up by the second week. He doesn't mind, and it's easy money.

When he was in graduate school, they walked around an outstanding practice in the business world: reverse engineering. That's where you start at the end and work to the beginning to solve problems. That's the method used to provide the name of the first real target, Dr. Jason V. Johnson. He was the attending physician in the emergency room over a year ago. He's as good as anyone to start with. Roscoe used the license plate list to practice; however, the bogeyman will visit if a new license plate list is compiled.

Chapter 3

Jason had just finished his dinner when his phone rang. It was his wife, Janet, wondering if he'd be home early enough to care for the children. Jason oversees the ER Room at Plant City Hospital. He told Janet that he couldn't just drop everything and come running home. Janet just hung up her phone.

Dr. Jason V. Johnson has been on the Plant City roster for over three years. Every month or so, a package arrives for Dr. Jason V Johnston with no return address. The package contains several ampoules of purified Sodium.

Dr. Johnston has been using the Sodium ampoules on several patients when he receives notification from NYC that a body is needed. No one ever survived these injections, and the diagnoses show the patients had cardiac failure.

Dr. Jason V. Johnston has traveled from New York to Boston, Chicago to St. Louis, and to Plant City. He graduated from Johns Hopkins with high honors in ER procedures. Just as his father had done many years ago. The senior Dr. Johnston was first contacted by mob bosses shortly after receiving his doctorate. They convinced him that they had stopped shooting people some time ago. Their new method now is to use lethal injections of Sodium in selected people. It didn't matter when a hit had to be made. They would ship them out to the ER, and a corpse would be delivered anywhere they wanted. The local ER would make an unknown person available for the burial. So you'll move around a little, they told his father. And about once every six months or so, the ER doctor would visit NYC and be debriefed.

His father did as he was told, and as he grew older, he needed his son to do the same. So, Dr. Jason V. Johnston has been averaging about a death by injection every six or seven months. The usual death rate in a local ER is about one every month or so. That's about 12 bodies a year coming out of the ER. In a big city ER, it's triple that. Plant City is between big and small. So if 24 deaths come out each year, nobody is going to raise a red flag.

So, Dr. Jason V. Johnston is living the good life in Plant City. He has a wife, two children, and a mistress. Every six months, he goes to NYC, where he gets debriefed. They put him up at the Essex Hotel and gave him an unopened Glenlivet bottle. After he finishes the bottle, he makes his report, and the next thing he knows, he's on the plane home in first class.

When he returns to Plant City, he contacts Mary, a nurse at the Plant City Hospital. She picks him up at the ER and takes him to her house for the evening. Mary will tell you the only things she likes to do is fuck. She stays with Dr. Johnson because he's pretty good in the sack.

Dr. Jason V. Johnson drives next to one of his five banks, holding onto his deposits. NYC pays very nicely for each body's ER services, equal to 1,500.000 USD. He doesn't get checks for services rendered; he likes to see the balances grow. He goes to the five banks where the deposits are made. The balance from all banks is presently 500,000,000 USD.

He drives a very ordinary Ford Taurus, while his girlfriend Mary, drives a very recent bright red Lexus.

Dr. Jason V. Johnson figures it's time to go home and see his children and wife, Janet. As he turns down his street, he notices the For Sale sign on the house on the other side of the street, a bit down the road. His children, for some reason he doesn't comprehend, seem to love him and come running when they see his car. As he exits his car, his children come to hug him.

He follows the children into the house, and Janet, his wife, begins to rail at him about not coming home when she asked, about going to New York without telling her, and about staying late at the Hospital and not letting her know.

He turns around, laughs to himself, and leaves. He heads to the hospital, where he has a comfortable cot in the back room of his office and a change of clothes available.

After a restful sleep, Jason gets a call from New York. They need a body, a female body.

Jason arrived in Plant City from St. Louis a little over three years ago. He grew up in a small town outside of Boston and aspired to be the best physician ever to take the oath. Jason grew to 6 feet 2 inches in his first year at Johns Hopkins Medical School. He excelled there, gaining a much-desired acceptance at Boston General as an intern and a full residency by age 23.

During his first year of residency, two unexplained deaths on his watch earned him a reputation he couldn't shed, and when his residency came up for review, he wasn't asked to stay. Stunned, he applied to New York Medical Center and spent a year there before being asked to leave. He followed Horace Greeley's advice and moved west to Chicago; he lasted there for three years and felt he had a home before three deaths became known, which gave him no reason that the review committee could be satisfied with. This time, he headed south and, for four years, worked the night shift in the ER of the St. Louis General Hospital. This time, he wanted a change of scenery, and the timing was perfect. Plant City Memorial was looking for an experienced ER physician. It can be said that Jason made it from Boston to the farming town of Plant City.

The Johnsons live in a fashionable part of town called Walden Hills. The use of the name Hills for a community in central Florida stretches the word hill to its limits. The terrain is slightly above South Florida, where the highest natural point is in Broward County, home of Fort Lauderdale, which is 7 feet above sea level. The Plant City area is around 70 feet above sea level, compared to the 700 feet in the Chicago area.

Chapter 4

A flock of Egrets, standing so white against the newly plowed strawberry fields that were ablaze with strawberries up until a few days ago, were bobbing along, looking for dinner. The weather was balmy and warm, as was usual for this time of year, three weeks after the Annual Strawberry Festival. This world-renowned festival is held in Plant City, Florida, about halfway between Tampa and Mickey Mouse. The Beatles were never here when they sang their song 'Strawberry Fields Forever,' but this is the place on the map that gets that name. For miles and miles, all that can be seen are strawberry fields.

Just up Main Street from the Strawberry Festival headquarters is the railroad caboose turned into a restaurant, and beyond that to the east is the Plant City Memorial Hospital. Jason V. Johnson is on duty in the ER on the late evening to midnight shift.

Ever since Roscoe decided on his course of action, he decided his first target would be Dr. Johnson. To ensure he wouldn't lose track, he made periodic trips to the hospital to ensure Jason's picture was in the rogues gallery that this hospital kept in the main lobby. The Dark Blue Oldsmobile Silhouette was in the Emergency Room parking lot tonight. Roscoe hoped to match Jason with a car this evening.

While sitting in the van waiting, Roscoe couldn't help but travel back to the evening over a year ago when he brought his wife to this place. Jason V. Johnson was also on duty that night. Afterward, Roscoe would try to convince the local DA that his wife's death was wrongful. He presented all the strange death evidence he was able to gather from Boston, New York, and Chicago, but no charges were ever considered. He took his cause to the Florida Department of Licensing for a malpractice case against Dr. Johnson. The official cause of death was listed as cardiac failure, and despite all her physical problems, she was never diagnosed with a weak heart. The Department of Licensing finally put the case down by sending a Registered Return Receipt letter to Roscoe informing him that they, the Department, found no probable cause to charge Dr. Jason V. Johnson with any wrongdoing. Roscoe firmly believes that something that wasn't kosher happened in the ER that night, and everybody seemed not to care. All Roscoe can remember is that he took her into those doors and never saw her alive again.

At around 2 a.m., Roscoe realized that when Johnson hadn't appeared, he didn't have the stamina to discreetly follow him without possibly making a mistake. He fired up the van and headed for the barn, but tomorrow was another day. He had arrived at the ER parking area around 10 p.m., thinking he'd only spend about 2 hours. By the time he got home after switching the van with the car, he barely had the presence of mind to get all the locks set before he crashed. Roscoe became a senior citizen last year. During the drive home, he decided to enroll in a fitness and stamina program if there was such a thing.

Jason finished his tour at 12:15 a.m., and later, he called home to his wife, telling her he'd been delayed at 11:30 and wouldn't be home until 3 or 4 a.m. Tonight, not knowing another was concerned about his whereabouts, he continued his liaison with the OR nurse, who had the same shift hours as him. They did this at least once a week, never picking the same night of the week, a pattern not too difficult for anyone who wanted to track it.

The OR nurse is named Mary. Her husband is an over-the-road trucker who is gone mostly between Monday and Friday. Together, Mary and the trucker make a decent living. They own a lavish condo on the 12th floor overlooking Lake Sheffield, just a 10-minute drive from the hospital. On these nights, she drives her Lexus ES 300 and brings Jason back to the hospital several hours later.

Roscoe woke up the following morning, somewhat disappointed with himself. He knew he should have been able to withstand the long stakeout these tasks would require. Part of the problem was that he got up each day as if he were going to the office when, in fact, the working part of the day was more likely to be 14 hours or more away. The other was building up his stamina to handle the long haul. While having coffee, he called all the fitness houses listed in the Yellow Pages and was not impressed. Young ladies answered everyone and made many promises that they couldn't keep. He wondered how to find a place that could cater to older needs.

Today, Roscoe decided to treat himself to a nice lunch with maybe a couple of Jack's. At about 11:30, he left for Floyd's, a lovely steakhouse lounge within 15 minutes of his flat. He was the first bar customer and asked the bartender, Bill, a fella in his late 40s by Roscoe's reckoning, if he knew of any places where he could get a trainer to put him into shape.

Bill said, "There's a regular lunch customer who works for a big firm in Tampa that has its fitness program for its executives."

"Thanks, that's great if you won't mind introducing me when it gets busy."

"No problem," he says.

Roscoe nurses a Jack' n water and waits. Twenty minutes later, Bill gives the high sign to Roscoe, motioning him to come to the other end of the bar, where he's talking with a woman who looks to be in her late 30s or early 40s.

Bill says, "Roscoe, meet Maxine; she's the trainer I mentioned before."

They looked at each other and shook hands.

"Nice to meet you," Roscoe says.

She spins around on the barstool, quickly eyes Roscoe up and down, and says, "Same here; Bill told me you're looking for a physical trainer."

"I'm not any younger and want to build up my stamina quite a bit."

"Have you tried the fitness places?" she asked. He called them all and was not impressed.

Maxine nodded in agreement.

"Would you like some lunch, my treat?" Roscoe says.

"Sure," is her reply.

They both head toward an empty booth in the bar area, which is usually the last to be filled by the hostess. As they slip into opposite sides, a waiter asks if they want something from the bar. Roscoe looks at Maxine, and she nods yes, and he says, "Yes, for both."

She says, "Beefeaters and tonic with lime."

"Jack Black and water with a twist," he says.

While the drinks are being filled, they look through the menus the waiter left.

She decides on the London broil, and he takes the stuffed shrimp practice. Roscoe mentions that it's an English combo, Beefeaters and London broil, to which Maxine smiles. As lunch is being prepared, Floyd brags that nothing is prepared ahead, so take your time. Roscoe asks Maxine what she does. She tells him she runs the executive fitness program for one of the aerospace companies that wants all upper management to be fit as a fiddle. Still, none of them have ever asked her to be available during lunch, which means none can do so after. They both get a pretty good laugh from that. She says that's why she comes here for lunch several times a week. They pay well; she has set her hours from 7 a.m. to 11 a.m. with no weekends or evenings. Roscoe tells her he's not trying to be the next Charlie Atlas; he wants to build himself up from being so sedentary for so many years, and he's recently retired and gets tired too quickly to be pleased with himself. Lunch is served, and they both concentrate on feeding themselves.

After they finish eating, Maxine says, "Join the 'Y' if you don't already belong, and I'll meet you there every Monday, Wednesday, and Friday at 2 p.m."

Roscoe tells her he'll join today and see her tomorrow at 2, since it's Tuesday. The deal is set. They skip coffee, Roscoe pays as promised, and they separate.

Roscoe stops by the 'Y' and joins, and by the time he gets home, he feels perfect about how today has turned out. His stamina problem has an answer, and he can easily care for himself, sleep later, and nap in the afternoon. Since it is afternoon now, he decides to lie down. As he lies there, his mind replays the pleasant lunch with Maxine. She is an attractive woman in an unglamorous way. Well defined and proportioned, standing about 5'5", he guessed. She had a lovely smile, and he enjoyed her laugh. He was glad, without realizing it, that he would see her the next day.

Maxine drove home thinking about Roscoe. He's the first man she's allowed to buy her lunch since she's been attending Floyd's for over a year. She was surprised when the bartender, Bill, told her that some old guy wanted to talk to her. She didn't find him old at all and was very surprised at herself for saying yes so fast when he offered to buy lunch. And she didn't mind his comment about the English; she couldn't help things British, having been born in London and raised in New York. Neither could she understand why she gave up her cherished free afternoons so freely. She was glad, without realizing it, that she would see him the next day.

The drinks at lunch took their toll, and Roscoe didn't wake up from his nap until half past 1 p.m. It makes no sense to try to rush to the hospital tonight. This would delay finding Johnson's car until Thursday because he knew the schedule gave a low life off on Wednesdays. There was nothing worth watching on the TV, so he picked up the latest John Grisham novel at the newsstand and began to read. At 2 a.m., he closed the book, locked up, turned off all the lights, and climbed into his vast, comfortable king-size bed. He wouldn't open his eyes again until 11:30 the following day. After getting ready and having coffee, he headed to the mall to buy gym clothes.

He got to the 'Y' with plenty of time to get a locker, change into his new 'sweats,' and wait for Maxine in the lobby to go to the gym area. Maxine appeared about five minutes early, looking like the British flag in bright red, white, and blue, depicting the official flag of England. Roscoe was sad that the U.S. flag had made it to this type of commercialization, but on the other hand, he thought she looked very nice and was glad to see her. Maxine caught his eye and waved.

She said when they got close enough to talk, "You look like you're ready. Today, we go over the steps I feel necessary to get you to a point of self-maintenance."

She motioned that they should go to the warm-up room.

"First, you'll spend 15 to 20 minutes on the walker each time you come to the Y." He sampled the speeds and controls of an available walker. "That should get the blood flowing and loosen up the muscles," she continued.

She then led the way to the passive weights and showed him the machines he would need to use to give him the maximum return for the effort given.

Roscoe wanted to try one of the machines, but Maxine wouldn't let him until he warmed up. He went back to the walker and started walking. Maxine told him he could bring a Walkman or similar device during warm-up and do it before the 2 p.m. start on the appointed days. That would be it for today's warm-up. After changing, Maxine suggested he buy her an afternoon toddy.

She drives a Jeep Grand Cherokee, joins him in the Town Car, and heads to Floyd's. She has her usual Beefeater and tonic while he orders a Corolla with lime. As they sit at the bar, Bill, the bartender, has the sense to stay away after filling the drink orders.

Roscoe begins awkwardly by asking if she's British.

"Only by birth," she says. "Dad was in the U.S. Air Force and met and married Mom, who was in the Women's Air Wing of the RAF. "I was born in a London hospital over Dad's objections, who wanted me delivered on the Air Base, which would have made me American at birth." She continued, "I'm happy it turned out that way; I've had fun with the limey thing all my life, even though we moved to New York before I was two."

"Dad was assigned to the UN, and Mom got work as a copywriter at an uptown publishing house."

"Which one?" Roscoe chimed in. I have a daughter working as an editor for an uptown publishing house."

She couldn't remember. That was a long time ago. They ordered another round, and Maxine continued her verbal essay.

"Dad's work involved a lot of travel, and he and Mom just drifted apart, and by the time I was six, it was just Mom and me. She took a job with Simeon and Roarster, a large downtown publisher, as chief copywriter, which she kept until she retired, and now she lives in New Port Richey, that place of the newlywed or nearly dead."

"I was a lucky kid growing up; we had a beautiful apartment in Upper Central Park East. I went to good schools, graduated cum laude from high school, undergraduate school at NYU, and finally, at North Carolina State, got a master's in sociology with a minor in Phys ed. And here I am, a nurse, mailing a bunch of eggheads who couldn't care less about what they're supposed to be doing with their bodies; they wouldn't give me the time of day unless they knew I must report to the executive committee each week."

"Was married once, during post-grad work. It didn't last a year out of school."

This was 100 times more than Roscoe wanted to know, but he was pleased he did. He suggested an early dinner, and she agreed.

Roscoe asked if she wanted the same drink, and she told him she never drank anything else; he told her he would switch from beer. He caught Bill's attention and ordered another for the lady and a Jackman for himself. He told her it was in honor of her stay in New York, and she blushed. Then he felt guilty and apologized, told her he only drank three different drinks, and she was now seeing the third. They slipped into the same booth as yesterday. Service was not what it was at lunch, which didn't bother either of them.

A waitress comes over, and Roscoe orders shrimp cocktails for them both. He tells the waitress they'll finish the order when the appetizers arrive. While they wait, Roscoe gives Maxine his story, omitting any mention of his current endeavor. They both order the house special, a butt steak with home fries, and another round from the bar. Roscoe mentions how it's almost coincidental that her mother works at a publishing house and his daughter does the same all these years later. Dinner arrives, and no other word is spoken except yummy. They both decline coffee. Neither seems to want heart-jumping liquid at the end of the day. Booze will bring you down, coffee will wake up the best of drunks, and there's nothing worse than a wide-awake drunk. Maxine admits she has an early call and asks to be returned to her Grand Cherokee. She tells Roscoe that she has thoroughly enjoyed her afternoon and looks forward to seeing him again, but she admits that her waistline can't be maintained on a steady diet like this.

Roscoe drives Maxine to her Grand Cherokee and waits until she gets in; the engine starts, and she pulls away. He has always waited for people he has driven to get into a house or car before leaving himself, old-fashioned maybe. He then heads for the van and drives to Orlando for the last item of renovation, the tinting. He's decided on the darker, and he'll risk it. Cecil, the mechanic, agrees with the darker choice. After the tinting, he treats himself to a visit to Epcot, the first place he's gone to that he and his wife shared. They enjoyed the World Showcase every time they visited the park.

Today, he enjoyed it differently. He got some French pastry, sat, and watched the laser light show, which ended with lovely fireworks in the last few years. He remembered Micky's 2+ birthday bash on the 4th of July; the fireworks that night were the best he'd ever seen. He woke up on Thursday morning feeling rested, something he hadn't felt for a while. Maybe it was because he knew what he wanted to do and had a plan to support it.

He watched Headline News while having coffee; he thought we weren't at war today, a sentiment he got from the day we watched that brave CNN newsman hide under a table, like it would do some good to do that. He couldn't help but go over and over the immediate plan he had to stalk the louse Dr. J. With nothing in the hopper till much later in the evening, he took care of some domestics, dropped the cleaning off, and a bag of laundry at the Laundromat, very convenient for the lazy single set. Roscoe never liked sitting in those places, wondering if that person or another person would get to "your" dryer before you did. To pass the time while picking up the laundry, he headed to the mall and the movie house, got a big tub of popcorn, and watched the latest Star Wars episode. After the film, which was good, He picked up the laundry, dropped it home, and picked up the van—stopped at a 'Chick-fil-A' for a sandwich and soft drink.

Without seeing him tonight, he would use the computer to get the doctor's name and address. He could see all the vehicles in the physician's parking area from his vantage point. The first was the Mercedes ES400 and belonged to Dr. Alan Griffen, the next to Bruce Clary; he did them all, not Dr. Jason V. Johnson. Was he off tonight? He picked up a phone and called the Hospital and paged him. When he came on the line, he told him he was from the local policeman's benevolent society, and he slammed down the phone. He's in there; how did he get there, or where is he parked? Come to think of it, he never saw him the other night either; maybe he parks in the other physician's parking area. Roscoe reversed the windbreaker, gray on one side and black on the other, and he intended to roam around the parking lots, so he didn't want to look like a spook, gray side out. He grabbed a small pad of paper, then discarded that for a small micro tape recorder, left the van, and walked around the hospital to the other physician's parking lot. When he saw the first plate, he began recording; seven cars were parked in the lot. He returned to the van and ran all the recorded plate numbers, but nothing. He couldn't figure it out. Was he parking somewhere else, and if so, why? He grabbed the phone and redialed the hospital; the page for Dr. Johnson was empty. Roscoe's intelligence wasn't that good; three days and nothing, he wasn't delighted. After he swapped the van and changed into regular clothes, he stopped by Floyd's in hopes of seeing Maxine. Tonight was not his night; she was nowhere to be seen, so he bellied up and ordered a Jack with water and a lemon twist. He needed to relax just a little before heading to the barn. There was a small jazz combo playing some old Jack Teagarden tunes, the kind of music he could listen to for the rest of his life. Louis Armstrong would agree that jazz is the only music played from the heart. Because of that, few jazz musicians can play a tune the same way twice. Roscoe left for home when the group stopped playing; he slipped a double saw in the snifter on the way out.

Today is gym day, and he's all warmed up when he spots Maxine, another flag of Britain; she looks great. Both give warm greetings. Maxine offers a quick turn and motions Roscoe to follow with the crook of a finger. The first machine is a leg press. She sets the weights and says, "All you got 10 times."

That's easy, he thinks, then she says, "Do it again."

Not so easy this time, and she says, "One more set of 10, please."

She has a sense of the macabre. He thinks this set is complex, and he slows considerably. They move from legs to arms, then abdomen, and finally back, and she declares that's it for today.

"I'm buying today."

Those last three words got him through the shower without passing out, which is all he thought he was suitable for.

Bill smiles at them as they walk in, has Maxine's gin and tonic sitting at a spot open, and asks Roscoe what he'd like.

"Jack'n."

Bill nods, gets the drink, and hands it to Maxine. The bar's full. Roscoe says, "Let's sit in a booth; I can't stand too long."

She spins around and offers her barstool, saying, "I'll stand."

"Let's sit, please."

She agrees. The Jukebox is blasting something current, which Maxine can keep up with. Roscoe mentions the jazz group playing in the evening, and she says she's heard them. Not last night, he thought. She says she likes them. He can feel himself coming down and asks if he can have a rain check, and she agrees, smiling. They drove their vehicles today. He leaves, and she stays. When he gets home, all he does is crash.

He wakes up at 1 a.m. and is angry with himself. The first week, all I accomplished was sore muscles and meeting a lovely lady, but neither was in the original plan. He promises himself to become a better time manager next week. The M-W-F gym thing is necessary, but if it keeps up like this week, those three days will not be productive evenings, and he will resign, saying that it just must be for the time being. He'd waited over a year to get this far, so there was no sense charging in with an empty weapon, and since he's the weapon, he decided to take it slow. He climbs back in and welcomes the sleep back.

Roscoe realizes that his quest requires him to do some things outside his usual comfort zone. He is aware that he must do every exercise Maxine gives him. While he may not like the work, he finds he does like the company he gets from Maxine.

Chapter 5

Long ago, Roscoe had checked the phone book on the outside chance that the doctor might be listed. He looked at it again today, hoping the listing might be in the wife's or child's name. He runs every Johnson listed in the Plant City directory through the reverse directory program and then through the license plate database. When that didn't produce any results, he expanded the search to all directories surrounding Plant City, but found nothing useful. He uses the phone again to call the hospital and ask for Dr. Johnson, but he's told that the doctor is not there. Today, he will get to the hospital early and be in place to observe his arrival. In all his early surveillance, he had noticed the staff, obviously by their clothing, entered the hospital through one door, which he assumed to be the staff door. They exited by the closest door to their cars when their shift was over, and it was this information Roscoe used to make his first assumption.

He isn't sure the van should be in the hospital parking area in broad daylight. This job could be accomplished with the Town Car. If he's in the car, though, he won't have access to the electronic toys he's come to depend on. The decision isn't hard at all, and he realizes his desire for true comfort is trying to convince him that a comfortable ride would be compensation for the physical beating he's been getting at the gym. The van is the right choice, and he goes to the van. By his reckoning, his surveillance should begin at noon to be sure he'll get to see the arrival of the evening shift. All his life, he's known better than to get anything requiring service at 2 p.m.; the shift leaving doesn't care, and the shift arriving doesn't know.

Everybody seems to drive themselves, and no carpooling is evident. The staff car park is on the far side of the hospital, right next to the other physicians' parking area. He has a vantage point, which took him around for almost an hour, where he can see the personnel door and most of the parking areas. It's obvious who makes the money; the fancy cars are in the physician area, with one exception in the staff parking; he watched this Lexus GS 300 roll up to the entrance and was surprised when it pulled into the staff parking. He sees the scumbag walking up to the door. How did he miss his arrival? Once again, Roscoe is puzzled. The one good thing is he has finally laid eyes on him.

He can leave now, and the target is safely ensconced in a place he can return to. He phones Floyd's, and when Bill, the bartender, comes on the line, Roscoe asks if Maxine is there. Bill tells him she has just arrived, so Roscoe asks him to give her the phone. He knows the bar uses cell phones from his previous visits. Maxine says, "Hello, Roscoe."

"How'd you know it was me?" he asks.

"Bill told me," she says with a slight chuckle.

"How about lunch with an old man?" he asks.

"That sounds good to me. Do you know any?" she says.

"I'll be about an hour; I still want to," he tells her.

"I'll just have a head start, that's all."

"Okay, I'll see you in about an hour, maybe a little sooner, and thanks, Maxine," he says and punches the disconnect button.

Maxine hands the phone back to Bill. She thinks back over the past two weeks, smiles, and is pleased on both fronts with Roscoe. He's shown good progress in getting himself to the self-maintenance level he asked for, and their thoroughly enjoyable, so far, frivolous relationship. He hasn't tried to pry or press himself, but she likes it that way. Maybe, she thinks, if he gets into good shape, she'll broach the sex thing. Forty-five minutes later, she gave the phone to Bill and Roscoe. Does he look better, she wonders, than he has in the past?

As he enters the lounge, Roscoe thinks Maxine looks excellent today. He walks up to her and gives her a quick kiss, which surprises them both.

"Made good time," he says, meaning the drive time, and she responds, "You're certainly trying."

They both smile at each other, and he orders a beer. It's not very busy in the lounge, so Roscoe says, "Shall we eat at the bar or a booth?"

"The bar," she says, almost finishing his sentence.

"Menus, please," he says to Bill.

They both order a special lunch: grilled swordfish with steamed veggies. While waiting, she tells him he's progressing well and should be pleased. The discomfort will disappear by next week, she announces. They have fun bumping their elbows while eating and go their separate ways after lunch.

Roscoe gets the van again and heads to the vantage point in the hospital parking lot. For the first time, he's going to use the bed. He sets an alarm built into the Silhouette's clock and stretches out on the futon bed. The alarm goes off at 8:30 p.m., and he jerks awake. Not as bad as he feared, but no bed you want to sleep in for too many nights in a row. He shakes the cobwebs and gives the best isometric stretch possible in the small quarters. Overall, he's pleased; the van is doing everything he wants. Last week, he installed a small refrigerator, which he opens to get bottled water and an apple out for dinner. By the time he's back online, it's 9:15.

He watches the next shift arrive, much smaller than the afternoon/evening shift. About one-half hour later, he starts to see the earlier shift leave. An hour later, the Lexus he had noticed rolled up to the door, and someone came out and got in the passenger side. Roscoe wasn't positive because the passenger side was on the far side, but he was sure it was the scumbag who got in the Lexus. He's unable to follow, and it happened so quickly that he didn't get the license plate number. It's okay, though, he thinks. A connection has finally been made.

The beginning of this quest should be easy now, Roscoe thinks as he prepares to go for the van and uncover the identity of the Lexus owner. Today is Friday, and Maxine would have liked a late lunch. He told her he had some business. She was correct when she said the sore muscles and stiffness would disappear this week. Roscoe can't remember when he felt better. He gets his thinking back to the task at hand. He cruises the staff parking area with the video on and records the license plate number of the Lexus.

It's registered to Mary Clement, with what looks like a condo address out on Lake Sheffield. Roscoe puts 2 and 2 together and realizes that the scumbag and this Mary must have something going on. It's mid-afternoon; he heads to Lake Sheffield and looks up the address. It's a condo, and he parks and walks to the entrance. It's a security entrance without a guard.

The marquee that shows all the names is inside, beyond his eyesight. He carries a compact digital 10- 50x set of binoculars in the van and retrieves them. With no one around, he scans the marquee and finds the Clement listing for G & M Clement in 12E. He believes the listing is for Mary Clement of the Lexus and Dr. Jason V. Johnson, who has just met his Waterloo.

He had told Maxine that if his business had concluded early enough, she would like to join him for a lovely dinner at Burns in Tampa. She seemed to light up at the question, but wouldn't commit to it. They hadn't exchanged personal phone numbers yet, and neither, it seemed, wanted to, so he said he'd swing by Floyd's, and if she was there and willing, they'd take it from there. He was dressed to the nines for a Friday as he entered Floyd's and spotted Maxine looking terrific. She had a pleased look on her face as she found Roscoe walking in. Roscoe was feeling excellent this evening. He ordered a Jack man, and Bill made some theatrics for it. When Bill delivered the drink, Roscoe picked it up, looked at Maxine, and said, "Happy New Year and a very nice evening with you, Maxine."

"Thank you very much," Maxine chimed in. "You look spiffy this evening."

He said, "1 was hoping you would be here, and when I saw the Jeep, I called a limo, which will be here in about half an hour, and reservations are made at Burns."

"After that," he continued, "the limo will bring us back here, and we'll enjoy some Jazz."

She winks at him and says, "This sounds like a great evening. Let's get it started."

As they're listening to the jazz combo, having returned to Floyd's after a usually good steak dinner at Burns, along with some good wine and even better conversation, Roscoe realizes he must make a decision and make it soon. Throughout dinner, he was subconsciously fearful that Maxine would ask a question requiring him to lie. If his relationship with Maxine were to go further, he would need to relay his plans to her. He was very reluctant to do this, and his children didn't know. He leaned toward Maxine and whispered in her ear.

"I have a confession to make. All the good lunches and dinners we've been able to enjoy lately will have to slow down."

Maxine looked sad and a little surprised. She said, "I knew this couldn't last too long, the way we're going about it."

Roscoe responded, "I want to continue to see you, but I'm not ready to bring a significant other into my everyday life."

Maxine leans into him and squeezes his hand.

"We've got about three weeks left until you're on your own; until then, I'll buy dinner on Friday nights," she says. "I enjoy our time together, and I'm not giving it up just like that," she continues.

"I accept," Roscoe says. "If any lunches work their way in, I'll pop." The combo returns from their break, and the beat continues.

Chapter 6

Driving home, he felt pleased with how his relationship with Maxine had settled down. He would never admit he knew where she lived or her phone number. He reaffirmed that there was no time to share anything he was doing. He was also thinking of a support group he could enlist without ever having to give up his reasons or methods. Tomorrow, he will check out his theory.

After taking care of the laundry, he stopped by the Acme Boot Company and bought a pair of flat black slip-on boots and a boot pull. He was unsure what terrain he would encounter in the future, so he wanted to ensure his footwear was up to the task.

Besides, where he was headed today was not sneaker territory.

Saturday was the best day for this. Roscoe entered City Limits, a local shot and beer joint with a general-type food menu. His reason for being here was that the local police hang out, and on Saturday at about 4 p.m., the chief arrives to hold court and get very, very drunk. Roscoe knew all this because he and his wife occasionally came for a late lunch and a beer on Saturdays. On those occasions, they would see this weekly play unfold. Also, some schoolteachers would show up on Saturday afternoons, maybe to get pointers on new discipline techniques. This was his first time here in over a year.

As will happen in neighborhood bars, regular customers will not remember how long it will be before it is removed. The bartender, Wally, hollers over the juke noise, "Roscoe! How are you? I'm sorry to hear about your wife. What can I get you?"

This type of establishment is about as far right in an uneducated way as you ever want to be.

"Bud," Roscoe says.

"Bottle, can, or tap?"

"Bottle," Roscoe hollers back.

Bud is the Red, White, and Blue beer, and except for a light here and there, they all drink Red, White, and Blue. When it gets serious, shots of one of the square bottles usually accompany the beers. Roscoe climbs onto a barstool and asks Wally how he has been.

"Same as always, you look good for yourself."

"Thanks," Roscoe says, and off Wally goes to serve another.

Wally is one of those old-timers who can manage a 30-seat island bar and provide service. He does this until the night crowd shows up, at which point he gets help on the service side.

After a short while, a conversation with the man on his right begins. The chief is enthroned across the bar and about six seats up the bar from Roscoe's position. The talk is mostly about sports, local politics, and the latest conquest made. The tongues wag a little loose after a few rounds and a big, juicy cheeseburger. Roscoe's bar mate is named Al, and he's a sergeant and very unhappy that he can't take the cruiser home every night. Al complains that it was a done deal until the newspaper got hold of it and reported it all out of proportion. Roscoe learns that Al works in the community relations section, and he tries to find out if they have dealings with the guys in Plant City.

"All the time," Al says, "Those guys are alright; they hang out at a nice place called Ricky's out past the hospital about two miles."

Having satisfied his thirst for information, Roscoe orders another round for himself and his new pal, Al. Al then seems required to buy a round. Roscoe tries to say no, but Al will have none of that. Roscoe can't leave on Al's buy, so he orders another round with three shot glasses placed upside down in front of Al and Roscoe. Roscoe excuses himself to go to the facilities. Al nods, and Roscoe heads straight for the door. The last thing he wanted was an all-night beer-drinking marathon. Getting Ricky's name was worth it. The ironic thing is that Roscoe knows he shouldn't be driving, but no policeman will be watching who's coming out of the City Limits as long as the chief is holding court inside. After a while, Al realizes Roscoe's not coming back. He leans over and slides Roscoe's unused shot glass to his position.

Roscoe is sitting in the hospital's parking lot with a good view of the staff door, paying special attention to the blind side he came up against the last time he was here. He's watching the Lexus. As the shift change starts, he turns on the camera and tests the video link. It works like the box said it would; whatever the camera sees, Roscoe watches on the computer screen. To test the printer, he freezes a frame and sends it to the printer; after all the mumbo gumbo of the color heads, a lovely color print slides out into the bin.

He spots Mary Clement coming out and going to her car. She drives straight out of the parking lot and leaves the hospital grounds. Roscoe is disappointed but knows he'll be back tomorrow. He feels good, and clear pictures are the first step. Back to the barn for tonight.

The camera starts recording when he sees Mary come out of the door, and it's pay dirt tonight. This evening, she pulls up to the door, and the scumbag quickly exits and gets in the car. Gotcha and Roscoe rejoice as each moment is recorded. He's ready tonight. As soon as the Lexus started, the van started. The Lexus left the car park and headed for the main road to leave the downtown area. Out toward Lake Sheffield, Roscoe guessed the location and stepped onto it. He wanted to get to her condo before they did. He had reckoned the area the first time he was there to determine the best vantage point to film from if he ever needed it, and tonight, he would. He got the camera back on when the Lexus entered the condo parking area. Roscoe's vantage was perfect; he filmed the entry to the car park, the lovebirds' exit of the car, and their entrance to the condo building holding hands. With a powerful zoom, he caught them getting into the elevator. This was everything he had hoped for once he found the out-of-wedlock liaison a reality. He was ready to cover a motel or some other place, not thinking they would use the condo, but here they are.

He returned to the hospital's main parking lot and ran every car through the database. Finally, he found the one registered to Jason V. Johnson, a late-model Ford Taurus, parked in the general parking area. He guessed it was to downplay the return ride, which would be in several hours. Right now, it was off to 856 Hidden Oak Lane. The house was one of those faux stone ones that appeared larger than it was. Hello, Dr. Jason V Johnson; your life now belongs to me.

Chapter 7

Roscoe now realized he had to solve two items he hadn't considered yet. The target has a family that will not be subject to the target's problem, and the paper and electronic files generated must be safe. Keeping the family safe from all the fallout will be impossible, but no direct action will be taken to harm them. The file problem will require as much thought and possibly much more action.

The temptation to print the images collected is strong and very simple. But it's not just the prints; it's also the electronic files. This hit Roscoe like a brick when he was in the office supply store to buy a small filing cabinet to put into the van. He could not answer the question of what would happen if something occurred beyond his control, and other persons besides himself were looking at the inside of the van.

Taking that thought to the extreme, he purchased five boxes of surgical gloves. He would wear these any time he handled paper going into or coming out of the printer, possibly ending up in a target's hands. Fingerprints and latent prints can easily be removed from paper. He also purchased a stamp-dampening device so his saliva wouldn't be present on anything. He would also wear gloves when handling any envelopes or media that could come in contact with a target or a person associated with a target.

He was delighted with the data collected so far, but he wants more, like getting them to leave the condo and arrive at the scumbag's Taurus in the hospital parking lot. This is the last Friday of the tutored physical education from Maxine, and her automatic dinner will be tonight. Roscoe must hurry so he won't be late for the gym.

Maxine was the British flag again today. She agreed to meet at Floyd's at 6:30 p.m. for cocktails and dinner. Roscoe used the time between stopping by the computer store and ordering encryption software. It would be 2 —3 weeks, according to the salesman. That wasn't good enough for Roscoe, now that he had data already stored; he went to the van, hooked up the antenna, and logged on to the site of his former company. Once inside, he checked to make sure his back door was still working. His replacement hadn't been on site the day he departed, and no calls for help had come, so he hoped he could still use his old passwords. Surprisingly, he was still employed with entire front and backdoor access. It was after regular business hours, so he didn't think anyone would be monitoring.

Nevertheless, he downloaded the encryption software as quickly as possible. Later, he would install the software; he didn't want to be late for cocktails. He would try for the remainder of the images after dinner, time permitting.

He entered Floyd's five minutes early, and Maxine was already seated at the bar. Her auburn hair seemed to shine more than he remembered at the gym. He slid up behind her and whispered, "Hello" into her ear. She hadn't seen him come in, so she grinned and returned his greeting, turning on her barstool to see him.

"And hello to you, young man. Can we do it all here?" she asks.

"Fine with me," Roscoe replies.

Bill sees Roscoe, and Roscoe gives him a thumbs-up sign, indicating a Jack man. Bill nods understanding and goes through his bar routine, putting together Roscoe's drink. Maxine says, "I told them we want to eat in the restaurant tonight, but not before 7:30 p.m. Tonight, Floyd's special is Surf 'n Turf, featuring one pounder from Maine and twelve ounces from Nebraska. They both ordered; Maxine liked her beef rare, and Roscoe ordered a medium. Floyd's famous home fries for both. Maxine brings up the inevitable subject: "This is the last of our planned dinners."

Roscoe responds, "I don't want to be the guy who eats and runs; I've given it much thought." He continues, "I was hoping we could use Floyd's as our meeting place, pretty much like we've been doing all these weeks."

Maxine smiles, indicating her agreement, and says, "I know we're both a little hesitant about our relationship, and I think Floyd's is as good as it's going to be for now."

Dinner arrives, and they enjoy their meals without further conversation. The jazz tonight seemed a little flat, as did Maxine and Roscoe. They leave Floyd's together; Roscoe walks her to the Cherokee, holding her hand. They embrace in the car without kissing, and he tells her, "Be well and happy."

She agrees, gets in without looking back, starts up the Cherokee, and drives off. Roscoe feels like he's lost something as he watches her drive away. He knows it can't go any further without consequences; he doesn't want to deal with it.

It's earlier than he thought, so he heads home, changes, gets the van, and drives to the hospital. The Lexus is there. A phone page for the target proves he's in. What he wants to catch is them leaving the condo together, so he leaves the hospital parking lot and drives out to Johnson's house to get a better idea of what he can accomplish in this neighborhood. He sees a for-sale sign but doesn't remember the last time he was out here. Maybe he can get a month-to-month rental before approval of the lease. He calls the number on the sign and gets a recording. He uses the recorder, which he now keeps in his jacket pocket, and records the number to call another time; he doesn't want to leave a message. He leaves Hidden Oak Lane and heads to the condo on Lake Sheffield. The Lexus is there, so he gets a good location to observe and wait, and waits and waits and waits. He sees a big Kenilworth tractor on the far side of the parking area that he hasn't seen before. He also hasn't learned that Mary's husband is home on Friday evenings.

After a light breakfast the following morning, he calls the real estate number again. This time, he gets a person who sounds like a young woman, describes the house, and asks if a month-to-month is available. The real estate gal tells him she doesn't have that information, but will gladly call him when she finds out. Roscoe tells her he'll call back later in the afternoon, but doesn't want to leave any phone numbers with anybody.

He takes the Town Car and drives to Rickey's to see what he can see. Rickey's is another shot and a beer joint serving chicken wings and catfish. These two food items are unique. Chicken wings used to go into broth for soup before someone in Buffalo put blue cheese and celery with them. Catfish was a junk bottom fish where Roscoe grew up, but a delicacy in the South. This place isn't as big as the City Limits, but it has similarities: an island bar and booths around the walls. He bellied up, ordered a bottle of Bud, and looked around. He was the new face, so everybody was looking at him. Just then, the phone starts ringing in his jacket pocket, startling him.

He's never given the number to anyone. He answers, and it's the gal from the real estate, caller ID, or something else he hadn't thought of.

The real estate gal wanted to tell him as soon as possible that the month-to-month arrangement was okay, asking if that was all right. Roscoe assured me it was, and yes, he would meet her and the principals out there in an hour. He makes a mental note to destroy this phone. He finishes his beer, pays, and leaves a slightly larger-than-normal tip, hoping to be remembered when he returns later.

He pulls up to the address and sees the Taurus across the street. He keeps his back to the street, so no prying eyes see his face. There are three people at the front entrance to the house: two women and a man. They all seem to be in their early 30s. One of them walks forward and asks if he's Roscoe. He identifies himself, and the real estate gal introduces the principles. Terms are straightforward: they'll give him 60 days to secure financing, and during that time, he will pay the real estate the monthly fee asked for, and no decoration of walls is allowed until a contract is signed; the vertical blinds will stay on the windows also. Roscoe agrees to everything and asks when he might move in.

"You can move in today if you'd like," the woman says.

"I'll do it on Monday as soon as I drop two months' lease payments if that's okay," Roscoe responds.

"Fine, the keys will be at the real estate," she says.

They all shake hands, and Roscoe follows them to block the view from across the street.

He hasn't figured out why the man was there unless it was to protect the women.

On his way back to Rickey's, he plans to stay in his flat and get an easy chair to make surveillance of the target easier. He asked if the garage door gizmo was made available when he picked up the keys; they assured him it would.

It's unlikely that no one has sat on the barstool since he left, but the one he vacationed at is open when he returns to Rickey's. The tip worked;

he no sooner got seated than a Bud sat before him. The bartender says, "Name's Kevin, and you?"

"Roscoe," Roscoe replies.

"First time in here?"

"Yes, I was just passing by; it occurred in Walden Hills on Hidden Oak."

Roscoe shares in hopes of getting a response of some type. Kevin nods and waits for another. Twenty minutes or so later, a fellow from the opposite side of the bar walks around and says, "You are a doctor, a lawyer, or something like that."

Roscoe looks at him, and this is precisely why he's in here.

"No, I'm retired. It's just taking the place until it sells; I wanted to test the area before I decide."

Roscoe responds. The fellow extends his hand.

"My name is Bobbie, and I'm the deputy police chief around here. Let me be the first to welcome you to Plant City."

Roscoe thinks, "I'm in."

"Can I buy you a drink, Bobbie, or should I say 'Chief'?"

"Bobbie's just fine, and yes, you most certainly can. Why don't you come around and join us?"

"Be glad to."

Roscoe says, "I pick up my beer and follow Bobbie to the other side of the bar." Bobbie introduces him to the three others he is sitting with: Ricky, James, and Earl, sergeants and troopers, respectively. The conversation stays light for several beers, and then Earl tells Roscoe, "I work that beat you're going to live in. I'll keep an eye out for you."

"Thanks a lot, Earl."

Roscoe says as he orders another round for the five of them and tells Kevin to join them if he can. That makes round six, which Roscoe figures several more will come before he gets any problematic information from them. He orders several platters of wings, two hot and one plain, with plenty of hot sauce. Everybody digs in, and he orders three more the same way, and those disappear just as fast.

Roscoe asks Earl, "Are most doctors and lawyers living out there?"

"Mostly"

Earl answers and continues, "There are a couple of strange ones out there."

Roscoe replies to keep Earl talking, but there's no more from Earl tonight. More wings and a couple more rounds don't loosen any more tongues. Roscoe shakes hands around, promises he'll return, and heads for the barn. He makes a mental note to be extremely careful of his goings and comings to Hidden Oaks Lane, never leave his car outside or the garage door open, and do things like that. While thinking about security, that phone still disturbed him; he would smash it into pieces as soon as he got home.

Monday was busy: going to the bank, getting a counter check for the lease money, getting a comfortable folding chair, and getting two new tripods, one for the camcorder and one for the binoculars. He's still bothered about the phone; he has to remember to block his number when he dials; with the cost of those phones, he'd better not forget. Picks up the key and garage door opener in trade for the check and signs a signature in the lease agreement at the real estate office. He drives by Floyd's but doesn't see the Jeep, so he continues to the rental house. The garage door opener works, and he pulls the Town Car in and closes the garage door behind him. The key works in the side door that opens to the kitchen. This house can't be more than three or four years old. All white walls were recently painted, and huge vaulted ceilings in the 'great room,' small dining and living rooms, three bedrooms, and a kitchen. Roscoe gets the tripods and chairs; the dining room is best for looking out at the target house. He plans to set the camcorder on a time-lapse when he sets it up; for now, it's just tripods. He opens and sets the chair to get a good view of the house. He sits for a while to get a feel for the surroundings.

Tonight, he plans to get the other side of his pictures of the ER/OR couple. He waits for them at the hospital to ensure it's done this evening.

Tonight's the night the Lexus pulls up to the staff door, and the scumbag gets in. He takes this opportunity to place a tracking device on the Taurus. Then, to be sure they're safely in the condo, he heads toward Lake Sheffield. He sees a car approaching at a very high speed. He's positive it's the Lexus, but he didn't see the occupants. The car was going so fast with bright lights on. Roscoe does a three-point turn as fast as he can and heads back to the hospital. Sure enough, the Lexus is at the Taurus. As he gets close, he quickly turns on the camera and hopes it will get this. Confused, he heads back to Lake Sheffield, and as he pulls into the parking area of the condo, he doesn't see anybody or a commotion, but he does see the big Kenilworth tractor on the far side of the parking area. As he slowly drives by, he sees the painting on the door, 'G & M Trucking,' and puts it together; it's her husband.

Chapter 8

Unexpectedly, which is why the ER/OR didn't happen last Friday, he saw the Lexus pulling back in without a passenger while leaving the parking lot.

Saturday rolls around, and Roscoe finds himself back at Rickey's. Last night, he had a nice leisurely dinner with Maxine; it was good to be with her. He greets Kevin and notices Bobbie and Earl on the far side of the bar. He goes over and asks if they'd mind if he joined them. They both shake their heads in agreement. Kevin brings a Bud over and asks, "Did you have a good week?"

"Sure did, Kevin. Thanks for asking."

Earl says, "Saw you were at your new place this week."

Roscoe tells them, "I got my stuff in on Monday."

Earl says as if last Saturday's question was still on the bar, "You know you got some strange neighbors living right by you."

"Really," says Roscoe.

Bobbie takes over, "Yeah, right next door is a lady's doctor, and he has a bad habit of taking advantage of his patients, if you know what I mean."

Roscoe tries to look concerned, hoping the scumbag across the street will come up.

Bobbie continues, "Across and down one, I believe; I think his name is Johnson; he's at the ER and sticks the nurse in the OR; we see them together all the time."

Bingo thinks Roscoe.

"He thinks he's clever. That one, one week it's Monday, next it's Tuesday, and so on, never on Friday though, her old man's home for the weekend, Friday afternoon, then they start it all over again."

Bobbie finishes his current beer, reaches for the one behind, and continues, "If her old man ever finds out, he'll probably kill the doctor 'cause they're doing it in his bed."

Roscoe orders wings again, and more beers, and the talk goes on. Roscoe listens to quite a bit more but stops taking mental notes when he hears the word 'kill.' He thanks them all and tells them he is getting too old for the long hauls anymore, and they laugh as he leaves.

Everything he's learned tonight confirmed what he's observed, doubled in spades and then some. He had toyed with the idea of bringing grief to the Lexus, but now discards that idea; it might get too many exciting events that might overwhelm him or dismount him altogether. Interestingly, the police think his scumbag is a scumbag also.

When Roscoe rejoins the human race on Sunday morning, he realizes that the perfect murder could be staged and committed, and the wrong person blamed. The Plant City police have already arrested, tried, convicted, and executed the truck driver's husband if anything happens to Dr. Jason V. Johnson. Diabolical, he thinks. He's never wanted to deprive anybody of life, and here it's being handed to him on a platter. He has no intention of planning or allowing, by any of his actions, the death of another.

He adds one more visual to his list for checking to determine if a rendezvous is on for the evening. He will ensure the Kenilworth isn't at the condo, along with finding the Lexus and Taurus, the last two he can view on his screen with the tracking software; last week, he got a device on the Lexus. The truck will be a visual; maybe on Friday, a tracking device will make it to the big Kenilworth. But if he pays attention to the Lexus about the Taurus, he should be able to do it without having any visuals. He has all the same software on the PC at home as he does in the van, so he brings up the tracking software; it can track anywhere in the US. A world map is available, but more money and disk space are necessary. Both devices are stationary, and he gets a good picture of the general location where they are by zooming in on each. He notes the map coordinates and stores them as both vehicles' bases.

He will start researching financial databases tomorrow to obtain information on Jason V. Johnson. Today, he heads out to Hidden Oak Lane to watch some birds. When he arrives, the target driveway is empty. The Taurus must be in the garage. About an hour later, a Mercedes sedan pulls into the drive, the garage door opens, and Roscoe sees the Taurus; he notices the scumbag at the wheel of the sedan, a woman in the passenger seat, and two small heads in the back as it pulls into the garage. So, momma drives the Mercedes; he manages to get the license plate number and will run it later. Figuring out that nothing more was to be gained here, he leaves and heads home via Floyds.

The Jeep is in the parking lot, which is a pleasant thought for Roscoe. Maxine sits alone at the big bar, looking fresh in a bright green jogging-type outfit.

"Hello."

Roscoe hollers as he enters. She turns and smiles, "Hello to you."

"Thought I'd stop in, think about you, and look at what the cat drags in."

The bartender is a young woman with Cheryl on her name tag. Roscoe orders a Corolla Extra with lime and sits next to Maxine. The Devil Rays baseball game is on TV in the lounge.

"I was up to see Mom yesterday and just didn't feel like sitting around at home today," Maxine says.

"Pretty much the same for me," Roscoe says.

Roscoe suggests they go to Busch Gardens, Epcot, or something for the day. Maxine says, "I'm doing all I want to do today, right here."

So, Roscoe orders another round from Cheryl, and the day goes on.

On Monday, Roscoe gets the van and drives to a county park, which is secluded and open. He wants to use the disc antenna and get good reception, as well as get as little attention as possible.

His first attempt is the local bank, First National of Tampa. He gets bounced right out on the first try. Maybe he'll have to start thinking about hacking into the banks. He spends several hours on the banks without any luck and gives up for today. He logs onto the tracking software and locates the Lexus and Taurus. Both are in their home position, so he pulls the antenna back and replaces it with the DSS disc. He uses the TV built into the van's back corner for the first time. The remote is in the armrest pocket, and he clicks the power button, and the TV comes to life for the first time.

He turns on Headline News to see if we're at war; with the trouble in the Balkans seeming constant, it's not certain that some conflict might break out.

All's well with the world today.

This week, he has gone out to the condo daily and made sure the Kenilworth wasn't visible, yet the Lexus was left alone every night. He put the van to bed, went by Floyd's, and saw the Jeep. Feeling like he needed a pick-me-up, he was glad to stop. This week so far has been a bust. He has had no luck hacking into the financial databases yet, and there have been no confirmation pictures of the naughty couple.

The Jazz combo is playing some lively Sleepy Time in the Old South tunes, which sparks him up as soon as he opens the door. He sees Maxine and then sees something he can't believe. Standing next to her and bending her ear off, it seems, is none other than the scumbag. How can this be? Roscoe is flabbergasted; he's been waiting for this bastard to go home with the L, Lexus all night, all week, and he's been here hitting on Maxine. Maxine doesn't see him; he orders a Jack 'n' water and watches through the mirror. Why is he feeling so angry? They've had nice times together, but haven't even exchanged phone numbers. Let it go, he tells himself. But he can't; it isn't that he wants Maxine for himself; he just can't let the scumbag get away with this. He tells the bartender with the name tag Mark to send a Beefeater's and tonic to the Auburn-haired lady down the bar and tell her it's from the 'Old Man.' When he does this, Roscoe watches it in the mirror. As Mark gives her the drink and tells her the line, she looks around immediately and spots him in the mirror, winks at him, and then smiles. The scumbag is impervious to these goings-on, so she excuses herself to visit the facilities and sticks a finger in Roscoe's back on the way by. On her way back, she slides a folded piece of paper into Roscoe's hand. 'Stick around, Old Man' is all it says or has to say. Roscoe orders another Jack and enjoys the music.

This opens a whole new perspective on the situation, and as Fagan of Oliver would say, 'I am r-e-v-i-e-w-i-n-g the s-i-t-u-a-t-i-o-n,' these thoughts are racing through Roscoe's head as he waits for Maxine to extricate herself from the scumbag. He decides to listen, listen, and listen when Maxine finally arrives beside him. This happens after his third Jack without anything to eat, so as soon as Maxine steps up behind him, he says, "Hungry?" and she replies, "I could eat a horse or a skewered doctor over a hot flame."

They get a table on the restaurant side, and she begins.

"What an asshole, excuse me, Roscoe, but I mean WHAT a complete asshole that man was. He told me he was single and a lawyer and then tripped himself over and over."

"When he went to the John, John, sitting next to me, poked me and said he was a doctor in Plant City. Can you believe the gall?"

Roscoe nods in agreement and empathy with her but says nothing.

She goes on, "I finally said you're a doctor, aren't you, and he then got cold and left; just because I'm female, some men feel they must lie to me, I'll go to my grave and never understand that."

She seemed spent, and Roscoe said, "I'm sorry you feel so bad. Let's have a great meal and try some good old-fashioned talk."

All she can muster at this time is, "OK."

Dinner was served; they had ordered the special butt sirloin steak and home fries with mushrooms.

Maxine has to unload, and Roscoe is there, unknown to Maxine, and very willing. "He's been coming in all week, Bill told me. Two nights ago was the first time I saw him; he worked his way up next to me, never offered to buy a drink, just wanted to hit. I was tired that night and went home early."

Still rambling, she says, "Tonight, I was hoping you would show up sooner than you did. He showed up about an hour before you and homed in on me like a magnet, still never even offered to buy a drink, just kept trying to get me to leave with him."

"Don't let the food get cold. You can tell me all you want to after you eat," Roscoe urges. She's getting over it slowly but surely. Roscoe orders Brandy Ice for dessert.

Maxine says, "I've never heard of Brandy Ice. What is it?"

"Trust me, I know I'm just a guy, but you'll enjoy this, or my name isn't Roscoe."

He hopes this will break her out of her reverie. They serve them perfectly, with flaming sugar cubes on top, and her eyes come alive. Roscoe feels like he has rescued Maxine.

After the ice is virtually inhaled, she says, "Thank you very much, Roscoe. You turned a bad experience into gold, thanks."

He feels like he owes Maxine, and partly because he wants to take the weekend off and wants company, he invites Maxine to Epcot over the weekend. He is pleased when she accepts. He promises her it's all right if she wakes up tomorrow and wants to change her mind. When they part, he calls and secures adjoining rooms at the Dolphin Resort at Epcot for the weekend. Reservations at Epcot are manageable at this time of year, and the service is just as good. She agrees to meet him at the Tampa bus station.

The weekend was grand. They wined and dined in a very relaxing atmosphere. Maxine let go and enjoyed herself. They went into all the shops in the World Showcase. It was the tail end of the flower show, and the blooms were still in their glory. She especially enjoyed a rock group at the Canadian pavilion that wore kilts and played bagpipes. Now, however, it's back to work. The financial databases must be cracked, and the ER/OR situation must be solved.

Chapter 9

Roscoe realized he was paying attention to the wrong vehicle last week; had he been monitoring the Taurus, he would have realized it was moving in different directions. He decided to follow it during the regular day hours to see where the doctor was going and coming. The van has become Roscoe's lab, and he has gotten into the habit of taking it out, going to parks, and spending several hours using the equipment. Today, he's got the Taurus on the move, the road map is large enough to follow the car through the streets, and he can pan the screen to keep the car reasonably in the middle. It leaves the Walden Hills area. It leaves the Plant City area and heads to Lakeland, about 15 miles to the east. The screen shows him eastbound on US92 and moving fast. Roscoe keeps the car in the center of his screen. The vehicle comes to rest in the middle of Lakeland. By double-clicking the mouse on the map coordinate, the software will give the address and name of the business or residential establishment. The Third City Bank comes up on the screen. Roscoe types a note tying the names Johnson and Third City Bank together.

He switches to the financial database and finds the bank in Lakeland; after about an hour, he sees the side door. He's cautious not to leave any telltale electronic trails and starts roaming around like the bank's president. He first tries to find the link the bank has to the other banks and gets lucky. The pathways to the state banking and federal deposit are right before him. Roscoe smiles to himself. The right decision has finally been made. No more secrets. He notes the pathway to the Third City Bank and all the others he's uncovered. Then, it switches back to the map to see where the Taurus is. It's back in the Plant City area, parked; the map says it's a restaurant lounge called Tony's; make a note.

He makes his notes in an editor of his choice on the computer. He installed the encryption software to get it right the first time or toast password setup. If he forgets his password, he's no better than someone trying to get in unauthorizedly. The hard drive will clean itself so fast that turning off the machine won't save anything; taking the drive to one of those places that brag it can get back will cause that person's machine to have a heart attack. Roscoe was extremely good at his job and knew all the tricks and traps.

Roscoe puts the van to bed and finds Tony's. He first checked the whereabouts of the Taurus and found it back in Walden Hills. Tony's is on the far side of town and, from the outside, looks fashionable. Inside, it's nice, with a lounge to the left and dining to the right, and in the back of the lounge. Today, there are six people at the bar, all couples. The bartender is dressed in a black tie and vest with a little brass name tag. Roscoe takes a seat and sees the name tag, says John. He orders Jack 'n water with a lemon twist. There's easy listening music piped in. Roscoe asks if eating at the bar is allowed.

"Yes," says John. "Would you like to see a menu?"

"Please," Roscoe replies.

The menu is general, with lunch and dinner in the same folder. And for that matter, most of the lunch items are just more expensive on the dinner side. Roscoe checks his watch; he doesn't want to get caught at 2 p.m. ordering. It's all show and no go, he thinks, so he orders a cheeseburger and chips. While waiting for the food, he asks the bartender if there's live music on the weekends.

"Every night," he says, and "Piano during the dinner hour."

Roscoe eats the burger, finishes the Jack, pays, and leaves. Other than trailing the scumbag, he can't think of any other reason to come back to Tony's.

He heads home and cranks up his home computer. It has protection with a different password; he won't fall for that one, either. The tracking software shows the Taurus still at his home. Roscoe stretches out for a nice, long nap. He wants to be ready to move if needed later.

He's having a root beer when the computer's beep signals a tracking device moving, and since he's deactivated all but the Taurus, he knows who's driving. It's 9:30 AM and a little early for the workday. The Taurus ends up stationary at Tony's. Roscoe's glad it isn't Floyd's, like he found him last week. He doesn't like his favorite places dirtied up with the likes of Johnson. While he's finishing the root beer, the tracker goes off again. He activates the Lexus, and it's on the go, also. They're heading straight for each other, at least on the computer screen. He deactivates the Lexus again and sets the tracking software to background mode. He's been anxiously waiting for nighttime to get back into the bank.

The Third City Bank should be ashamed. The poor security they've installed isn't worth one-tenth of what they paid for it. It takes hardly any time to find out that Jason V. Johnson has four accounts in this branch. He also searches for anything for Janet M. Johnson, the name Mercedes is registered under. There is one account in her name. He dutifully makes notes of all the account numbers. Then, he checks the balances of all of them and begins to understand how he will protect the family after he destroys the good life for Jason V. Johnson. Just before he shuts it down for the evening, he checks for connections to other branch banks.

Roscoe wakes up early, gets cleaned, and heads for the van. It's off to Tallahassee to do personal checking of the printed records in the Bureau of Licensing. It's a five-hour drive to the state capitol, and he gets there before noon. He knows it will take several hours to accomplish what he wants, so he takes a room and gives the license plate number of the Mercedes on the form with J. V. Johnson as the sign-in name.

Using the freedom of information as his power, Roscoe demands that Dr. Jason V. Johnson see the original documents. He'd seen copies of all this over a year ago when he tried to convince the DA and this agency to act against Johnson. The attendant is reluctant; whenever someone wants to see the original documents, the attendant has been instructed to be unhelpful. Roscoe brought all his tools for this task, including patience and perseverance. Seeing the front of a document after it's been through a copier is to look at what someone wants you to look at. When the requested records are made available, he can review them at one of the tables in the area. He found light penciled notes on the margins and the reverse of each sheet. One of the reviewers knew about the applicant's past and noted it. No initials, date, or name to identify the note maker. This information angered Roscoe because he knew someone had to get this file with these notes to make the copies he received. He looks at the person at the counter, who is supposed to be watching him, and notices she's talking on the phone.

Roscoe takes a pencil out and prepares to end, at least as far as this form is concerned, the career of Dr. Jason V. Johnson. He dates the note to be about one year old and writes lightly but firmly enough so the note can't be erased without being noticed. 'New evidence uncovered indicates this person should not be kept on the lists of accredited physicians. See claim made by Roscoe Find.' Now, let some future review board swallow that.

He's finished his business sooner than he thought, but doesn't want to make that long five-hour drive twice in one day. The van performed flawlessly, purred right along, and blended right in with all the other vans on the road, invisible. As he rolls in the van, he remembers his friend Jeff, who lives in Chipley, several miles further to the west. He pulls into a supermarket parking lot, checks Jeff's number, and gives him a call.

Janis, Jeff's lovely wife, answers. She's excited when he says he's in Tally, "Come on over and stay with us," she urges.

"Not this trip, Janis, but I would like to have dinner with you both, my treat."

"That sounds great, but we'll buy; Jeff is at the market right now."

He suggests Bouffard's Mansion as the meeting place, which she readily agrees to.

"It'll be so good to see you, Roscoe. How about 6:30 in the lounge?"

Roscoe agrees, and they disconnect. It's about 4 p.m., so Roscoe heads to the motel and parks the van in a quiet part of the parking area. Thanks to GM, the van's security is the best money can buy, and no one without the key can start the van. He destroyed the second set as soon as the mechanic finished.

Relaxing a little before calling a taxi to take him to dinner, he recalls how he met Jeff and Janis. They had a very profitable bean-counting business covering the entire panhandle when Roscoe's firm acquired them lock, stock, and barrel. Roscoe had seen them around the office several times and was always friendly in greeting them. They had taken a condo close to the offices and kept their place in Chipley. One day, Roscoe saw Jeff just standing in the hallway like someone had shot him or something. He approached Jeff, and Jeff told him he had been sacked. Roscoe just stood there like a lump himself. He shook Jeff's hand and wished him all the best. Jeff mentions that he has some furniture to sell, and Roscoe remembers telling him, so he did. Later that evening, Roscoe mentioned it to his wife, and the mention of the furniture and his response. She had looked at him like he was a moron or something. As it turned out, the then-college girl's daughter needed stuff, and Roscoe called Jeff and asked if any of the furniture was left. They bought most of Jeff and Janis's stuff and became fast friends. The southern district manager had been overheard bragging that as soon as they got all the client base that Jeff and Janis had brought turned over, he dumped them and got a commendation from the national office. His name was Allen or something like that. Roscoe was sure they would toast his very slow, painful death many times this evening.

The taxi got him to the mansion about five minutes late, and Jeff and Janis were at the bar with an empty stool between them. He walked up behind them and hugged them as best as he could. They both exploded with happy cheer. How are you? It's good to see you; what brings you here? He squeezed into the stool they saved. Very wise, that was too. The bar had filled as if someone had flipped a switch. There was a piano and player over in the corner playing and singing George Benson tunes, an adorable background; Jeff said they were living well in their semi-retirement, forced as it was. Roscoe ordered his Manhattan straight up as usual, and Janis commented that he hadn't changed that much. When the drink arrived, Jeff picked up his drink and said, "To our best health and happiness and the death by ants eating Allen very, very slowly."

So, the evening began.

While driving home, Roscoe reminisced about the enjoyable evening with Jeff and Janis and made a mental note to keep in contact with these lovely people. He also allowed himself the feel-good of taking the first covert action toward Jason V. Johnson.

Chapter 10

Roscoe realized he needed more information about the Johnsons and wouldn't be able to gather what he needed through the electronic method without spending the next several months querying all the databases. He purchased an additional camcorder with a time-lapse feature and placed it at the Walden Hills address.

The database at the hospital wasn't difficult to access. Discerning passwords for the financial section took a little time. He entered the personnel files and found the entire list, placing the people by department. He compared this list with the ones slated in the financial section against the one for clerical and eliminated those that matched for the time being. He then printed out all the pertinent information about each person in his current list. White pages were used to find phone numbers and addresses from this information. From there, I queried deeper and found dates of birth, number of children, and birthdates of children. Most people use one of these in some fashion to create their passwords, even though the MIS section has probably told them not to do that very thing. People who have their phone numbers unlisted are wiser.

After about two hours of playing front, backward, combinations, and so on, he got what he wanted. The lady who runs the payroll section used the first three letters of her middle name reversed and the last three letters of her middle child's middle name reversed—no more secrets. Once in, he found that Johnson split his take-home pay among three banks, one of which he trailed him to. Roscoe made notes of the other two, the Second National of Tampa and the First Centurion of Tampa. He also found the disbursement to a 401K plan; he thought he needed to find the provider.

The tracking software comes to life, and the Taurus is on the move. Roscoe calls the Johnson home and says he is performing a survey for a local marketing company. He finds Mrs. Johnson is easy and agreeable to talk to, so he asks several questions: "What brand of laundry detergent do you use in the household?"

"I don't do laundry; we have a service that picks it up," she responds.

"Do you own one or more passenger cars?"

"We have two."

"Of the two, are they American-made?"

"One is, and the other is a Mercedes."

"Do you or another person in the household go grocery shopping?"

"Which food store do you use?"

"Food Lion"

"Do you shop once or more times a week?"

"Most weeks, it's two times."

"And one last question, Mrs. Johnson, if you don't mind, do you use cash, bank card, or credit card at the Food Lion?"

"I always use the bank card."

"Thank you very much, Mrs. Johnson. This survey is being done to determine the food shopping habits of people like you, willing to take a few moments out of your busy daily routines."

Roscoe takes a tracking device and heads to the Walden Hills rental.

He replaced the tape in the camera, and he'll view it later. From this vantage point, it's impossible to tell if anybody is home at the Johnsons. Roscoe has a lunch date with Maxine, so he leaves, taking the finished tape. While on his way to Floyd's, he thinks about how difficult it might be to get a tracking device for the Mercedes. Mrs. Johnson's trips are likely all-purposeful and short, especially with small children. He remembers when his two were small, and Mrs. would complain about how hard it was to get anything done or go shopping with two of them hanging on all day.

The Cherokee isn't in Floyd's parking lot, so he must be early. Bill, the bartender, greets him as soon as he's inside the lounge and asks, "What'll it be, a cold one or Jack?"

"Jack," Roscoe replies.

He continues to think back to the early years and can't help but get a tear in his eye. Maxine appears just as the tear starts to roll down Roscoe's cheek, and she asks, concerned, "Roscoe, are you alright?"

Grabbing a bar napkin, he says, "Sorry, I'm fine. It's just a fond old memory revisiting; see what you get when you leave me alone."

She laughs lightly and kisses him on the cheek. She takes the seat next to him, and Bill sets her drink in front of her. Roscoe raises his glass and toasts.

"Happy New Year."

Maxine clicks her glass and says, "You called this meeting. Is there something you want to talk about?"

"Nothing other than to share a couple of hours of enjoyable time with you. Maybe I'm becoming a sentimental old fool."

"Roscoe," Maxine says, "that's one thing I don't think you'll ever be accused of."

Bill holds up a couple of menus and says, "Take any booth you want, or stay right here."

Roscoe grabs the menus, swings around, and walks to the corner booth, where lunchtimes are quietest and evenings are the loudest. Maxine follows, bringing the drinks. Someone in the bar starts a CD of the "Velvet Fog" on the Juke. That suits both their moods just fine, they agree. They both order fish, and neither enjoys it. It's probably not the chef's fault, so they agree they'll give Floyd's one more chance and make a date for dinner this Friday night.

On his way home, his heart feels heavy; he can't get his family out of his mind. Instead, he heads to the cemetery to place a stone on her headstone and chat about the kids. He's been here at least once a week, sometimes three or more, in the past year. He always feels a little better after sitting and chatting; This will go away when he hits the road to continue his quest. Roscoe sits on the cold concrete bench for over two hours thinking about this, and isn't entirely convinced he should continue this new adventure. Then, he gets up to leave.

The resolve returns before he gets home. He inserts the tape into the converter and inserts it into the VCR; the PC is blinking. He has mail. What to do first, he decides on the VCR. Watching time-lapse takes discipline; for most of the time, all that can be seen is the static scene; fast forward until something changes, stop back a little, and play and watch. After a while, his other curiosity gets the best of him, and he goes to the PC. It's from NY, and his daughter's note is short and sweet. She says he'll read an e-mail but never answer the phone. She's right, and he knows it. He replies that seeing was on his mind today, to be well and happy, and the fond 'I V U's'. He finishes the tape cataloging six comings and goings of the Mercedes in 24 hours, all daylight. After the gym tomorrow, he will sit it out in the Walden Hills rental, he resolves.

His arrival at the stake-out location is just in time to see the Mercedes pull in, and he only sees one little one because she didn't go into the garage, which he noticed while watching the tape. She uses the front door when she leaves the car in the driveway. No packages were carried in, so he concludes the Food Lion hasn't been visited yet. He had two days of surveillance on the first tape and didn't notice any packages, although it could have happened during a lapse, but Roscoe didn't think so.

She said, "Most weeks, it's two times" when he talked to her. By his reckoning, today would be a Food Lion Day; this is the only place he feels he'll be able to get to the Mercedes without too much risk. He had taken the precaution to back the Town Car into the garage when he arrived to be sure he could leave quickly without her getting too far in front. He knew where the Food Loin was, which meant he couldn't just go ahead and wait.

It takes about an hour and a half, and here they come: Mrs. Johnson and the child are out the front door and into the Mercedes. Roscoe gets to the Town Car, starts the engine, counts to ten, and opens the garage door. The Mercedes has passed, and he falls discreetly behind. The Food Lion is today. He parks quickly without looking at his way because he knows she's seen his car over the last several weeks. With the device in his hand, he strolls over to the Mercedes; just as he's getting ready to lean down and tie his laces, he sees Maxine talking to Mrs. Johnson like they're old friends. What's going on here? First, he finds Maxine with the scumbag and now with his wife; what is he oblivious to that Maxine knows and is involved with the Johnsons. He doesn't think Maxine has seen him; he gets the device set, crawls back to the car, lies down in the back seat, and hopes like hell he hasn't been spotted. After what seems like an eternity, he looks up and doesn't see Maxine looking down at him like he's some degenerate or something or anybody else. He slides out of the back seat, starts the car, and escapes the Food Lion. The good news is that he can now track Mrs. Johnson without risking exposure, but how does she know Maxine?

At the PC at home, he deactivates all but the latest device and sets it in background mode, only to beep when it starts moving. For the next several days, he collects information on the goings-on of the Mercedes, and he realizes he wouldn't want her schedule. I went back and forth to a private school at least twice daily, almost 2 hours for each trip. There is one more Food Lion and three banks, but none are on his list. This is paying off 1000 times over the risk at the Food Lion parking lot. First Florida, Carolina Central, and Tampa State Bank.

Dinner with Maxine could turn into a disaster, Roscoe realizes. He gets to Floyd's on time, and the Jeep is there already. Is she waiting for the slaughter? She spots him entering with a warm smile; she's decked out to the nines tonight, Roscoe comments, "Wow, you look great!"

"Thank you. You don't look too shabby yourself."

Roscoe has taken to wearing turtlenecks with blazers. After Bill has served Roscoe and refreshed Maxine, she starts, "I thought I saw you at the Food Lion earlier this week."

"What's a Food Lion? I've heard of Mountain Lions and Jungle Lions, but never Food Lions."

"It's a grocery store; you must know what they are. They're all over."

"Can't say as I do," he lies.

"Oh well," Maxine continues, "Do you believe it's a small world?"

"Sometimes it seems that way."

Roscoe responds, knowing what's coming and not wanting to seem overanxious.

"I met a sorority sister at the Food Lion, which I hadn't seen since NYU, when I thought I saw your car. I looked around the car park and didn't see you, and didn't see you in the store, and when I came out, the car was gone."

Roscoe is getting a little nervous with Maxine continuing to ponder his presence at the Food Lion offers.

"My car isn't unique, you know. I think only about 100,000 of them are the same color as mine. If we go outside at 1911, I bet we see a car like mine before one like yours."

"I guess you're right," Maxine says.

Just then, Maxine turns white, and Roscoe comments, "Maxine, are you all right? You look like you saw a ghost."

Bill, the bartender, sees her and also comments. She says very quietly, "I just realized a connection that's so bizarre it's hard to believe I don't know if I can."

"Do you remember," she says, "a couple of weeks ago, that guy was hitting on me?" Roscoe nods.

"If I remember what John said, he told me the guy's name was Johnson, and he was the doctor at the Plant City hospital."

"If I remember, it was something like that. Why don't you ask John again? He's about five stools down," Roscoe says.

Maxine gets up and talks to John, then comes back. She's still visibly shaken up. As she returns to her seat, she tells Roscoe, "That's what John said; he works in the ER."

Again, Roscoe nods.

She goes on, "Janet told me her husband was a doctor at the Plant City hospital, and her married name is 'Johnson.'"

Roscoe whispers lowly, "Wow, that's almost eerie," knowing full well that is the situation. He feels bad for Maxine; she's going through a traumatic time right now, and he knows he must be reassuring and sympathetic for her sake.

"I wonder if she knows," she says. "Does Janet know what kind of man she's married to? She gave me her phone number, so I think I'll give her a call."

Roscoe, not wanting Maxine to disrupt his plan, cautions her to be careful: "Don't you think it might be better to sleep on it before possibly being the bearer of bad news?"

"You're probably right," she says.

Roscoe tries to cement it, "Remember what Queen Elizabeth or one of the Queens of England did to the bearers of bad news; first, the hands came off for carrying it, then the feet for bringing it in, and so on."

"Stop already, that's enough," Maxine mockingly cried. "I give up, I won't call her." Roscoe noticed, though, that Maxine was quick with the phone number for an old friend she hadn't seen in many years, but not him. They settled down and ordered another round. Maxine began to reminisce about her relationship with her old sorority friend, how she'd be glad to renew it, and what a shame about her husband.

Over the following weekend and for several weeks to follow, Roscoe kept shaking his head at how small the world was and how close he had come to being discovered. He hated having to deceive Maxine, but he felt she was deceiving him. Wouldn't she be surprised when the doctor got defrocked soon? Progress was very slow in getting the information he needed to bring down the scumbag. His option on the Walden Hills property lapsed, and he retrieved his equipment shortly after placing the device on the Mercedes. He didn't have to leave the house or van to keep tabs on their whereabouts. Every once in a while, he would check on the Lexus, out of curiosity more than anything else.

Maxine was convinced Roscoe was holding something back. She was positive it was his car at the Food Lion, regardless of how he tried to make her believe otherwise. Why would he do this, she wondered, and what would she do about it? To date, they had not truly entered each other's lives. This wasn't good enough, and she wasn't sure why; maybe that original attraction was growing more than she realized. Breaking off with Roscoe didn't seem like an option she wanted; she resolved to confront him the next time they met, which had been over a fortnight now, more ammunition that he must be hiding from her. And what about Janet? Her call was not met with the warmth she felt at the Food Lion. She had tried to make a lunch date to review old times, and Janet was evasive and non-committal.

62

Chapter 11

Maxine called her mother and told her she was driving up to spend the weekend with her if that was OK. Mom said no problem, always glad to have Maxine visit, as long as neither of them had to do any cooking or cleaning. That sentiment of her mother's always made Maxine chuckle. There weren't any Food Lions close to her mother's, but there was a Publix with a nice deli section. It was about 4 in the afternoon of a Friday when Maxine arrived at the store. Enough deli throws away for three days, she is thinking, and Mom eats anything. Sliced honey cut ham, deli roast beef, smoked turkey, a rotisserie BBQ, Lemon Pepper Chicken, and deli-style rye, white, and wheat bread, some Kaiser rolls, and some Swiss Lorraine cheese, everything sliced super thin, including the bread. Over to the liquor store, Mom likes Tanqueray and Beefeater for Maxine, some tonic, and a couple of lemons and limes for the limeys.

Maxine's mother's house is one city block from the water on an East-West Street, which means the sun never really shines in the front or back yards. Maxine's mother's name is Margaret King, Margie to her friends. She was waiting for Maxine on the bungalow porch. Many yards in the older sections of Florida are not improved, and cars park anywhere. Also, driveways are not well-defined in these types of yards. Maxine pulls right up to the porch.

"Hi, mom, wanna give me a hand here?"

"Better hurry," Margie says. There's a big storm sweeping in. I can see the black clouds crawling across the sky from the south."

The two women get the deli and booze in the house, a nice one-story with two bedrooms, an eat-in kitchen, and a nice-sized living room.

The rain started just as the last packages were being brought in. They put all the deli packages into the refrigerator and then hugged and kissed each other on their cheeks.

"Good to see you again," Margie tells Maxine.

Maxine asks, "Are you hungry? How about some smoked turkey sandwiches and a gin and tonic with lime?"

"That sounds great. I'll turn on the news, and we'll eat in the living room."

"White or rye?" Maxine asks.

"OK," is the response.

Maxine makes one sandwich with one side white bread, the other rye for her mother, and a rye on both sides for herself, some chips, and a crisp kosher spear for each. After they finish eating and the local news is over, Maxine says, "I've got a couple of things I'd like your input on."

''Figured something was on your mind when you called, you don't have to bribe me with food and booze to talk to me, but I like it."

Margie jibes, "Anytime you feel comfortable, let it roll."

They watch a couple of sitcom reruns, and as Maxine is bringing in another drink for each of them after she's 'cleaned up the dishes,' she tells Margie, "I've met a fella."

"Why am I not surprised by my Peacock lady?"

"Mother, you know I've never been fond of that term."

"Well, it's your name, Maxine," Margie kids. "Tell me about him. What does he do? Where is he from? Is he nice? Will I like him?"

"Not so fast, all in due time. His name is Roscoe, and he's a retired accountant; he likes good food, wine, booze, and me."

"You say 'retired.' How old is he?"

"I helped him get into shape a while back. I've never asked him, but I believe around his mid-50s. You get a feel for the ages by how they respond and react to certain stimuli."

"I know you never like to talk about this, Maxine, but I've never understood why you do that when you have so much talent in other ways."

True to what Margie has just said, Maxine ignores that last comment and continues: "He's a decent-looking guy. He's not handsome, but he's not bad-looking either. I know he colors his hair; I guess it's to look younger."

Margie is paying close attention and shaking her head up and down.

Maxine goes on, "I think I caught him in a lie."

That stops everything for a while; the TV drones on, and neither of them hears it.

Margie breaks the ice. "So why are you pining about this 50ish colored hair liar?"

That question hangs over the rest of the evening. Margie has one of the DSS units, so they find a nice love story and snuggle up together.

One of the nice things about being with her mom is that she can 'hang out,' sipping her heavy cream and sweetened coffee, while Margie is loyal to tea. The following morning, they are both still in their pajamas.

"I don't know why," Maxine answers last night's question. "Something has drawn me to him in an outside way, if any of that made sense."

"Perfect sense," Margie inserts. "Guys like that gnaw on you."

"Then you don't think I'm nuts?"

"Not at all, baby; I wish you had it easier with men."

"Thanks, Mom. I've decided to confront him about this the next time I see him; it's been a fortnight now."

"What if he doesn't come clean?"

"I've convinced myself that if that happens, I will drop him like a hot potato."

"Good for you."

Silence prevails for a while. Maxine speaks next, "Do you remember my sorority friend Janet from so long ago?"

"I think so. Was she the blonde with the skinny legs and big blue eyes?"

"That's her to a 'T' except her legs aren't sticks anymore; they've held her up for two kids, and her eyes looked sad. I ran into her, literally, a couple of weeks ago."

"Oh, what's she doing now?"

"Married and raising a family."

"Her husband is still around; maybe she's doing it the hard way."

"He's still around, from what I could get out of her. I bumped into her at the grocery store, and we chatted for a couple of minutes and exchanged phone numbers. I called her the next day, and she sounded so different. I wasn't able to arrange a get-together or anything."

"That's strange."

"Much stranger than that is what I believe to be profound and is the main purpose of coming to see you."

"You mean this Roscoe fella plays second fiddle?"

"To this, yes."

"What could be so strong to override a fella?"

"I think I want a little courage. Do you have anything against getting started early today?"

"You know it's always OK with me. I have nowhere to go, and I'm not hurrying to get there."

Maxine gets up, clears the mugs and other items, and mixes two strong gin and tonics. She sits for a while and then begins.

"You remember how strange Daddy died? You always said you thought something was wrong."

Margie looks at Maxine very carefully and slowly responds, "What's going on here, baby?"

"I remember you crying a lot when they came and told you he was dead, but mostly I remember you getting so angry later when you talked to somebody on the phone. I never knew what that was about at the time. I was very young, about 11 or 12, but I remember you screamed, 'That damn Doctor Johnson', well Janet is married to that Doctor Johnson, I believe."

Margie stares at Maxine for a long time without a sound.

"I never knew you heard any of that; I remember telling myself to shield you from my feelings back then. I guess I didn't do an outstanding job. I've always loved your father and still do. That's why I never remarried."

Silence again, and tears welled in both their eyes.

"I begged him not to take that job with the UN. The people he worked for were nasty folks, and they had him flying all over the globe with the most unsavory types." Margie continues, "We argued a lot then, which is why we separated; neither of us liked each other much after those times. When he came home that last time, he called me and told me he'd been injured and was going to the New York Medical Center to check it out. He never got out of that hospital alive."

All the talk stopped again for a while. This was complex territory for them both. Maxine got up to refresh the tonics, and as she passed her mom, Margie reached out and pulled Maxine to her. Maxine fell to her knees under the pressure, and they embraced, each letting out deep sobs for what seemed like an eternity. Then, the tears exploded. Finally, Maxine got up to get a new supply of tissues.

As the tonics were set on the table, Margie went on.

"I called so many people at that damn place and finally found out the attending physician's name. That's the call you heard. Further, it was found that his full name was Jason V. Johnson. I followed his career, and that's why I'm here in Central Florida; it's where he is; I only found him at the Plant City Hospital. It's taken this long. I never knew he was married till you just told me."

"What are you going to do about it? You can't sue him for malpractice or wrongful death here in Florida," Maxine asks, concerned that Margie sounds like a vigilante.

"I don't know, Maxine, I've just been so tied to him physiologically; I've followed his career, there's a lot of dead people associated with him; every place he's been, people die in his care. I haven't been able to find out if anybody was killed on his watch here, Florida, but I've got my sources out there checking for me."

Maxine sits there with her arms crossed, slowly shaking her head from left to right, and she says after a pause.

"I never realized any of this, and I lived with you until I left for North Carolina."

"Like I said, I tried to keep this from you, and except for that one phone call, I think I did a good job. Let's leave this alone, but I want to probe where this new information can get us."

"It's time to get cleaned up and ready for lunch," Margie declares.

They sit out on the porch after devouring the BBQ chicken for lunch. It's a relaxing afternoon. They sip their tonics, and Maxine resumes the Johnson thing as dinner hour approaches.

"About a month ago, a guy tried hitting on me in the lounge where I met Roscoe; it was him! It wasn't until Janet told me she was married to a doctor that I put any of this together. He sure thinks he's a lady killer, but he comes off as a slob."

"I'm sorry you had to deal with that, but I'm glad you know what he looks like; I've never seen him; that was one thing I had hopes of getting accomplished this time, and now I have, through your eyes."

"I think I'll pursue the Janet connection next week. She probably knows about his philandering."

"Ok, this makes you a co-conspirator, you realize."

"It's all right with me, it makes life a little interesting, and if this bastard killed my father, I want him as much as you do."

"Thanks," is all Margie can muster.

After a while, she says, "Now, tell me more about this Roscoe guy."

"It's funny, I've never asked him what he does all day, I guess because I didn't want to know until this very second! The more I think about him, the more I think I'll break it off, I still want to confront him and hear what he says about lying to me."

"Good for you; I'd feel different if he hadn't lied to you."

They finished the other chicken for dinner, and the following day, they just lay around as two women can do. Most men would say they wasted a day, but they thoroughly enjoyed it, and Maxine left for her place around 6 PM to get home before dark.

Chapter 12

Roscoe always went home via Floyd's, looking for the Jeep, not stopping; today, he decided to have a cold one and pulled in. Bill, the bartender, had a message, "Maxine will be in for cocktails on Friday. Would you please join her? Haven't you guys heard of the phone?" he says, laughing, and gets a cold one for Roscoe.

Roscoe thanks him and tells him to have one. That's the best news Roscoe has had in weeks.

He hasn't had much luck getting the bank information he wants, but that doesn't matter today. He pulls into Floyd's parking lot at 6:15. The Jeep is not there yet. He orders a Manhattan, Bill goes through his ritual, and at 6:30 on the dot, Maxine walks in. She looks a little tired, he thinks. She greets him without a touch and suggests they sit in a booth. Once they're settled and the drinks are brought over, Maxine begins, "Roscoe, I haven't been around lately because I've been hurting."

Roscoe looks puzzled but says nothing; she continues, "I'm convinced you lied to me for no good reason, and I'd like to know why."

Roscoe's look changes from puzzled to shocked. A few long moments pass before another sound is made. Maxine looks at him anxiously, hoping he won't pack another lie on top of the one already there.

Roscoe starts cautiously. "Maxine, it's never been my intention to deceive you, and I sincerely apologize and ask for your forgiveness."

"That's it! No, why did I do it? Was it because of anything? I won't accept that, Roscoe. You've got to do better."

After more silence, he flags Bill for another round of drinks and has to wait for the show, which he welcomes right now. He's confused: Should he tell her the whole story? If he does, he has to quit, and he's not sure he wants to just yet. On the other hand, he doesn't like losing Maxine like this.

When the drinks arrive, he begins. "It's a long story. Are you up to this?"

"Fire away," Maxine shoots back.

"It started a little over a year ago." He recounts everything to her, including his frustration, and finishes, "Now that you know all this, I'm going to give it all up. I have to. No more secrets."

Maxine's demeanor has changed from anger to sadness to joy. She gets up and comes around. The booth slides in next to Roscoe, hugs him, and kisses him fully. Roscoe is a little taken aback, but finally gives in and joins the embrace and kiss. When the kiss and hug end, she slides back out and returns to the other side.

"Now that I know all this, you are not going to give it up or anything of the kind. Now, you sit there and listen to this." Maxine recounts everything she and her mother have discussed, and Roscoe sits there, his mouth open in disbelief. He thinks the world is hell; he thinks it's a microcosm.

"I have to call Mother, and I think we need some dinner," Maxine says and gets the waitress's attention. When she returns, she announces, "Mother wants us up there pronto. Skip dinner here, she told me. She'll have plenty, and she'll get a jug of Jack. She wants to meet you and plans on you staying the weekend."

"Well, let's get organized and go," he says. "You might as well drive," Roscoe tells Maxine.

"Okay, where shall we meet?"

"Here's my address; I'll be outside, and here's my phone number if you get lost."

Roscoe gets home, quickly checks his messages, and packs an overnight bag with enough for several days. He gets outside just as the Cherokee is pulling in. He tosses his bag in the back, and they're off.

"It'll take about an hour to get to Mom's, her name is Margie."

"What's her last name?"

"King."

"That's odd, I got all the names of the bereaved at the hands of the scumbag, and there never was a King, and I never found one in New York."

"I'll let Mom fill you in on those details."

"Okay, I'll wait; it's not like we're in a hurry."

"By the way, have you got one of those bugs on my car?"

"No."

"Do you know where I live?"

"Yes."

"Have you driven by?"

"And what about my phone number?"

"Yes, guilty to all, but I abused none."

"I'll accept that."

"Speaking of security, the way I got your information was off the Internet; I suggest you get a completely unlisted phone number and don't buy any real estate; that's the only way you won't be listed."

The time passes pretty fast, and they're at Margie's. Roscoe is impressed: no neighbors are within reach, it's close to the Gulf, and our buildings look out back.

Maxine introduces Roscoe to Margie. Margie, never to be embarrassed, jumps in, "I told Maxine to dump you, and here I am buying you expensive booze; speaking of which, let's get inside and have some. By the way, Roscoe, you sleep on the couch in the living room."

"We'll see about that." Maxine gets in.

Roscoe lets the talk go on. He's not about to touch any of it with a ten-foot pole.

They all settled around the kitchen table. Margie announced she has a special dish she wants to serve the group at their first meeting.

"It's something that goes along with what we're endeavoring to do," she says as she passes out shallow bowls. "What we are doing is defined as a dish best served cold, so here it is."

She ladles what looks like tomato soup into each bowl and places a platter of chopped condiments, such as peppers, onions, cheese, olives, and a few others, on top.

"This is called Gazpacho for those who are uneducated or cold tomato soup; it doesn't become Gazpacho until you add some of those."

Pointing to the platter, she just sat down.

"If we're going down this path of no return, we might as well do it with knowledge aforethought."

They all nod their heads yes. When the cold soup is finished, they adjourn to the living room.

"Margie," Roscoe asks, "would you tell me how you latched onto Jason V. Johnson and why there's no record of Mr. King dying at his hands at New York Medical?"

"I'll answer that backyard; it will clear itself up. Maxine's dad was involved with the government, flying strange cargo all over the globe. That's why there's no record, I've always supposed, as to how I found him; I hounded two of his associates at the UN complex until they released his medical records; officially, it said he died of heart failure. They kept arguing that we weren't married, so I had no right to any of the records; I used Maxine as my authority, saying as his daughter, she had a right to know, and there he was, the attending physician Jason V. Johnson."

"Thank you, Margie, and you too, Maxine. It is never easy revisiting painful memories, but these items must be known. He marked my wife with health failure, also, and she never had a problem with her heart. Thank you again."

"You know we want this guy, Roscoe; we want him to feel the pain," Margie insists.

"I won't have any part in killing anybody!" Roscoe also insists.

"That's the last thing we want; that would be too easy for him; he must feel the pain every day he gets up for the rest of his long, long life!! Tell me more about this Mary character, the OR nurse, I think we send some grief through her."

Roscoe relates how the big green truck, which he assumed was Mary's husband, spooked them. Margie suggests that he bug the big green truck.

"Won't that be counterproductive?" Roscoe asks.

"Look at it this way: if anything happens, we can always use his travels as an alibi."

"That's great thinking, Margie; I think the three of us will make a great team."

"Tomorrow, why don't you go and get the van? We can hide it here in the back."

"Okay, but I think all three of us should go; there's not a passenger seat in the van, and there's no sense either of us riding back alone. Lunch at Floyd's is on me; the vans are within a mile."

"Sounds good," both ladies agree.

Maxine gets up and announces that she's bartending, then refreshes everybody's drink. When she brings Roscoe's, she sits in his lap and says loud enough for Margie to hear.

"You'll sleep with me tonight, okay?"

Roscoe nods his agreement, and Maxine stays right there.

Margie comments, amused, "The things I allow in my own house."

As Maxine leads Roscoe into the guest bedroom, Roscoe whispers in Maxine's ear.

"This isn't going to be rape and plunder, I hope."

"No, Roscoe. I know it's been a long time for you. We'll go very slowly."

The bed is full-size and not the biggest for two full-grown adults. They manage to get comfortable with a mutual embrace and a goodnight kiss. Maxine comments, "We fit okay lying next to each other in bed."

In the morning, after a light breakfast, Margie tours the premises. The shed in the back is big enough to house the van, and the grounds are amazingly private.

Margie notes, "When you start traveling to these targets, will you give up your flat?"

"I figured I would, but that was calculated from a single man's position. Now I'm not sure if traveling alone will be the way," Roscoe says, looking at

Maxine, who responds, "I have no plans to give up my position to go anywhere, but I might join you occasionally."

"Just a thought," Margie says. They all pile into the Jeep and head for lunch.

The weekend crew is at Floyd's, and it's nice and quiet when the three of them walk in. When the waitress arrives and leaves menus, they order two gin and tonics, different but similar, and a cold Corolla with lime for him. They take turns heading to the facilities, he alone, and the women together. When they're back, they order cheeseburgers with fries. The talk centers around the OR nurse, Mary, and the ways she can help with the first target.

Roscoe explains, "I staked them out for a week and got nothing; that's when he found you, Maxine; if they're a team again, I'd still like to get the finishing shots. I guess I can stake them out again. I have all the vehicles except the big green one, bugged. I'll take your suggestion, Margie, and get a tracking device. It's probably at the condo now; after lunch, you want to go on a mission with me; watch from a safe distance?"

"As long as it's a safe distance, okay?"

The big G & M Kenilworth sits right where he last saw it when they get to the condo. Roscoe had told the girls where to park and watch. He remembered a spot he could park that was blind to the condo building, and parked there. He took the device and, staying on the blind side, planted it under the running board on the driver's side. It took almost a minute, and he was back in the van and pulled alongside the Jeep and goads.

"Ya wanna race?"

"That was sure quick. Mom and I were thinking, can't we two sit on the futon on the way?"

"I don't see why not. Let's get the Cherokee into the storage bin and get going. We can retrieve it when we return."

So, they leave the condo and get the Jeep tucked away.

"I'm setting the tracking software to signal if the Johnsons or Clements move."

The ladies settle in on the futon with the TV on and head to Margie's place.

When they arrive, it's almost dinnertime. Margie goes behind the house, wheels out a kettle grill, and says, "Roscoe, I hope you know how to use one of these; I've got three beautiful porter houses waiting for the perfect cook. There's ready-to-burn charcoal where the grill came from, and one of those lighter guns to get it started. I'll fix the cocktails."

"Come, help me. Maxine."

Inside, Margie holds on to Maxine and quietly whispers to her, "He's a keeper."

Maxine replies, "I think you're right. Besides you, I've never been so comfortable with anybody as him."

Margie cranks open one of the back jalousies, a window type fast disappearing from the Florida scene, and hollers, "How's it coming out there, chef?"

"Just about ready to burn the house down, is that all right with you?" he laughs.

Maxine whipped up some greens, and Margie heated some home fries she had, and they all had a feast. After dinner, they ate with real silver and good paper plates, so cleanup didn't take too long.

Margie requests, "Let's have a real tour of that van. We just saw the fun stuff."

Roscoe is like a kid showing off; he opens the bonnet and shows the powerful engine, which is muffled to sound like a kitten. All the computer stuff, the beeper had gone off while they were eating, so he showed them from all these miles away. He could tell who was on the move and where they were. Both Maxine and Margie were amazed at these toys. He showed them the images he'd collected so far of the ER/OR connection. He printed a couple of them and warned them about destroying them and not leaving them lying around. He explained his security system and the need for complete secrecy in the business of their choice. They wanted to watch the tracking some more; it was the Lexus moving and the Taurus. Roscoe told them they were heading to the hospital to work.

They were sitting in the living room watching the History Channel when Maxine grabbed their attention and announced she had something to say.

"The last twenty-four hours have been a tremendous whirlwind for me. I've seen and heard everything, and it almost seems surreal."

She looks at them both and continues, "If we're going to go forward with this, and I haven't heard otherwise, I think we should form a company whose name should be M.R. Associates. That's M for Margie and Maxine, R for Roscoe, or what I've been thinking about Measured Revenge. Associates."

Margie jumps up and runs to the kitchen, and Roscoe looks puzzled again. Margie comes back in with a bottle of bubbly and three champagne spoons. She hands the bottle to Roscoe and gives each of them a glass. Roscoe pops the cork and pours. Margie raises her glass and toasts, "To the three kindred spirits who have all lost a loved one by the hands of another, let us come together stronger by this association and take our measure of revenge."

"Hear," Maxine and Roscoe echo, and M.R. Associates is born.

Chapter 13

One of the M's and the R head to the guestroom. Once the door is secured behind them, they embrace and kiss with a newfound passion that each of them has held at bay without being aware of it. Their arms tighten almost too much, and they must loosen up for air. Maxine whispers ever so lightly in Roscoe's ear.

"I know I'm ready for you."

He's had mixed emotions all day long about the closeness without intimacy they shared last evening. He knows he likes her company more than he ever thought he would. For several weeks that slipped by before Friday, he knew he missed her company, as infrequent as it was. He was sure of only one thing: he wasn't sure about anything.

"I hope we live up to both our expectations, Maxine. I'm ready for you!" he whispers back to her.

Maxine squeezes Roscoe and steps back to let him watch her remove her blouse, exposing her creamy white skin and full bosom; she wore no brassiere. She reached out and gently selected his arm, slid her hand to his hand, and pulled it to her breast, holding it there until he squeezed her. She unbuttoned his shirt, removing it from its anchored place and sliding it off his shoulder. She's pleased at what she sees, a soft pillow of graying hair on his chest still cut from his days at the gym. She can tell he's continued the regimen after the last tutoring. Both half-clothed, they once again embrace and kiss each other deeply. Urgency takes over, and they fumble with the remaining clothing and get between the sheets quickly.

Margie is in the kitchen making as much noise as possible in the morning. If she were up, everybody else would be soon enough. While neither wanted to open their mouths when the racket started, finding themselves still snuggling together was nice. A good fit, they both thought. Roscoe was first.

"Good morning, Maxine; you go first."

She wiggled beside him and said, "No, you go first. Take care of us both, and good morning to you, you tiger."

She did slide out first, and as Roscoe lay there, he watched her waddle, swinging her hips at him. He remembered how soft and smooth her skin was to the touch of his hands, and the length of his body, which sent a chill down his spine. He then recognized a sensation he had not felt for a long time. He softly called to Maxine, and when she came over to him, he threw off the bed covers, and Maxine extolled, "Oh, how nice, a piss hard," and she climbed on.

It doesn't take her long to reach her climax. When her breathing comes back to something resembling normal, Roscoe says, "That was a pretty one-way street."

"OH NO, Roscoe, don't ever feel that way. If you didn't get it, nothing would have happened. If you didn't share the moment with me, nothing would have happened if you weren't lying.

Therefore, I don't think anything would have happened for me to watch and enjoy. So, you see, my darling, you were a part of it. And I'm glad to say it's still there."

She started moving again. This time, Roscoe joined, and Maxine reached her heights twice more. Afterward, she leaned forward and kissed him hard, whispering, "Thanks, I needed that more than I realized, and I want to do it repeatedly; please don't ever hide one of those delicious treats from me."

"I promise."

He said, nibbling her earlobe. Maxine slides out of the bed and heads again to the bathroom, increasing her wiggle and waddle. Roscoe rolls over, feeling good about himself.

Maxine joined her mom in the kitchen while he was preparing for the day.

"Well," is all Margie said.

Maxine said, "Like I told you, Mom, he's a keeper; he doesn't leave the lid up."

They both have a good laugh at that. Roscoe enters at the height of the laughter and gives him a puzzled look. They did not explain, but Margie handed him a steaming hot cup of coffee with a wink. As he sits at the kitchen table, Maxine says, "Besides what we're doing right now, what does anybody want to do today?"

The other two look at her and say nothing. Roscoe offers, "The van is a night vehicle basically, so we have all day."

Margie offers, "We could walk to the beach."

Neither Maxine nor Roscoe wants to put themselves in the frying pan. Roscoe goes once more, "Well, we have a few business decisions to discuss and decide on; today would be good for that while we're all together."

Both women simultaneously say, "Boo."

But then, I agree, because no one knows when the three will be together in this mindset again.

The only bugged vehicle moving on a Sunday afternoon was the big green one; all the others were in the barn. The Kenilworth was stationary at a trucking dispatch yard, which meant he was picking up a trailer or looking to do so. They all reconvened in the kitchen, sitting at the table. Maxine reached over and covered Roscoe's hand, and Margie said, "We'll have no hanky panky at the table, please."

Almost embarrassed, Maxine withdrew her hand, and Roscoe reached behind her and covered hers. Then they all reached out and held hands together.

"May all of our highest expectations be met at the beginning of an earnest endeavor." Roscoe offers as they hold hands. Maxine looks at him with warmth and squeezes a little harder.

"Okay," Roscoe the businessman says, "Let's call the first meeting of the Board of Directors of M.R. Associates to order. The first order of business is the third and fourth 'W 's of five."

Having worked for a publisher, Margie knew he was talking about the When and Where.

She says, "It's already started; you and I have been actively working on it for several months, and I for many years. The Where, as far as I'm concerned, is wherever the van is today, it's here."

"Okay," Roscoe continues, "Should we incorporate, subchapter S, or partnership?"

Margie again counters, "Why don't we just trademark the name, so we can sue if we have to, and just form a local partnership?"

Roscoe again: "Let's incorporate out of Delaware. We'll never go public or anything like that. Still, with a corporation formed, we can immediately eliminate all our expenses, lease equipment, get a line of credit, and do so many other good business things. I like the trademark thing, too."

"Then let's do it," Maxine offers, her first foray.

"I'll take care of the filing and paperwork. How about this structure?" Roscoe says, "Margie, you'll be the chief officer, I'll be the CFO, and Maxine, you'll be everything else. I'll forge all signatures as necessary to protect the guilty."

Both women agree. Roscoe declares the business meeting over. Margie suggests, "Let's see if something's on the dish."

Maxine agrees and offers to pop some corn and get some sodas.

The afternoon drones are on, and they find a good mystery to watch and cuddle together on Margie's oversized, comfy couch in the living room. Maxine in the middle, with her always love on one side and her new love on the other. Around six o'clock, Maxine announces sadly, "It's been a great weekend, but I have an early start, and there's a lot of driving and stuff to do tonight before I sleep." Borrowing a line from Robert Frost.

Maxine lies on the futon watching TV during the van ride and calls Roscoe.

"Some of my muscles are sore, and it's all your fault."

"I'm not ready to run the mile myself, but it's all warm and fuzzy-like."

"Oh, you sweet talker," she says. "By the way, Roscoe, has this vehicle ever been christened?"

"No, it most certainly has not," he replies.

"Well," is all she says.

As soon as he finds a rest turnout, he pulls in, removes the window screen curtain, and snaps it in place, making the inside of the van almost dark.

"You've had this planned for, admit it," Maxine chides.

"I knew there would be nights and sometimes long drives where I might want to rest. These things I have anticipated and have provided them," he rambles on.

"I'm impressed," says Maxine. She says as she pulls her slacks off, exposing strong, slender, creamy legs. The van's interior is smaller than the bed they shared at her mom's, but they made do, and about an hour later, they headed home again.

Chapter 14

The following week, Roscoe made some headway on the fronts he was working on. A new dimension has been added to his daily life: phone calls. He's done without them for so long; it was a novelty at first, and now he lets the machine pick up everything. Margie calls twice as much as Maxine. Tonight, he's going back to his hospital stakeout position. He's convinced the ER/OR is alive again. His suspicions are paying off tonight; he sees the nurse, Mary, walk to the Lexus and drive it up to the staff door to collect the scumbag.

Mary is a little miffed tonight. Three weeks and not even a hello, how are you from Jason, and tonight it's all lovey-dovey, want to do it, and all that crap. She's half a mind to call it off; it wasn't her fault that big George was home the last time. Hell, she thought, maybe she'd call his wimpy wife and tell her—all the promises he's made and never kept, one of them. Early on, he told her he'd get a divorce, and they'd get married. He told her that for six months, and nothing. She'd never considered leaving Big George; he'd been good to her and helped her through nursing school. And he was a gentle giant, never laid a mean hand on her, but the sex with Jason was so good. He'd shown her things that she tried to teach big George, but the big lug couldn't catch on. As much as she was angry with Jason for being such a liar, she hoped Big George wouldn't be home. He never called when he had a short run 'cause he hated the people at the hospital except her. All these things ran through her head while driving up to get Jason.

Roscoe was elated; he raced to the condo for the same reasons Mary worried, to see if the big green Kenilworth was there. Not tonight. He's like a little kid with the cookie jar open and no one counting. He parks the van at a good vantage point to get them going in; he gets them at the staff door, and wants it all to have the same date imprinted. Later, he'll get them coming out and deliver the scumbag back to the Taurus. Tonight's the night. He feels like he's about to go on his first date. Yesterday, he placed another stone on the headstone, chatted for a while, and felt sure she agreed he was doing the right thing. Maxine was okay, and maybe Margie was a little bossy.

At about half past two, Roscoe heard thunder that shook him to full alert. A widespread central Florida phenomenon is usually heard in the afternoon, but is no stranger to any time of day. Maybe it will pass, he hoped. He didn't want it to rain on his parade. But it did; in torrents, it came down as if it had a vengeance. Shortly after the rain began, he noticed the umbrella-clad couple standing in the dry, lighted foyer of the condo. He could barely make them out through the rain and realized the party was over for today anyway. At least he could listen to good jazz on the local NPR station during the wet drive home.

He met Maxine for cocktails at Floyd's on Friday. He thought she had a glow on and told her so, which she shamelessly told him was still left over from last weekend at Mom's.

"How about my place tonight, tomorrow, and the next day?"

"Hmmm, that is all she can do."

"How was your week?" she asked.

"Not as good as I wanted, but some progress."

He explained how he filed the incorporation papers. He continues, "Got into the fund account for his 401 plan. I haven't gotten intense, though; it gets tricky once you get involved with the SEC. I've got something I'd like to pass by you and Margie."

"Shall I give her a call now?" Maxine says.

"No, we can do that later if you want. There's no rush."

He relays how he got rained out for the phase two images, "Now I've got two sets of phase one. They have different dates, so there's no waste, but I wanted to finish it, and I will."

Maxine says, "I accept. Shall we eat first or just hibernate for the weekend?"

He signals Bill, orders another round, and then asks for menus and a table.

They each find themselves studying the menu like it's the first time they've seen it. He says, "I don't see it."

She says the same thing. Roscoe asks Bill if he can get the food man up front, but he and Maxine want to ask a question. The food services manager is named Roxanne, a very business-like-looking lady. Roxanne appears in the lounge dressed in business attire. She looks to Bill for guidance, and he walks over to Roscoe and Maxine, signaling her over. Bill makes introductions, and Roscoe asks if she can join them for cocktails. She agrees, and they take a booth, but it's the only one that is still open. Roscoe suggests Bill have one on him in absentia, and Bill nods in agreement. Roscoe likes to pay for services rendered whenever he can.

Once they're all settled with coasters and glasses, Maxine takes over, knowing full well what the objective is.

"Roxanne, we're regular customers here and consider ourselves common sewers." Roscoe almost breaks out laughing, and Roxanne's official aura melts somewhat.

Maxine continues, "Recently, we were introduced to something that seemed bizarre to us, but we liked it very much and want to know if we could get it here at Floyd's on those occasions that we would like to have it."

Roxanne was a good listener. She commented, "What is this bizarre item you're talking about?"

"Gazpacho," Maxine responds.

"That's high-flying French cuisine; we're pretty much steak and potatoes here."

"Yes, we noticed it isn't a menu item, but after all, it's just cold tomato soup, and the hot version is on the menu," Maxine tells her, not wanting to show her up because the dish is Spanish in origin.

"We could chill some tomato soup if you give us advance notice. What about the condiments?" Maxine responds, pleased she has successfully negotiated the cold dish.

"I'm sure whatever is handy on any day we ask for it will be fine, even bread cubes will do. Will one day be enough time?"

"Plenty," Roxanne acknowledges.

Roscoe offers another drink, and Roxanne declines.

"Thanks for allowing me to help you, and please stay here and enjoy dinner on Floyd's compliments of me."

Neither Roscoe nor Maxine expected this, and they both accepted it graciously. Roscoe mentioned they had reserved a table; she asked if they wanted to move, and he indicated no, so she told them not to worry. Bill also comped them tonight; the waitress brought another round, telling them all drinks were on the house. Roxanne begged them to enjoy themselves and departed to thank the duo. They truly did enjoy butt steaks, medium, Floyd's special home fries, steamed veggies, and a good bottle of California Beaujolais. The jazz combo started right after dinner, so they stayed longer to enjoy the music.

During dinner, Roscoe had told Maxine his idea, and when they got to Roscoe's flat, Maxine suggested they call Margie. Roscoe suggested they wait till morning; he had something to show her. He leads her to his bedroom, and she exclaims, "What a big bed."

"All the better to ravage you on," he says, pinching her behind.

She reacts to the pinch by jumping away and vaulting onto the bed, which is higher than any she's been on before. She rolls around, realizing it's also possibly the most comfortable.

In the morning, after hot coffee, she called Margie. Margie wanted to know everything, but she would only get what they wanted her to hear. The speaker feature of Roscoe's desk phone always sounds like everybody's in an echo chamber. Roscoe greets Margie and begins, "I've been thinking that we should allow all the other bereaved to partake in us Gespatos, as long as they agree with us."

"I don't know."

Margie fires right back with a little bite in her voice. Roscoe looks at Maxine, puzzled, and shrugs his shoulders.

Maxine takes over: "Mom, how are you feeling? Have you been okay? Is anything wrong?"

Margie, still with the irritation, still in her voice, says, "I was hoping you would have called last night, sorry."

Roscoe cautiously continues, "Until I met you, I thought I knew all the folks who've lost a loved one to Johnson; you add to the list. I've talked to every one of them. When I was trying to get the law and government to take a look at my wife's death, I found all that could be found; you, I believe, were the only one I missed. They all, including you, expressed the anger we all feel. How committed they would be, I don't know, but I'd like to find out. Extremely discreetly at a minimum," he promises.

Margie seems reluctant but agrees. They tell her they'll be up to see her tomorrow. He sets the tracker in the background, and they return to the big bed.

Chapter 15

It's a little after noon when they get to Margie's; he convinced Maxine the Town Car was the perfect choice; it hadn't been christened yet. Margie was glad to see them and had already made lunch. Roscoe told them that five people he had contacted about a year ago, all of whom said they wanted to hear if there was any news worth reporting. They are Nancy Fuller, Andrew Leverling, Anne Callahan, Laura Dodsworth, and Michael Buchanan. Fuller and Leverling live in Boston, and Callahan, Dodsworth, and Buchanan are from Chicago.

"If you agree, I plan to keep us anonymous and untraceable even when we receive iron-clad RSVPs."

He explains that it will require a complete weekend and a lot of individual travel. Will next weekend be good for them? Maxine looks at Margie; they both shrug their shoulders and agree.

Mary is anticipating tonight, just like she has for these weekly encounters for the past year. Jason suggested it earlier this evening, and she was pleased. Last week was a little strained, especially when the heavy rains came just as they left, and she hated driving in the dark rain. Something strange happened in the OR tonight. A trauma was radioed in, and the OR was told to gear up and be ready, but nothing happened. They waited and waited; she'd ask Jason tonight if the ambulance had ever arrived at the hospital. Twice, she tried calling the ER and gave up after five rings. No answers were at her house either, or George would not surprise her tonight.

About halfway home, she asked Jason about the mix-up. He seemed like he didn't know anything about it. She jogged his memory a little by relaying some of the details, and he finally told her it was just about a DOA, heart failure as soon as the ambulance arrived.

Tonight is the night; no rain, and the cameras are rolling as they walk out of the condo, arm in arm, with the condo logo in the frame, perfect. Roscoe has been lucky tonight; he's been staking out this possibility for weeks. He found another route from the condo to the hospital or vice versa. He uses the power of the big engine in the van to be first to the hospital and be parked at a good camera position when the Lexus pulls in, the camera running all the way. At least this week, he'll have something positive to report to his new board of directors; the incorporation papers have arrived at Margie's. She had called and left a phone message earlier. He headed home, tempted to print the new images, but he kept his discipline; he wouldn't do something so foolish. He stops at Floyd's to catch the last call and have a private celebration. Bill is in the closing routine and backs him up once on the house.

The next day, Thursday, he doesn't wake up until noon. It was a late night waiting for the lovebirds to make their move and provide all the pretty pictures. He had a lot of work to do before tomorrow's meeting with the girls, and Maxine left a message saying she'd be at Floyd's by Chinese dentist time. Roscoe wasn't sure he was up to all this; somehow, he was going to have to manage. It's his chosen field of work, and he allowed Maxine entry. He made his first queries for the upcoming weekend, and the beginning was done before leaving for Floyd's.

Maxine was sitting and sipping her gin and tonic when Roscoe showed himself. They exchanged warm kisses and hugs. Roscoe told Bill, who looked much better than Roscoe felt, a cold one. Maxine got right to the point.

"I'm not sure about these other people being involved. The more I think about it, it scares me."

He asked, "Have you talked to Margie about this?"

"Yes, she thinks I'm paranoid. She says they should be informed; they've all suffered at his hands, too."

"What can I say or do to help you with this? At this point, it's all or nothing, or we don't do it. So, I ask again, how can I help you with your dilemma? You wouldn't have asked me to lunch if you didn't want my input."

She reached and grabbed his arm and squeezed it hard.

"Can I stay with you tonight? If I wake up feeling this way in the morning, I'll tell you; on the other hand, if I wake up feeling different, I'll also tell you."

"Fair enough," Roscoe replies.

They ordered lunch, the special crab cakes with béarnaise sauce, which was an odd couple but very tasty.

"I've taken the day off tomorrow," Maxine says as they're finishing lunch. Roscoe thinks what a predicament he's in; if she says no, no problem; if she says okay, he'll have to pay full fare, hell, he thinks it's full fare no matter how we do it. He decides to get the arrangements done this afternoon.

He looks at Maxine and says, "That's nice, what's for breakfast?"

She laughs and says, "I might ask, big spender, what's for dinner?"

"Order a pizza with everything, including the fish."

"After crab cakes, that sounds awful; I'll let you know later. I've brought all my travel things just in case."

They drive to Roscoe's separately, and she parks where he indicates no one will bother her Jeep over the weekend if it turns out that way. When they get inside, she announces, "I'm tired, I guess, from all this heavy thinking. I haven't done this much since I was in school. Even then, it wasn't like this; since I've met you, I've had to do much more thinking. Most of it was fun, but it's all tiring. You don't mind, do you?"

"Not at all; go right ahead; you know where it's at."

Roscoe thinks he'll have time to finish the reservations for tomorrow while she naps, which is precisely what he does. When he finishes, Maxine is still sleeping. He makes a sandwich and watches some TV. She's still sound asleep when he's tired, so he snuggles in next to her and nods off himself.

He wakes up at about seven in the morning. Maxine is watching him.

"Been awake long?" he asks.

"About a half hour, I guess. Can't remember the last time I slept through like that."

"You must've needed it; the body just does that to us now and again; you know that better than me."

She nods in agreement.

"Coffee?"

He says as he puts his feet on the floor. Again, she nods in agreement. Roscoe feels she's setting him up for a negative; if it is, it is. She doesn't join him while the coffee is brewing, so he brings two steaming cups back to the bedroom: she's still sitting there like a statue. Concerned somewhat, Roscoe hands her the hot cup and inquires.

"Are you feeling all right, Maxine?"

She lets out a profound sigh and smiles.

"I guess I'm mostly worried that one of these people will blow the whistle on us before we complete our quest."

"I thought I'd wait until we were together before going over this, but now is the perfect time if I think I know what I'm doing."

"Okay, are you ready? This will take a few minutes to explain."

"Convince me I'm nuts," she says.

"Here goes. There are five of them: 2 in Boston and 3 in Chicago. I've written a generic letter using Mail Merge, so they're all very personal; you can read the letter later. I've signed the letters 'Concerned,' sealed them, and set the postage for first class. Each letter will be mailed from a different city outside of Florida. That's where the trip comes in. We will carry one Chicago, and Margie and I will split Boston. Your ticket will take you to Pittsburgh and then to Islip, New York. Your layover in Pittsburgh is two hours; a mall in the terminal has a private post office. You will open a box in a fictitious name I've chosen before heading to Islip. Once in Islip, you'll be laid over for four hours. You'll take a cab to the same private Mailbox Company and open another box in a fictitious name. Mail your letter in Islip. The return flight will go through Raleigh, North Carolina. Your layover there will be four hours. One more mailbox here catches the plane and comes home to Tampa International; you'll be the first one back. Your excursion will take 16 hours with no flight delays. The most important part is the mailboxes."

"Why so elaborate?" she asks.

"Remember I said, 'anonymous and untraceable?' This is how that's done. It takes a little time to set it up, but it's virtually foolproof and will stay in place as long as the boxes are maintained. Each can be rerouted with a phone call from me should someone get noisy. Now, how do you feel?"

"When's my flight? Where are you going, and where's Mom going, or shouldn't I ask?"

"No problem. I'll tell you on the way to your mom's. She leaves first and gets to stay overnight in LA. So, let's get going. We'll stop for chops and eggs on the way."

During breakfast, he explained that Margie would take off this afternoon, going through Dallas, Las Vegas, and Los Angeles before laying over and returning through Denver and Little Rock, mailing Boston in Dallas and Chicago in LA, and opening mailboxes in every city. While in the final part of the drive to Margie's, he told her he was heading to Atlanta, Chicago, Minneapolis, Cleveland, and home. With Chicago from Atlanta and Boston from Minneapolis. Maxine was impressed with the planning and asked how long it took.

"While you were napping yesterday."

They had called Margie while driving and told her to be ready with an overnight bag and two days' clothes. When they arrived, she was waiting on the front porch. Roscoe put her bag in the trunk and went off to Tampa International. All tickets are e-tickets, so no, but Roscoe's mailbox instructions need to be carried out by any travelers. Margie is excited about traveling. All three are waiting when they call for first-class passengers and those requiring assistance. Roscoe had purchased 1st class for both women and a coach for himself. As Margie walked down the Jetway, Roscoe and Maxine departed the airport and left for home. Both of them will go at 7 AM tomorrow, but they will depart from different tramways at the airport.

Tonight, they ordered pizza without the fish; they didn't want upset stomachs on the plane rides tomorrow. Roscoe relayed his success with the Mary front as they sat eating pizza. He wore protective gloves and printed several frames he had downloaded from the van. Maxine was amazed at the sharpness and clarity of the images. She stared at one in particular that showed the entire front of Jason V. Johnson and whispered to no one in particular, although she was thinking of her long-dead father, "We're going to make you feel the pain."

He took all the prints, slipped them into plastic protectors, and locked them in a file drawer. He noticed the answering machine blinking. It couldn't be Margie; she was instructed not to call home tonight. The Oldsmobile dealer, the woman who sold him the van, told him that next year's model would have an optional TV built in behind the driver's position. Would he be interested in a test drive when the new models arrive? They both got a good laugh out of that message.

Margie was having a great time; she enjoyed every minute on the plane, having everything handed to her with a smile. And the food wasn't half-bad. Dallas was a blur, and she followed Roscoe's instructions to the T. She had to admit she wasn't optimistic about all this mailbox stuff, but he seemed pretty sure of himself. She couldn't believe her good luck. It wasn't luck at all, and she was convinced of that. Roscoe was brought into her life for a purpose she was sure of. How strange the world turns, she thought over and over. Roscoe was making her daughter's wish come true, a good, decent man, and hers, her private avenging angel. Good things come to those who wait, she thought of often, and she had waited quite long enough. She managed to leave $100.00 in Las Vegas, which she didn't plan on, but pulling handles was fun; most of the time, it was easier to push the button. Now she was relaxing in a very nice suite at the Hilton airport. She had ordered gazpacho with a rare New York strip steak and mushrooms, and a split of Dom Perignon from room service, and there was the knock.

The alarm was set for 4 AM, so they got to bed early; Maxine reminded him they hadn't christened the Town Car yet; he snuggled up closer and nibbled on an ear. The alarm went off before they got to sleep, they both agreed. He was the first to put his feet on the floor and get coffee brewing. It was still dark out when they left for the airport. He chose the short-term parking and gave the ticket and keys to Maxine. He told her that you'll be back first, so you might as well have them as a precaution. She protested a bit, but he prevailed. He hugged and kissed her, watching her go to the tram for her flight. He turned and went to his side of the departure area.

It started raining in Raleigh while she was cabling back to the airport. It wasn't hard, but she hoped it wouldn't delay the flight. As luck will sometimes do, all flights are canceled; Raleigh thinks it's a large southern city; it's actually quite rural where the weather is concerned, and everybody still gets inside. The airline picked up the hotel, but Maxine was laughing inside because she had the car keys, and Roscoe had insisted that Margie arrive in Tampa right on schedule. She is looking for Maxine. Roscoe said she should wait for her when she got off the tram. There is no sign of Maxine. Plan 'B' is to stay by the tram coming from Cleveland. One hour and six minutes later, Roscoe appears looking about as tired as she's ever seen anybody. She's feeling pretty good.

"No sign of Maxine," Margie says. What have you done with my daughter?"

"Her flight was canceled. She'll be in the morning. I booked a couple of rooms in the Marriott over there," he said pointing to the airport hotel sign.

"How do you know all this?" Margie asks.

"It's easy; use the attendants for something besides getting you a drink," he winked.

"Let's get checked in, have a toddy, and call Maxine."

"You know where she's at?"

"Sure, like I said, they'll tell other things than 'do you want another drink' on those flying machines."

She punched him in the arm.

Maxine seemed surprised to hear Margie's voice when they called. Maxine said she was okay. Roscoe had said there could be travel delays, and besides, she told Margie, you've got to stay in a hotel by yourself, it's only fair that I also do. She warned Margie to keep her hands off Roscoe. When Roscoe took the phone, Margie pinched him, making him squeal like a pig. Maxine swore she'd get Margie for that. Both Margie and Roscoe were waiting for Maxine when she deplaned. Roscoe declared a significant victory when they were all together; he told them that what they accomplished as a team was tantamount to the most precise military operation he had ever been involved in, read about, or heard of. They deserved a celebratory dinner together, he told Margie. She had better know the best restaurants in the upper Sun Coast area because we'll have a great dinner and sleep at your house tonight.

At the dinner table after drinks were served, Roscoe picked up his Manhattan and toasted, "To a task well done and a job well started."

Maxine responded, "Thanks, but could you explain what we did this weekend?"

Margie indicates she's just as confused. Roscoe begins trying to keep it as brief and concise as possible.

All five letters had instructions to mail their response to a P.O. Box that was given in the letter. When each letter is received at its given location, it will automatically be forwarded to the next P.O. Box and again to another before reaching the one I've opened here in the Tampa area. I'm not telling you where the mail drop is to protect you."

Maxine was thinking about what she had gotten herself into; her life was pretty uneventful before being introduced to Roscoe. While she enjoyed her time with him, she wasn't sure if she wanted to be in this clandestine operation they were all in now. She liked the idea of getting her dad's killer, but for her, it could be a TV show or a news program that someone else did. She never considered being involved with Margie on anything more complex than what's for dinner. Yet here she was asking questions and toasting accomplishments as an actual co-conspirator. Where will all this lead to? Should she consider a career change? Roscoe seems ready to do this to somebody for the rest of his life. If she wants to stay with him, she might have to. She's the one who forced the issue, and she could have dropped him before she knew anything. So, in reality, it's her own making, wherever it goes. For the time being, she decides, she'll just let it ride. She reaches over and squeezes Roscoe's forearm.

Roscoe takes this opportunity to cover some other business.

"What about Mary?" he asks as a general question. It was Margie who was interested in getting Mary rolled into the mix. She says, "We've got hard data on the two of them, don't we?"

"Yes, we do," Roscoe confirms.

"What I want to know is what do we do with her? Do we confront her with what we've got and ask her for help? I know from conversations I've had with the Plant City police that if her husband gets wind of any of this, he will probably kill Johnson and maybe Mary." Margie takes the initiative and suggests they eat without any more business discussions.

Which is what they do.

Maxine continues the Mary issue in the car on the way to Margie's.

"Early on, I mentioned my acquaintance with Janet, Mrs. Johnson. Maybe I should show her the data and see where that takes us."

Roscoe says, "Everything is risky at this point. I haven't uncovered enough financial information yet to have Mrs. Johnson start anything that might result in account freezing. I'd like to wait a little longer."

Maxine says she'll try to renew her friendship with Janet without mentioning Jason. She also asks if Roscoe and Margie would mind if she stayed at their house; she has an early start tomorrow.

Chapter 16

On the way back from Margie's, Maxine repeated herself regarding Janet. Roscoe mentioned he could track her and let Maxine know where she was, and they could meet again by chance. Maxine isn't sure she wants it that way; it might taint how she talks to Janet when they meet. Roscoe reminds her that Mrs. Johnson seemed a little strange when Maxine called her. Maxine said she would think about it. He offers to follow her home if she wants, but she says not to bother, and he says it's no; she tells him not to worry. When they get to the Jeep, he gives her a phone, telling her that if she decides to use the locating Janet service, he will call her on this phone. Reluctantly, she puts it in her purse. They embrace and kiss, bidding each other a good night. She gets in her Cherokee and leaves; Roscoe counts ten and follows her home, ensuring he sees her enter her building okay.

When he gets home, he's exhausted. He logs on to the computer. There's mail from both children; he'll read it in the morning. He launched the tracking program and turned off every device except Janet Johnson's Mercedes. He sets the beeper to alarm strength and crashes. It's been a long and productive weekend with his two new accomplices.

After an hour, he's wide awake, sitting in bed, concerned about Maxine.

Maxine couldn't sleep; she saw Roscoe in her rear-view mirror and decided not to acknowledge him. She keeps thinking about how her actions will affect others, some completely innocent. Take, for instance, Janet and the children she has; they've done nothing to be affected by what the three of them are setting up to do to her husband and their father, respectively. Nothing in her upbringing, training, schooling, or life has prepared her for this. Maybe a night's sleep will help her out. She still can't get to sleep, and to add to her confusion, the phone rings. She looks at the clock, and it's showing 2:35 AM. Who will be calling at this hour? She always believed that any emergency would be out of her hands, so if her mother were in need, she wouldn't be able to get to her fast enough to make a difference. She gets up and checks her caller ID; it's Roscoe!

"Hello, Roscoe," she says as she picks up the receiver.

"My apologies, Maxine; I can't sleep tonight because I can't shake the feeling that you want to distance yourself from our quest."

"Is it that obvious?"

"I've picked it up here and there over the last several days," Roscoe responds.

"Why don't you come over and we'll talk it over," she says.

"I'll be there as soon as I can."

When her doorbell rings, Maxine makes sure it's Roscoe before opening it. Once inside the closed door, they give each other a warm hug and kiss, with the radio playing jazz from the Riverwalk in San Antonio. A nice, quiet tone is set for the long-awaited chat for them.

Roscoe begins, "I watched and listened to you carefully from the first time you learned the truth about me."

The radio was wailing Fats Waller's "Ain't Misbehavin'," and they allowed the music to carry the moment. Maxine picks up the conversation.

"I'm just very confused. In my whole life, I've never given a moment's thought to avenging Daddy's death until just recently. The other day, when I whispered to no one in particular that another person should feel pain I would help inflict, it scared me very, very much. Roscoe, convince me this is right."

Roscoe just leaned back in the chair and looked up at the ceiling. With Dick Hyman caressing the ivories, he said, "I won't try to convince you, Maxine. This was a very singular thing with me when it began. It took me a long time to come to my current conclusions. My wife was gone for a year before the realization struck me. I didn't recruit you, nor will I encourage you to do something against your good will."

"Please, Roscoe, tell me how you realized you need to do this."

"It started slowly after about six months; something in my mind kept tickling me. I couldn't quite put a handle on it, and I don't believe I came to understand it fully until the mourning was over. At that time, I truly missed everything that my life had been and hated those who, because of their incompetence, were mostly uncaring, or possibly criminal behavior, made that happen. You know the lengths to which I've gone to derail Dr. Johnson, don't you?"

"Only that you've tried to have him defrocked and jailed to no avail."

"Maxine, I don't want to belabor my beliefs on you because I admit they're self-serving."

"I have to know all these things, Roscoe. I'm at a crossroads in my life, and I know it. I'm not sure if I'm ready for it. Mom has a new life breathed into her, but I can't be doing this for her or you. It must be for me, or I'll be lost to me and you."

"Maxine, I think we should sleep on this. You are here, and I am in your place."

"No, Roscoe, you stay here with me; I don't want to be alone tonight any longer, please."

In the morning, Maxine has coffee for them. She's ready for work. She tiptoes into the bedroom where Roscoe sleeps and watches him for a minute before leaving. She doesn't want to be late after taking Friday off. She leaves a note for Roscoe by the coffee cup in the kitchen. It is strange for her to go home with a man still in it.

When Roscoe rose and stumbled to the kitchen, he saw the note. It said simply, "Thanks, Roscoe. See you for lunch."

After drinking coffee, he left for home to clean up and write the children.

Lunch with Maxine sounded nice; about 1:30 should be good.

The Mercedes was on the move, but he wasn't interested. After showering and changing into clothes suitable for lunch, he sits and begins to communicate with his children. There's nothing but everyday chatter, so he mentions to each of them he's seeing someone and enjoying retirement. The Mercedes is still moving around, so just before leaving for Floyd's, he makes a note on the whereabouts of the car, noting the outside changes.

Maxine will agree to the stalking.

Bill greets him and asks, "Jack or a cold one?"

"Jack, thanks, Bill; I'll take it over in that booth."

About twenty minutes later, Maxine walks in. He thinks she looks a lot better today than she has lately.

"Hi, good looking," she says as she slides into the booth next to him.

"Do you mind?" she asks.

"Be my guest, by all means, and welcome. How are you today? I'm sorry I missed you this morning. The coffee was great, and it was nice getting a note," he rambled.

"I've been thinking hard about all this, as you know, and I've got just two burning questions. First, will we have to fly nationwide whenever we want to mail a letter? And second, can I move in with you?"

Roscoe slides around so he can get a better view of Maxine.

"Must I answer them in the order asked?"

"Anyway, you want to," she says.

"YES, and we gave the post office company instructions at each location, remember?" She nods agreement to the last, puts her arms around him, and plants a big juicy kiss on him for the first answer, then says, "Finish that, I still don't understand."

Roscoe says, "In the instructions, they were told to forward. They will re-envelope the letters to the one where we mail them and then forward them. To the casual or not-so-casual observer, there is nothing to see. That's why we use private mailbox companies; they will provide special services for a fee. Does that muddy the water anymore?"

"I think I understand now. Correct me if I'm wrong. Do we never have to leave on an airplane again to mail a letter?"

"You've got it. WHEN?"

"How about today? I promise not to cook or have wild parties you're not invited to."

"Sounds okay to me, but may I ask two questions?"

"Let's have lunch first and enjoy what we've got here and now."

They order shrimp cocktails to start, and the special is monkfish.

After they finished lunch, Roscoe continued his request and asked, "What happened that makes you want to live with me? I'm practically old enough to be one of your parents."

"Last night after you came over, it hit me like a brick; I enjoy your company; time not including you has become lonely. I've had enough of that for my lifetime. I look at my mother, and she says she enjoys herself; I don't want that to be for me. You give me the missing link in my life. As long as I have something to do about it, I will grab it while it's there to be grabbed, so consider yourself grabbed! You've said OK, but do you think I'm being a little pushy?"

"No, I don't believe you are. I've thought about you and I living together; frankly, I couldn't imagine how long it might have taken me to get the courage to ask you. I'm glad I don't have to know. On the other hand, I like to cook, but I make a mess of it. I firmly believe all meals will be delivered, carried in, or eaten out. How long will it take us to move you in?"

"I took the liberty of loading the Cherokee before coming here. All I need to do is follow you. We'll get the rest as time permits. I haven't decided what to do about my lease yet."

"In that case, Bill, two more please," he says, trying to get the waitress's attention.

On the way, Roscoe stops and picks up some cold cuts and bread for later. Maxine has most of her clothes in hanging bags. It only takes a couple of trips to get it all in. Roscoe cleans out half the bedroom closet and makes the hall closet available for her. He offers to help but is shooed away. He turns on the TV and relaxes for now. There are no wars on the tube today. Just as the news channel begins to repeat itself, Maxine joins him.

"Do you play gin?" he asks.

"Never have, but I've heard it's a cheater's game."

"The very best, and I'll be glad to introduce you to it and challenge you to beat me."

"What other games do you play?" Maxine asks.

"Most of the board games, but I haven't played any since the children grew up. If you want to play some, we'll need to get them, and the gin cards are in that drawer over there," he says, pointing to a small drawer chest next to the TV.

"There are special cards for gin?"

"There are when Roscoe plays gin," he says, laughing as he does.

After several hands, she remembered that the game of gin resembled one she had played in school. She beat him by the fourth hand. They played 'for real,' and a good rivalry instantly developed.

Maxine lets out a deep sigh and sits quietly for the moment. She tells Roscoe, "I'll call Janet tomorrow and see if we can get together. She hasn't been a part of my life for all these years, and I feel no true attachment to her. I'll call you to get her location before I try."

Roscoe looks at her solemnly, assuring him she's doing this of her own free will and not by misguided loyalty.

"Are you certain this is what you want to do?" he asks.

"As you know, I've done some soul-searching about all this. I've come to realize living with you is what I want, and doing this goes along with that. After Johnson, which is my only personal involvement, there will be others for you, and I want to be with you; it's really that simple when I look at it like that. I just thought of this: Mom can't be part of the Johnson thing from where she lives; I'll tell her to move into my place till we're finished with him."

And so, Maxine and Roscoe became a team. They found an old B&W film on the dish called 'Hobson's Choice' and enjoyed it with microwave popcorn and soda. Their first evening as a live-in couple passed smoothly.

Roscoe would have to get used to the alarm again, but Maxine announced the big bed took no getting used to at all. She beckoned him to stay right where he was; no sense in his being up just because she had to be. She was as quiet as possible and kissed Roscoe when she was leaving. As she left, she thought this seemed normal to her, like everything before must then have been abnormal, and this didn't bother her. She felt at ease and at home with Roscoe, a warmth she had never experienced before. Despite their age difference, she figured they'd have many good years ahead of themselves. She thought marriage didn't matter to her; if it does to Roscoe, she'll not object at all; it's just not necessary for her.

Roscoe's phone rang at about 10 AM. It was Maxine, and she wanted to know the location of the Mercedes. At home, he told her.

"I'll call you on the cell in ten more minutes to give you more time to compose your intro and check the phone. Call me in fifteen minutes if you haven't heard from me," Roscoe told her.

"I must get used to this James Bond stuff, but I'll do it cheerfully," she chuckled as she said it. Roscoe called her in nine minutes and suggested she make all calls on the cell just to be sure.

"Hello, the Johnson residence," a young voice announced.

"Is your mom home?"

"I'll get her."

Maxine pulled the phone away from her ear. The phone on the other end was set down as if dropped into the canyon.

"Hello," it's Janet Johnson's tentative voice.

Maxine tried the side door this time with Janet; last time, Janet was curt and cold.

"How lovely to hear such good news on the phone. What's the little one's name?"

"Thanks," Janet acknowledged. "That's Rosie; she's six," she said in a much warmer tone.

"Just thought I'd try again to say, 'Hi.'"

Maxine says very carefully, making sure not to ask any more of Janet, keeping her out of the corner. The line stays quiet for a long moment. Maxine fears the same coldness from her old friend as before.

"I'm sorry, Maxine. I've just been having a little female trouble. I'm okay now."

"I'm sorry about that, Janet. Are you sure?"

"I think so, can we get together?" Janet asks, and Maxine lets out a long, quiet whistle.

"I was hoping we could do lunch or something easy so we could play as much catch-up as we want to," Maxine says with her fingers crossed.

"That sounds nice, I'd like that."

"What's a good day and time for you?"

"I'll get a sitter for the children, and I have to pick up the other children at 3 PM."

"You've got a busy schedule, how about an early lunch close to the school?"

"I go by a place called Martha's, can't vouch for it, I've never been in it."

"That's fine with me; all we need now is when."

"Tomorrow will be fine with me; I can get a sitter on very short notice."

"Tomorrow's fine, I'll make the arrangements and see you there at 11:30 AM."

Maxine wonders why Janet volunteered the bit about the 'very short notice'; she's proud of herself, her first James Bond solo. Janet acknowledges, and they both hang up.

Maxine can't wait to call Roscoe with the good news.

"I did it, I did it" is what Maxine says when Roscoe picks up.

Roscoe suggests they meet for lunch, indicating he doesn't want any details spoken over the phone, even if they're supposedly safe. They agreed to meet at Floyd's for lunch.

"Just a minute, Maxine," he says. "Why don't I get some Chinese takeout, and you come home for lunch?"

Maxine says she can hardly wait that long, and Roscoe assures her she can.

After Maxine relates her story about Janet and the food is eaten, the two slip between the sheets for what Roscoe calls a 'nooner.' They both dozed off and woke up rested and hungry again.

Roscoe says, "Why is it every time I eat Chinese, I'm hungrier than I was before? You want to go to Floyd's for dinner."

"Sounds good to me. Would you like to accompany me to the Jimmy Buffet concert this year?"

"I don't know, never been to one, when's he going to be here?"

"Next month, I dragged Mom to them, and she didn't care; I've mostly gone alone because I've always been a big fan."

"Well, no sense wasting a perfect ticket, count me in; I've never disliked him, just never have been a live concert man."

"When you go down south to the Miami area, I'll go with you so I can get to Margaritaville."

At dinner, they discuss tomorrow's lunch with Mrs. Johnson. Roscoe suggests, "Be careful not to be too pushy, listen a lot, and you learn much more. My pa always told me I'd never learn anything with my mouth open."

"I thought I'd get it started by having her tell me about the children, how, when, all that stuff, and see where it goes. We won't have a lot of time, building her confidence in me is all I want to get started tomorrow."

"Sounds great, Maxine. Do you feel comfortable with this?"

"Yes, it's a new adventure for me; you coach me, and I'll do fine, I'm sure."

Chapter 17

Roscoe raises his glass and offers, "Happy New Year."

"Thanks," she says, "Is that the only toast you know?"

"The only one that never gets me in trouble."

"We're a couple of Jimmy Buffett's pearls."

"How so?"

"In one of his songs, the world is full of oysters but only a few pearls."

"Thank you for that nice compliment."

"You're most welcome."

On her way home, she comments on how nice it is not to think about driving home.

Maxine waits outside Martha's when Janet Johnson pulls her Mercedes to the valet station. They smile at each other, shake hands, and kiss each other on the cheeks.

"This is your find, Janet. I'll follow you."

"Your guess is as good as mine."

Janet leads to the marquee station, where a snooty-looking character wants to know if they need anything. Maxine tells her that I'm in charge and that there's a reservation for Peacock for two. With a finger acting like a wand, the effete one announces that there is one for the two birds and snaps his finger for a captain to escort the ladies to their table.

Once seated, they almost broke out laughing. It was a tremendous ice breaker, Maxine thinks. She couldn't have done better if she had planned for three weeks, and it wasn't her call, but she got a hint when she made the reservation yesterday. She had thought of taking Roscoe here, but didn't want to poison anything.

"Can you imagine the gall of that guy?" Janet says.

"Janet, I thought I would laugh in his face."

"Call me Jan, and if I remember correctly, you were always Max at school."

"That's true, but no one has called me that since. It's okay if you do."

Janet takes the lead.

"It seems almost funny, but I had the outside feeling the day we met at the Food Lion, but it wasn't a chance meeting."

"What do you mean, Jan?"

"I don't know. For the last couple of days, I felt that someone was following me, and then there you were, and no one was following me anymore. Do you think there's some connection, Max?"

"I haven't got any idea, Jan," Maxine's first lie; she continues, "Why do you think someone was following you?"

"Don't know, Max, maybe it's women's intuition or whatever. There was this house across the street, and some guy who drove a big Lincoln seemed to move in. I may be off my rocker, but I thought he was watching our house. A couple of times, my departures were his. Also, I never got a good look at him or the courage to go over there and confront him. He moved out, and my paranoia stopped. That's the frame of mind I was in when we bumped into each other; it was one of those times I knew he was behind me somewhere."

"Wow, that's some tale. Were you able to get a license plate number or anything like that?"

"I tried a couple of times, but I'm lousy with remembering numbers."

"Anything, a couple of numbers, the color of the car, the color of the hair, that kind of stuff."

"Just that it's a big Lincoln; I like the big cars, and those I remember, I can't help it." Relieved that the cover isn't completely blown, Maxine asks one more leading question.

''Did you check with the realtor to see the guy's name?"

"That I did, it turned out to be a dud, nothing real, I mean, phony as a three-dollar bill. So, you tell me, Max, would you be paranoid?"

"Absolutely," is all Maxine can respond to. She continued, "I was amazed to see you at that store; I just stopped to get some gum. Then, when I called and you blew me away, I figured I'd said something rude or something. I have a bad habit of being blunt, and sometimes people tell me it's like being rude; Mom always tells me that. She sends her love. I told her I bumped into you literally."

"How is she? I remember her as being pretty feisty."

"She's in great shape, always complaining that I don't come to see her enough. Your folks, are they still in the Northeast somewhere?"

"No, my mother passed six years ago, and my father went a month later."

"I'm sorry."

"Don't be. I was the youngest of five; they had full lives and weren't very young when they went."

Before they realized it was time for Janet to leave, they walked out together, promising to meet again next week. The food and prices were okay, as was the service, but the marquee was worth another trip.

Maxine was honestly flabbergasted. Roscoe will have a heart attack when he learns that the watcher is being watched. She stops and picks up a roasted chicken with the trimmings for dinner. Roscoe is busy at the computer when she walks in. "You're going to be perplexed by my report, Coach."

"How so? That smells good. What have you got with you?"

"Thought we'd munch on some BBQ chicken and beans."

As they eat, she relates what Janet told her about feeling that she was being followed when, in fact, she was.

"Now you see why I'm so paranoid about some things, like mailing, and even in her stakeout. While she felt my presence, I was cautious about exposing nothing but the car. The plates were phony, also. I don't think I ever mentioned that little detail."

"I never realized how difficult this kind of work is." She continued, "I think I've broken through to her, and I hope we can set a regular lunch date to 'catch up.' I called Mom earlier, before lunch, and mentioned she might want to inhabit my place for the duration, but I followed your advice and didn't mention any details over the phone. She said she'd be there this weekend."

"That sounds great, we'll all get together and formulate the next phase. I got one answer today from the mail-out. This one is hot to trot. We'll keep them all informed when the proper time comes."

A little gin was played, and some TV, and their second evening passed nicely. Roscoe had picked up a bigger automatic coffee maker; this one has a timer, so it will be ready for Maxine in the morning and still be warm when he gets up. He has gotten into the habit of leaving the tracking software with all the current devices active with a low-sounding beeper; nothing short of skipping town would be of interest to any of them. In the morning, Maxine informs Roscoe that the computer is beeping and won't stop. He checks the movement and sees the Mercedes has left the map area, and the Taurus is not at home either. The Lexus is home, and big George isn't in the picture and isn't sending a beeper signal. So, where are the Johnsons? He tells the software to center around the Mercedes. It's in the Orlando area, stopped at a Denny's on International Drive. Maybe it's no more than an excursion to one of many amusement parks in the Orlando area. Roscoe tells Maxine he'll call her when he discovers the destination of the Mercedes.

Maxine leaves for work, and Roscoe settles down to the serious work of finding the keys to the banks where the scumbag hides all the marbles. To date, he's located five accounts and passwords out of the twenty different accounts that Johnson has spread around the area, including several he's found offshore. He knows none of this will work unless he can absolutely cripple him financially. Until he's broke, and he knows it, he'll never be vulnerable enough to inflict the pain the women want him to feel. So, it's back to the grind for Roscoe.

Margie was pleased to get the call from Maxine, which means they're playing house, and that's okay. Moving into Maxine's will be all right for a while. Maybe she'll be able to get somewhere with the OR nurse. She called the Post Office and asked them to forward her mail until further notice. The carrier brought a form to fill out, which he waited for. Margie thought that was decent and made a note to be generous during the holidays. The rest of the utilities she'll leave on, the bills won't be big, no one to use them. She called the fella who trims the yard and had him come and do it, and paid him double, told him to check next time it needed it, and just do it. She told him she was going to be on holiday. She's been looking forward to seeing the 'kids' as she's begun thinking of them. She hopes they go to the place they had lunch at, it was a nice place. She makes a note to check with Roscoe concerning the security of the place.

Roscoe called Maxine, the Mercedes is in the parking lot at Universal Studios, and the Taurus is at the Condo with the Lexus. All's well and quiet; they got an early start. Maxine tells him Margie will be in her place this evening and wants to go to Floyd's for dinner. Roscoe suggested she pick her up on the way home, we'll have cocktails here, and then go to Floyd's for food.

"Sounds good to me," Maxine says and hangs up.

Roscoe gets the prints of Mary and the scumbag out to determine if they're good enough to scare someone into doing something they don't want to do. He reviews the tapes he has and prints several more, making sure he takes all the precautions. If Margie wants to go through with the Mary thing, they'll have a three-pronged attack plan in action. He spent several hours carefully thinking of all the possibilities that could present themselves to Margie when she confronts Mary. Having given it enough thought, he heads out to the store to replenish the liquor cabinet for the cocktail party he has planned for this evening. He goes to the mall and picks up three crystal decanters, a marble cheese board, and a good decorative knife. He then goes into the music store and gets the Jimmy Buffett CD with the song 'Changes in Latitudes, Changes in Attitudes' on it.

He's ready for the party. He'll be a bartender and probably a host, because Maxine doesn't know about any of this. When the girls arrive, they're almost taken aback. The lights are low, candles are giving off a glow, and over on the counter are decanters catching all the flickering light from the candles. There's what looks like an inverted cut glass bowl on the far end of the counter, also catching the candlelight. Jimmy Buffett's music is playing, and there's Roscoe smiling, saying, "Welcome to the party."

"What's the occasion?" Margie and Maxine ask almost in unison.

"Tonight" is all he offers. "Come on in and make yourselves comfortable," he adds.

Maxine comes close to Roscoe and says in a low voice, so Margie won't hear, "When did you do all this?"

"This afternoon, I wanted it to be nice for you and your mom."

"Well, you certainly did that. Can a girl get a drink around here?"

"You betcha, had to put cheaters on the gin bottles to separate the Beefeaters from the Tangary, the brown stuff was easy enough. Your usual, Ma'am? There's some ham rollups and cheese and crackers over there," he says, pointing to the other end of the counter.

The three of them settle down with some munchies and a drink. After a while, Roscoe gets up and says, "The real reason for having cocktails here versus Floyd's is this. I want the group to think and decide this evening whether we continue or disband, that would make dinner celebratory or consoling."

"I've come to this crossroads," he continues, "because my original time estimates have been totally blown, what I thought might take days is taking weeks, what I thought would take weeks is taking months. I don't want you two hanging around waiting for me with nothing to do."

Maxine speaks first, "My contact with Janet looks like it's going to take much longer than I thought to begin with, but I'm sure I will get through to her and get the information we need and want. I've spent a lot of soul searching recently, as you know, I'm not ready to dump it."

Margie chimes in, "If the bartender can refill my glass, I have something to offer also." Roscoe quickly gets up and, with a smile on his face, refreshes Margie's glass.

Margie goes on, "I'm here to investigate the Mary connection to see if that will bring us any benefits. I've moved from my home to be closer to the command center for this project, so don't go thinking that a little more time will be required; I'm going to fold. I've been waiting for this for many years; nothing will deter me now. How about that for an endorsement to continue? And Roscoe, remind me to ask you about the security at my place."

"Thank you both," Roscoe says. "I'll update you on what I'm working on. By my best guess, the matured values of his investments will exceed five hundred million." Both women give low whistles.

"I'm currently digging out the account details and discerning passwords for the diverse network he's set up to hide his funds. The names of his children will be needed to see if they got any blind accounts using their names."

Maxine reminds him that the child's name was Rosie. She adds, "That will be my next priority when we have lunch next week."

Roscoe refreshes Maxine and his glass, passes the cheese around, and then continues. "What I would like to set in place is a coordinated attack plan that will deprive him of all his access to the money. At the same time, we lower the other booms."

Both women nod their agreement.

After they finish their drinks, they all pile into the Town Car and go to Floyd's for dinner. On the way, Roscoe suggests that Margie stay with them tonight, mostly because he doesn't think he'll want to drive over to Maxine's place when dinner is finished. She agrees only on the condition that someone makes breakfast in the morning. Roscoe agrees that cereal is considered breakfast.

During dinner, Margie asks Roscoe some questions about himself. He says his standard bio as briefly as he can, but she probes deeper with every statement. He's not sure he wants to go in this direction, but he doesn't want his compatriots to think he's evading them.

"My life isn't exciting, really."

"We'll be the judge of that," Margie inserts.

"The most important and satisfying thing I ever did was get married; we were a great couple in love for the better part of thirty-three years together before that scumbag Johnson ended her life. I was a happy man all during those years. Of course, we had our ups and downs, but there was a tremendous imbalance in them on the high side. I met her when I was in grad school, and we became famous friends from the first moment, but you don't want to hear all this ranting."

"Every word of it," Maxine asserts.

"To pay for everything, I worked two jobs during grad studies; one job was at the steakhouse just off campus, and the other was at the campus library. The first time I ever saw her was in the library; she was book learning with a co-ed. Several nights later, I was waiting tables, and she and her friend sat at my station. She told me she remembered me from the library and that I was following her. I accused her of the same thing, and we had our first smile together. That moment I will always carry with me. I've had a lot of good ones, but that one has always been at the top."

Dinner was served, they all ordered the butt steak again with home fries, and Margie gave him a reprieve, "to be continued."

Chapter 18

They ate in pretty much silence. For dessert, he ordered for them a delight he taught.

Floyds to make just for him and anyone else who wanted it.

"Three brandied ices, please," he told the waitress.

They were served just the way he taught them, with flaming sugar cubes. Both ladies wanted more. He then told them that he had prepared a gallon of brandied ice cream in addition to fancy cocktails, and it was waiting at home. He even had sugar cubes to flame. He told them he was being presumptuous, but he was hoping it would be a celebration dinner, which it is.

As they finished their delicious, brandied ice, Roscoe had made, Margie told him to continue. He tried to beg off, but she insisted. She even told him that as long as she was staying here, she'd take over as bartender, "Nobody has to go to work early tomorrow, so let's keep going," she said.

So, Roscoe continues his litany.

"We had two children, a boy and a girl; they both grew up well mentally and physically, which I always felt was a parent's primary duty, in addition to loving them. The girl lives in New York, and the boy is on the West Coast. I've been thinking of having them down here for the Thanksgiving holiday. My birthday falls in that week every year, so it's my favorite holiday time. Whether I invite them or not, you'll get to meet them; it's just a matter of time. I'm getting tired. I'm going to turn it in," Roscoe finishes.

Margie says, "Thanks, Roscoe, but there's more I know. We'll continue again sometime."

Maxine and Margie keep each other company for a while. After all, Roscoe says, they don't see one picture of his wife anywhere, and Maxine says she doesn't think there's one anywhere. There are pictures of the children at various ages here and there, but none of Roscoe or his wife.

Margie wants to know everything; this time, Maxine gives her more than just crumbs.

"Like I said earlier, I'm in this long term. It didn't come easily for me, and Roscoe and I talked about it several times. He's never been pushy, and it wasn't he who asked to live in. I finally realized that I love him, and I don't want him to slip away because I'm afraid to make some changes. Neither of us has yet used the love word in each other's presence." Margie got up, joined Maxine, and gave her a warm motherly hug.

Roscoe was first up and got the coffee brewing, which he figured would wake Maxine. Then he had water boiling for Margie's tea. He also did breakfast shopping yesterday, anticipating Margie's demand for breakfast. Today, he will order hash browns, ham, eggs, rye toast, and raspberry preserves. He only cooks on weekends when there are no time constraints on anyone. Margie is the first woman to show up. "It smells good. Thanks for the tea."

She sits at the table and snuggles up with her hands around the steaming teacup. "Roscoe," she says, getting his attention. "I don't have any electronic security at my place, and I told two people that I wasn't going to be home for a while."

"You want me to go up there and set something up?" Roscoe asks.

"I don't know, what do you think?"

"I have always believed that 95% of the people we know are honest until allowed to be otherwise. You, Margie, have given these two the opportunity, in my estimation. So, yes, to answer my question, I think we should do something. After breakfast, we'll talk again."

Maxine comes into the kitchen, wondering what smells so good.

"I didn't know that cereal could smell this good," she chides.

Roscoe hands her a hot cup of coffee and kisses her.

"Ham'n eggs with hash browns and rye toast and jelly will be in the cereal bowls this morning, or would you rather have corn flakes?" he says.

"No, the first type you said sounds just fine," Maxine comments.

"Eggs to order this morning, Margie, you're first."

"Make mine scrambled?"

"Over medium will do me just fine."

Roscoe busies himself as a cook for the morning, careful not to burn the hash browns, beating eggs for Margie, toasting the toast, and heating the ham. Margie is served first, and she claims, "This looks great."

He serves Maxine and himself together, and they have an OK breakfast.

"Okay, Margie, let's talk about security in New Port Richy. I've been thinking, maybe we should take a camera and the van up there for the next week; I wouldn't think that anyone is going to do anything, it would be later than that."

"If you think that's good, let's do it," Margie agrees.

"Okay, after we clean up, we'll haul the van up north."

"Do you think the van will be safe all by itself, unprotected?" Maxine inserts.

"We'll hide it in the back; it just needs to be close to the camera; I'd leave it here, except there'd be no communication," Roscoe comments.

"Maxine, you can drive the Town Car, can't you?"

"I'm sure I can," she responds.

As they get everything set up at Margie's, Roscoe comments

"It's like fly paper. What are we doing here? I hope for all our sakes it's clean when we return. If somebody does get in, we'll catch him or her with the camera."

Roscoe was satisfied with the camera placement; he used both to be sure; he didn't feel he'd need either one in the coming week or weeks, and the same for the van. He was less concerned about the van than the cameras. He told Margie she was on for lunch since they were doing her bidding. She took them to a lovely little English-type pub, and they had authentic style fish 'n' chips.

On the ride back from Margie's after lunch, Margie renews her probe into Roscoe's life. "Why don't you continue, Roscoe? You left off telling us about the children."

"Well, you know I was an accountant for all my working years except Uncle. Sam owned me."

"Tell about the Uncle Sam part," Maxine says.

"I was very young, I'd just finished grad school, my deferments were all expired, and some strange-looking people with official credentials were nosing around a lot. They put it bluntly the last time I saw them. I could do it their way or the hard way. I did not want to find the hard way, so I took their way. Within the week, I was in Providence, Rhode Island, attending an indoctrination into the world of the Military, Naval intelligence, to be exact. I had to buy three uniforms, two I never wore, the blues and whites."

"I would have liked to see you in the pretty boy uniform," Maxine says.

"After two months of learning the Navy way of doing and not doing, eight other guys and I, pretty much like me, were hustled cross-country to Coronado, California, where they tried to kill us all. We spent another two months there, learning two things very well: how to stay alive and take life from another. I was taken to the island of Guam in the middle of the Pacific Ocean. It was here that I first met my team. Twelve highly trained men in all facets of modern warfare; during the next two years, we traveled all over South Asia doing things to people and places that I signed an oath never to tell another living person. That pretty much concludes my military story, except I'll say that I don't believe I've ever performed better at anything in my life. On my return, I left those twelve men in good health back on Guam. I met up with two of the guys I was with at Coronado, and they both had teams like I did, and neither one brought back all of their team. Once here in South Florida, I met one of my team members; he remembered me, but I didn't recognize him. He told me he got out a couple of years after I left; the new guy, he said, wasn't much fun nor nearly as professional, and the team suffered casualties during the next two years. He got out while the getting was good, he told me. He put rice paper in one of our new office buildings when I saw him. Said he got work hustling magazines by phone. It was good and got promoted fast. He oversaw the southwest territory, with 80 people reporting to him. Went home early one day and found his wife in bed with some guy. Calmly walked to the closet and got the 45 special he didn't have. Shot the dude between the eyes, took a bead between his wife's eyes, squeezed, and just nicked her ear. He said the State of California kicked him out without prosecution and just never came back, they said. That's more than I've ever said about that time before, sorry if I bored you."

"Are you nuts, boring? Hell, that is one of the most fascinating stories I've ever heard," Margie says, and Maxine gives a hearty second.

"How did California let him go like that?" Maxine wants to know.

"I asked that very question myself. He said the Navy interceded, and as long as his wife wasn't dead, they listed it as a break-in caught in the act of burglary. That's what he said; he couldn't believe how he ever missed his wife. His specialty was weapons. He could shoot the eyes out of a fly at fifty yards."

"That's got to be one of the wildest stories I've enjoyed listening to. Take us to Floyd's, I'm treating the driving storyteller to a drink," Margie announces.

Chapter 19

Monday morning, Margie presented herself at the volunteer desk of the Plant City Hospital. She inquires whether they have late afternoon or evening shifts. She's told that most of the work is done early, in the morning and afternoon. Margie tells the woman at the desk.

"I don't want to give up my days, but I will do my evenings. Since this is voluntary work, shouldn't I be accommodated?"

The woman stammers a little. She's never been in this position before and doesn't know what to do. She gives Margie a telephone number and suggests she call and talk to the supervisor. Margie thanks the woman and leaves. Some, but not much, progress was made today.

The woman's name on the card is Nancy Beggs, a local number. She calls Roscoe and asks if he can do some research on her. Roscoe calls, saying she lives with Mr. Beggs, about four blocks from the hospital. Margie calls Nancy and explains the same story she had told the woman earlier. Nancy says, "You have such a nice accent, Margie; I'm sure we can accept your offer to volunteer. Let me check our roster of volunteers and see what I can come up with for you."

Margie thanks her and hangs up.

Roscoe checks the locators he placed on the cameras at Margie's after she calls about the volunteer lady. No movement is good movement. Maxine calls to tell him she's scheduled for lunch tomorrow with Janet. He's become the central clearinghouse for this operation; he thinks about that for a while and likes the idea.

Mrs. Beggs calls Margie to congratulate her on becoming a volunteer pink lady for the 8-12 shift. Does she want the work? Margie says, "It's got the hours I asked for. What will my duties be?"

"I've got you penciled in to assist the unit coordinator."

"What's a unit coordinator?" Margie asks.

"It's the position that shuffles all the paper, the ones who keep the hospital rolling. From my understanding, you'd be doing some of her running, allowing her to get more done."

"Okay," Margie says, "When do I start?"

"We have an indoctrination this coming Thursday. If you make that, you could start Thursday evening."

"I'll be there on Thursday. Thank you, Nancy." Margie calls Roscoe with the news. "I'm a pink lady now," she tells him.

Maxine meets Janet at Martha's, and they get a good internal laugh at the host, which they acknowledge by winking at each other.

"How have you been this last week?" Maxine probes in friendship.

"I took the children to Universal for one day, and the rest of the week just happened."

"First time to Universal for any of them?" Maxine asks, hoping to get some names.

"First, for Rosie, Junior was there with his father last year." Janet volunteers without giving it a second thought. "I assume Junior is for his father's name?"

"Oh yeah, I guess I never mentioned his name; sometimes I try to forget it, which is why I always call him Junior."

"I'm sorry, Janet, I didn't mean to be nosey."

"It's okay, and I'm sorry I'm bringing doom to our second luncheon. So, how was your week?"

"Mostly same old stuff; mom is staying over right now and has a friend close to me she likes to visit occasionally. Work is work, boring men every day who all think they're God's gift to us."

"I've got a husband who knows he is and tries to prove it to everyone he meets. Let's get some strong liquor today; I've got a sitter with the children whom I can trust."

They get drunk and eat heavy food to try to work it off. They should have eaten before, but nobody can convince them at this point. They both have the intelligence to call a taxi to get home. Since their cars are there, Janet suggests they have lunch again tomorrow, and Maxine accepts wholeheartedly.

When Maxine waddles in, she tells Roscoe she has a great story to report, but she wants to call in sick for tomorrow and then crash. Roscoe can smell why she'll be sick tomorrow and calls her to take some aspirin before crashing. She thanks him for the thought and does take a few. He checks the coffee maker and adjusts the start time from six to eight. He sits back at the computer and continues his search. He's first up in the morning and gets a couple of aspirin and an ice bag ready for Maxine, thinking she might need them. When she makes the first sounds of life, he carefully sits next to her with aspirin and ice. When she can focus well enough, she whispers he's an angel, takes what he has to offer, and then requests he wake her no later than noon.

Maxine is first to Martha's and waits for Janet in the lounge, taking a little hair of the dog that bit her yesterday. Janet walks in looking as if she had never felt anything from yesterday.

"I want to do it again today, but I'm afraid to." Janet says, "I've got the sitter living in right now. My husband didn't come home until seven this morning with a very lame reason, but he believes that I accept them without question."

"Are you all right, Janet?" Maxine asks.

"Maxine, I'm so sorry I had any bad thoughts about you. I'm so happy to have found you again, so I can talk to someone without having to be so guarded."

"We were good friends once, and there's no reason we can't be again," Janet says.

Maxine pronounces, feeling a little guilty. They eat at the bar and leave after sharing many of their old memories, laced with current events, and promising to meet again next week.

Roscoe is dosing when Maxine arrives, filled to the brim with information to give. She realizes she hasn't been taking very good care of herself and lies down. Roscoe wakes and composes himself. He wakes

Maxine and tells her some startling news. One of the cameras has grown feet and left Margie's! He's got the phone on repeat and can't find Margie.

"Are you going to be sick again tomorrow because we have to get to Margie's place with or without her today? It'll mean a late night getting back," he says.

She makes the "I'm still sick" speech and tells Roscoe to let's go. He takes a mobile phone with him and keeps trying to call Margie. Halfway there, Margie answers. Roscoe briefs her and suggests she get home as fast as she can.

They wait for Margie in the van. Roscoe replays the time-lapse films the cameras were taking. Just before going blank on the missing camera, a very sharp image of a postal uniform appears. The other camera gets good images of the uniform and the face. Margie knocks on the door, and Roscoe replays the films for her.

"That S.O.B. and I were going to give him an extra at holiday time."

Roscoe switches to the tracking software to locate the wandering camera. He gets the address, and they take the van after Margie checks the house for what's missing: all the easily carried electronic gear, VCR radios, and the small TV she kept in her bedroom.

Roscoe finds the address, and the three of them discuss what to do. Roscoe decides to just walk up to the door and knock. If a woman answers, he'll just ask for the guy; if the guy answers, he'll start his spiel about how he's going to jail and all that. The women aren't sure but can't come up with anything better on the spur of the moment. So, Roscoe knocks on the front door, ready for anything, really, wishing he had a weapon right now to give him comfort. The face in the video answers the door. Roscoe, in his most belligerent voice and manner, says to him, "You're under arrest for the burglary you performed while in the uniform of a postal worker earlier today."

The face soiled himself; Roscoe could see and smell it. He asked him if anybody else was in the house, and the smelly one just shook his head negatively, indicating no. Roscoe then told him to clean himself up and not try anything funny because they knew all about him. The house was a virtual warehouse of stolen goods. Roscoe recovered the camera, VCR, radios, and the small TV and took two very nice notebook PCs for the trouble. The face was more than pleased to let Roscoe take what he wanted as long as he didn't blow the whistle on him.

Back in the van with the returned merchandise and the two PCs, Roscoe printed out the best pictures of the face and mailed the local postmaster a set. They returned the equipment to the house, reset the camera, and parked the van in the back again. Margie said she was staying here tonight but would be back for the pink lady indoctrination. On the way home, Maxine relayed Janet's story completely, leaving out nothing, including Maxine's own interpretations of some of the nuances. Roscoe comments that it sounds like Janet is indeed prime.

After being introduced to the staff of volunteers working with the new ones like her, Margie felt right at home. No one she meets will be working the same hours as she will. Nancy Beggs introduces herself, "I'm so glad to meet you. You said you'd be here, and here you are. As you can see, we get fewer and fewer volunteers these days."

"Will I meet the person I'll be working with now?" Margie asks.

"No, that won't happen until you actually get up to work, if that's tonight, ok, or tomorrow or next week; it's up to you; after all, you're a volunteer, and no one can order you around. I need to give you a key to our supply area. All the daytimers will be gone when you arrive in the evening, so I don't want you to wear your clothes. Just remember, don't wear the stripes, just the solid pink. The girl you'll be helping works on the ground floor at the OR nurses' station, and her name is Beatrice Jones, Bea for short."

"Thanks, that's a lot to remember," Margie says.

"I'm so sorry, Margie. I have it all written out here. Let me find it."

She rummages through her purse and produces a 3x5 card neatly printed with all the information she has just given Margie verbally.

"Will you be willing to start tonight?" Nancy asks.

"Yes, I've planned on it since we talked earlier this week."

"That's great, I'm sure Bea will be pleased as punch with your help."

She shakes Margie's hand and gives her the promised key.

Roscoe has configured the two notebooks he scammed off the postal crook to give to each of his compatriots. They may not like it, but it's time they joined the 20th century before it becomes the 21st as far as electronics are concerned. He plugged the Johnson children's names into his search queries to see what there was to see, and voila, he got hits immediately. Each of the children had trust funds established at birth, and neither parent can draw, but they can add. This is great news for Roscoe; his plan is coming together.

Maxine called and suggested dinner at Floyd's tonight. Sounds good.

Knowing that the evening staff reports at seven because of Roscoe's research, Margie is dressed in her pink uniform and mingling around the OR nurse station to get her first look at Mary. Bea spots Margie first, hard to hide in a pink dress, and introduces herself.

"Hi, I'm Bea. Nancy said you'd be here tonight, didn't expect you so soon."

"Well, you know, first day and all," Margie lies.

A young woman dressed in a nurse's uniform, matching the pictures she's seen wearing a name tag of M. Clement, walks into the nurse's station and asks Bea if anything is happening tonight.

"Nothing on the board yet, Mary, but meet my new slave, Margie."

Mary looks over and smiles, walks over, and warns Margie that Bea's bark is just as bad as her bite as she shakes her hand. Margie's thinking, the connection is made, and the beginning of the end has begun. Bea has Margie running all over the place for the next two hours. Mary catches her rounding a corner and mentions where the cafeteria is and that she'll be in there in about half an hour if Margie wants to join her.

Mary is sitting with another nurse when Margie enters the cafeteria, and Mary motions for Margie to sit with them. She introduces herself to the other nurse, who says she must return to the station and leave. Margie has her tea, and Mary drinks a Coke. They chat around each other, learning family stuff. Margie asks, "Do you have any sports interests?"

"Just fucking," says Mary as one would tell someone the time.

Margie smiles, and Mary laughs, "Thought I'd see if I could shock you, guess not. Did I offend you?"

"Surprised, yes; offended, no," Margie responds, wondering how shocked Mary will be when she looks at herself in the movies.

As Roscoe and Maxine are having seconds made by Bill, they both think about Margie almost simultaneously.

"Wonder how she's making out?" Maxine muses.

"I just hope they don't wear her out," Roscoe comments. Thanks to Bill for the round.

Around 11:30, Bea asks Margie if she would come in three nights a week.

"I'm sure I can, provided they're not Thursday, Friday, and Saturday."

"Oh no, I'm thinking Tuesday, Wednesday, and Thursday."

"That's fine with me."

Margie answers and asks if there's a phone she can call locally. Bea hands her the handset and tells her 9 to get out. Margie calls Floyd to see if the two lazy birds are still there. She's said they've left, she calls Roscoe's and gets the machine, "Pick it up, please."

But no one does; in her nicest voice, she suggests they get together tomorrow evening.

Maxine picks up Margie, and they all get together for cocktails at Roscoe's place. He makes libations for all and passes them out along with some yummies he picked up during the day, such as apricot nut rugalas, traditionally a morning food. Roscoe could eat them all day. Both women enjoy them and say so. Roscoe says after everybody's set, "Margie, you called this meeting. Do you want to start it?"

Margie relayed her conversation with Mary from the OR and her thoughts that she is a very naive person who loves her husband and thinks she can live a double life and escape it. Roscoe asks, "Do you think she'll react in our favor when the time comes?"

"I think she will miss her outside activity, even though she does it at home. Maybe we should play Cupid for her," Margie responds.

"Wow, that's a scary thought; I don't think I want to get into the pimp business," he says.

"I wasn't thinking of a pimp as much as the stud service," Margie adds.

"She seems not to like the physical side of her loving husband."

"Her job doesn't sound too demanding," Maxine inserts. "She could accommodate daytimers and a late night; it would appear."

"You two sound vicious. Listen to you, making decisions about another's love life without discussing it with her." Roscoe amusedly says, "It's certain we'll need to do some form of management regarding her physical wants. We will try to use her against her stud without any reward. Do you get what I mean?"

Maxine says, "I sure do. If she's getting it regularly from Johnson, then we are responsible for replacing it."

"We could always let her visit him in the poor house, couldn't we?" Roscoe tries to stay light. "I don't have a clue how to go about this," he says.

"I do," Maxine says assertively. "I work in a building full of them. They're constantly hitting on me, and I could string one along long enough to meet Mary and see what comes of it."

"Kind of like mating at the zoo," Roscoe throws in.

"Don't be part of the problem; we're trying to come to a solution," Maxine says, a little testy. Roscoe winks at Margie, who's playing bartender, and says, "Will that coming to a solution be an extra or just another hand job?" Maxine snaps around, stops momentarily, and laughs; the other two join in.

"When do you go back, Mom? Next Tuesday, did you say?"

"That's right."

"Okay, let's sleep on it before going any further. Are we going to get some food?"

"What's your pleasure?" Roscoe invites.

"Take me to Floyd's," Margie demands, "and what's for breakfast? I don't want to stay by myself tomorrow."

"How about some breakfast burritos ala Roscoe?"

"Never had one," both Maxine and Margie say.

"Then it's about time," Roscoe finishes with.

The jazz group is playing by the time they get to Floyd's, but they're lucky to have gotten a booth. They order quickly since the cocktails are over. Roscoe takes this time to get his two cents in.

"I realize we need to keep Mary happy to do our bidding. I don't want us to become linked to her; it could be a nasty arrangement if anything goes wrong. Big George is just that, Big George. My friends at Ricky's told me he could easily be a killer if Mary were at stake, if you get my drift."

Dinner is served, and all conversation is halted. After they finish eating, the waitress brings over three brandied ices.

"I'm never going to eat out again, except here. You have spoiled me rotten, Roscoe," Margie says.

When they get home, they scan the dish for a good movie, pop some popcorn, and get comfortable. Tonight, they catch 'As Good as it Gets,' one of the great ones. They all agree.

In the morning, Roscoe is busy preparing the burritos when the girls join him in the kitchen.

"Coffee, tea, and me," says Roscoe.

They sit down, pick up a knife and fork, and hold them upright.

"What kind of joint is this? No service," they say in unison.

Roscoe had turned around while they were saying this and smiled, "It's the no-frills kitchen. Didn't you see the sign on the way in?" as he poured coffee for Maxine and hot water for Margie.

"Breeders in a couple of minutes, they can be messy, depending on how you eat them," he warns. Almost like magic, he delivers each of them a wrapped burrito of egg, peppers, ground sausage, cheese, and salsa. Hold them straight up, suggest they keep them in that attitude, and eat top down. They're about halfway down, and he delivers two more. They look at him, bewildered; he motions for them to take these. Several minutes later, he joins them with two of his own to devour. Both women are amazed at how good the burritos are.

"Where did you learn to cook like this?" Maxine questions.

"I told you I like to cook; I just make such a megilla of it," he says, stretching his arm across all the pans he used to make breakfast.

After breakfast, Roscoe updates Maxine and Margie on his progress and gives them his new toys.

"I don't want this," Maxine protests.

"Neither do I," Margie adds.

"No questions. If you need lessons, I'll pay for them. If I try to teach you, we'll have bad blood. You need to learn email and stuff like that. The e-mail is encrypted, while the voice phone lines are still questionable, in my opinion. So, the discussion on this issue is over."

Mary is spending the weekend with Big George. They went to SeaWorld and stayed over in Kissimmee. She has told George about the pink lady who worked on Thursday.

"She seems nice, and I love her accent."

"If you're going to make friends with her, just remember: The last one just up and walked out when you thought she was becoming your friend," Big George reminded her.

"I don't like seeing you hurt," he tells her again.

He told her that from the first time they met. Mary hugs him and tells him she loves him, which she does, if only he could be a little more aggressive in bed. Big George suggests they head to the big water, and she agrees gleefully. They head to Singer Island on the East Coast.

Driving long distances comes to George like walking to the mailbox does to some.

Janet has taken the children and gone to Naples for the weekend. Anything to get away from that lying, cheating husband. She's suspected he at least took care to keep it out of the house all these years. He broke the camel's back the other night when the hospital called to locate him, and he didn't get home until seven in the morning, blaming a hectic run on the ER. She didn't confront him. She didn't want this on his terms. She was happy to meet Maxine then; she was like a shining ray or something. She can tell her anything and not worry about her telling anybody who cares, and she's looking forward to lunching next week.

Margie reports to work early; she has been an early arrival all her working years, and she doesn't know another way. Bea is waiting for her.

"It's sure nice to know someone will be here when they say they will be. It's been my experience that it's mostly lip service, not clockwork. I stockpiled plenty for you to do if you're ready, Margie."

"I'm as ready as ever," Margie replies.

She takes the stack of work and begins to make the rounds. About halfway through her stack, she finds herself heading to the ER. When she gets to the coordinator's desk, she spots the scumbag leaning on the counter, talking to one of the nurse assistants sitting at the desk behind the counter. It's the first time she's laid eyes on him, and her initial feeling is to attack him. She takes a deep breath, composes herself, and delivers without saying a word. She's surprised that there isn't any activity in the ER. Margie asks Bea, "There isn't much activity in the ER here, right?"

Bea responds, "We're not a Trauma Center, so we didn't get the first call. The EMS dispatchers only use us when overloaded, mostly on weekends."

When she gets back to the OR, Mary is there. Margie asks Mary how she is.

Mary smiles and says, "I'm just fine, thanks. Do you want to join me during break time?"

"It would be my pleasure."

Mary enters the cafeteria while Margie gets tea, so she grabs a soda. They sit at a table by themselves. Mary says, "We went away for the weekend, George and I."

"Where to?" Margie asks.

"Friday, after I got home, George told me he had reservations in the Orlando area, and we left immediately. Saturday, we went to SeaWorld, that whale is something, then we went to Singer Island and got back early this morning, so George wouldn't be late for a pick-up."

"That sounds like a week of traveling to me."

"We don't do it often, but we go when George wants to take off."

"That sounds so romantic."

They finish their refreshments and head back to work. Mary tells Margie, "I enjoy talking with you. Would you like to come over and visit sometime?"

"I don't know, Mary; I'll see you tomorrow night."

Margie gets up bright and early and calls Roscoe after her first cup of tea.

"She wants me to visit her house," she tells Roscoe. "What do you think of that?"

"I'm not sure, Margie. Why don't we meet somewhere for breakfast, and we can discuss this?"

"Fine with me, where's a good place? I'm not all that familiar with this area."

"Let's go to Lenny's; it's right by you. I'll pick you up in half an hour." It's about 40 minutes by the time Roscoe shows up.

Margie gets in and apologizes, "I'm sorry, Roscoe, I forgot about not talking about business on the phone."

"No damage done, but I'm glad you're thinking about it."

While they're waiting for food, he asks, "If you go with her, what will happen?"

"Don't know, but I think it would be nothing but girl stuff; I'm probably a mother figure to her, and she doesn't even realize it."

"Well, I'd string it out until next week. Her rendezvous with Mr. Scumbag is going to be tonight or tomorrow. I checked their whereabouts on Monday, and they both went home separately last night. If they were on for tonight and you said okay to your girl, it might put her in an awkward place. I'll check again tonight; they seem to have a pattern; if it's Monday this week, Tuesday next week, and so on."

"Maxine should be meeting Janet this afternoon. That was a close call, wasn't it?" Margie tells Roscoe.

It was a perfect idea to have Mom stay at my place, Maxine thinks as she drives to Martha's. Monday evening, Janet called to say she couldn't make lunch. Tuesday was okay, and Wednesday was okay, and Mom was there to take the call—lucky for us. Janet waits for Maxine in the foyer and enters the dining room together. Janet looks a little distraught.

"Are you okay, Janet? Something must be bothering you."

"Is it that obvious? I'm having some trouble at home, if you don't mind putting up with me."

"That's what friends are for," Maxine says and believes in herself; this is the hard part for her, but she's decided to stick it out.

"Children or otherwise."

"Otherwise, he always kept it out of the house, but it jumped right in last week with both feet, wearing biker boots. It was so bad, I took the kids and went to Naples for the weekend, came close to calling you to see if you might want to join me. I was surprised to find your mother still with you."

"Yeah, she decided to stay a little longer; it's one of those good times, bad times if you know what I mean?"

"I think so."

"Anyway, I would have enjoyed the trip, but maybe not the company," she lies. "By the way, let me give you my mobile number, just in case you want to talk to somebody instead of something like a machine."

"Thanks, I appreciate that," Janet says. I'm not sure what I'm going to do, Maxine. All my instincts tell me to scream and run, but I know I can't. If I let him know I will do something, I'll be outside looking in with the children, a half-paid car, and half a house. He'd make it happen so fast I don't want to think about it."

"Do you have anybody you can turn to?"

"I'll hire a good divorce lawyer, I know a good female one, and she loves her work. This is such a small town, I'm afraid to call her, lest the word leaks out somewhere and Jason finds out."

"That's his name?" Maxine slides in, positive. Janet has never used it since the meeting. "Yeah, I thought you knew that for some reason. Maxine, would you mind terribly if I asked you to make the call for me and set up a meeting, maybe the three of us, for lunch next week, he knows I am coming here for lunch already, but he hasn't mentioned with whom I'm having it with though, probably feels since it's not a man it doesn't matter. I've never given him cause or reason."

"Can I think about that overnight, Janet? I mean, I've grown into a cautious person. I always like to sleep on major decisions, and this is one of those."

"It's okay with me; I'm the one asking, and I'll buy tomorrow whatever way you decide. Want to know how I know he knows I'm coming here?"

"Yes, I do," Maxine says, genuinely intrigued.

"I've had him followed for the last year on an intermittent basis. The firm I use is the same one he uses. I told you this is a small town since I was first and pays more, the guy that works for me has never told them about our relationship, so he gets to see the reports about me, but they don't get to see mine of him, so he says."

"That's wild. What a double-dealer your guy is." They finish lunch by agreeing to meet again the next day.

Maxine is just about through briefing Roscoe on the lunch today when she says, "You think I should agree to be her go-between?"

"Maxine, I don't want to sound strong, but we couldn't have asked for a nicer platter than this. If her lawyer is half good, we'll get her to do all the dirty work and feed her everything one way or another. If she's as good as Janet feels, he won't have a pot to piss in when she's tough. We'll get our objectives met and stay in the background completely. My fingers are crossed that this gal is good at choking the blood out of turnips. He'll never know what hit him. Janet won't ever know it was her long-lost friend, Maxine, who allowed it all to happen. Maxine, this is the stuff they write books about." He makes them both a toddy and toasts to their success.

Chapter 20

He fills Maxine in on Margie's night, and Maxine just shakes her head slowly from side to side.

"It's almost mind-blowing, thinking about four women so wound up with one useless man, all conspiring to reduce him to rubble," she says.

Continuing, she tells Roscoe, "I got the Jimmy Buffett tickets today; still want to accompany me?"

"A deals, a deal; I said I would, and I will; when is it?"

"Saturday night."

Maxine is in the lounge at Martha's, and her pocketbook begins jumping.

She realizes it's her phone and answers, "Hello."

"Maxine?"

"Yes, is that you, Janet?"

"Yes, I'm terribly sorry, but I can't make it today. Can I rain check for tomorrow?"

"I don't see why not. Is everything all right? Can I do anything for you?"

"You're doing it; I'll see you tomorrow."

Maxine detests eating alone, so she calls Roscoe and tells him she'll be at Floyd's within half an hour if he'd care to join her. Roscoe is waiting at the bar when she walks in. He can't help it, but he thinks back to when he first met Maxine, which was lucky for him. He orders Maxine's drink and tells Bill to have one, too.

"What's the occasion?" Bill asks.

"Just feeling good today, is all."

Lunch is on for tomorrow, she tells Roscoe. She doesn't have a clue and couldn't get a good enough read from her phone's voice to decide. Roscoe says, "That's too bad. If she gives you the lawyer's name tomorrow, you'll have to wait until after the weekend to call her. What I mean is, if she gives the name to you during lunch, grab the cell phone and call. I just don't think you'll make contact on a Friday afternoon," Maxine agrees, and she signals Bill for another round.

It's Margie's first full week of volunteering, and she can see why many people don't take to it. It's more complicated than it looks; knowing she has to be in uniform later takes the edge off her days. They better be ready to turn Mary in by next week. She's not sure she wants to do much more of this; she's getting too old to be working, even if it's for a good cause. Big day for Maxine tomorrow, she thinks, and a good dinner at Floyd's, Roscoe promised after cocktails at his place; it's getting to be a habit she likes.

This time, Janet is waiting for Maxine, "Thanks for the rain check, Maxine. Business first: Will you or won't you? I want to know so I can decide if it's sober or otherwise."

"Yes, I will!"

"Great."

Janet reaches into her purse and produces a folded piece of paper with her name and number on it. Maxine doesn't even look at it. She gets the phone out of her purse, punches the numbers in, and stores them in the phone's memory.

"Law offices" is the crisp answer.

"Harriet Suzanne," Maxine asks.

"I'm sorry, Ms. Suzanne is out until Monday," Roscoe was right, Maxine thinks as she tells Janet.

"Monday, I'll call you as soon as I know."

"No, I can wait until lunch. Make sure she understands. She needs to be discreet, and she must meet us at Martha's on Tuesday."

Maxine nods her head approvingly. Janet orders another drink, telling Maxine she got her answer just the way she hoped she would. Maxine must coast, it's going to be a very long day for her. Maxine couldn't believe how ragged her Mom looked when she picked her up.

"Mom, you've got to quit. This looks like it's killing you."

"Just a couple more days, Hun; we'll discuss it tonight."

"You bet we will, and we're not running a slave camp here."

Roscoe is not prepared for the dynamic duo that walks in tonight, even with Jimmy Buffett music; it is somber.

"This looks like doubles or nothing," he says.

"Doubles for me."

Margie gets in before her sourpuss daughter can get a word in edgewise. Roscoe, sensing doom, quickly makes a drink for Margie, one for Maxine, and one for himself. Today it's aged New York cheddar and wheat thins for the hors d'oeuvres, which he passes around briskly. He says to no one but aimed directly at Maxine, "Is everything all right tonight?"

"I'm fine and ready for a good dinner," Margie sneaks in. Maxine finally speaks: "I'm just concerned, is all. I want to have a good time tonight and a great time tomorrow night. When I looked at you, Mom, I got a little shaken. I don't think I've ever seen you strung out like this before."

"I'll be okay; Roscoe told me I should quit when we had breakfast the other day; he could see the strain in me then. I told him then, and I'll tell you now. I haven't come this far carrying this cross to toss in the towel; if I collapse, my only request is don't, under any circumstances, allow me to be taken to the Plant City Hospital. Can I have another drink, please? That was the weakest double I've ever had." Maxine relaxed for the first time today.

"So, how was lunch?" Roscoe asks.

"I'll tell you all about it at dinner."

"That's it," Roscoe says. "All anybody wants is food, so let's go."

When they're all set at Floyd's, Maxine begins, "You were correct, Roscoe. The lawyer wasn't available. Janet wants me to be her go-between, make the appointment to be with her at the meetings, the whole nine yards."

"What's this 'whole nine yards' thing? American football is ten," Margie questions.

"It's a construction term," Roscoe inserts, "it deals with the amount of concrete in a rotating drum of the mobile concrete delivery trucks. If you were a contractor buying concrete from a jobber, you would want the 'whole nine yards' delivered when you had already paid for it."

"Anyway," Maxine continues, "she wants the first meeting to be our Tuesday lunch. Janet also told me she has had her husband tailed on and off for a year and knows he's having her tailed, too. What do you think about that?"

"A trusting group if I ever heard of one," Roscoe comments. In my surveillance, I haven't noticed anyone milling around beside me. If they know about me, they won't be able to identify us. Your lunch should be enjoyable. Remind me to see what there is to see about the lawyer."

"Margie, let's discuss Mary," Roscoe continues. Next week, they will meet on Monday if our observations are correct, which means she'll be available for your visit any night you're scheduled."

"Can we do it on Tuesday? I'm really tired of wearing pink," Margie pleads.

"Do you think she'll honor her offer on Tuesday?" Roscoe inquires.

"I had the feeling she would have the night she first asked me, so I think all I have to do is say okay."

"Then let's do Mary next Tuesday. Are you up to it? What if she turns sour?"

"I don't feel she will. We have a very good profile on her. I think she'll be shocked to find out others have been nosing around her private life."

"Do you think she'll be able to do what we want?"

"I'm pretty sure I can make her believe me."

"Then it's set for Tuesday evening. You'll stop by our place on your way in, and I'll give you the package. Afterward, you come back to our place, no matter what time it is. Brief me. I'll include a mobile phone in your package with my number taped to it. If you need to call, don't hesitate."

Chapter 21

"Wow, I can hardly believe it's begun. All the planning is over. I didn't tell you how I felt the other night when I first got to see him. My first reaction was to do him harm. I wanted to walk over and swing a baseball bat at him, but I couldn't find one," Margie unloads. All this happened before they ordered, so Roscoe ordered Gazpacho for the group as an appetizer. They will also have more brandied ice for dessert tonight.

Maxine felt a little silly. She told Harriet she'd find a yellow hat so she would be easily recognized. Standing out on the walkway in front of Martha's, she felt vulnerable.

Harriet came up beside her without Maxine seeing her, "Maxine, I'd know you anywhere," Harriet said quietly.

Maxine spun around and smiled, "Harriet?"

"Yes."

And they shook hands. Maxine immediately took the yellow hat off and jammed it in her purse. Harriet was very business-like. She wore a dark gray pin-striped suit with a green silk scarf around her neck. She wore low heels in an expensive-looking leather shoe. Her eyes were steel-cold blue, and her severe blond hair was pulled straight back in a bun. "I signed out for the afternoon based on what you told me."

Harriet says, "Good, let's get inside; the marriage is a real joke for Janet and me; see if you agree," Maxine says as they enter, and she announces their reservation. As they're seated, Harriet has a grin on her face.

"I wholeheartedly agree with you both on that one," she says. Maxine orders her usual, and Harriet has ginger water.

Harriet begins, "So, how long have you and Janet known each other?"

"We were classmates at NYU so many lifetimes ago. We just bumped into each other about two months ago, and since then."

"You must have been very close to doing this for her."

"I don't know for sure. Maybe we're just two ports in a storm about to happen, and we know we can lean on each other."

"Nice to have friendships like that."

Janet shows up at the table, puts out her hand, and introduces herself to Harriet.

"May this acquaintance be very beneficial for us both," Janet says as she shakes Harriet's hand and sits at the table.

Janet orders a drink and, while waiting, says, "I only have two questions for you. How much and how long?"

"This lunch is on the house, fee-wise. I'm $50 an hour in research, $75 an hour in conference, and $150 a half hour in court. No matter who picks up the lunch tab, the next lunch is a conference for billing purposes. The State of Florida governs the other, and they're very kind to the state of marriage. What's yours is mine if you get my drift. It's a 50/50 state. Is there a prenup?"

"Do you work for wages?"

"Do you hold any measurable amount of anything that is liquifiable?"

"No."

"Did you ever enjoy being married?"

"Yes."

"Okay, I'll stop when I get my first yes answer. We're going to do everything alright, you and I. I checked the public records before coming over and found he's in good graces with everybody but you."

"What's that supposed to mean?"

"All that means is he's got all the wrong people happy with him. If he kept you happy, the rest wouldn't matter, and I wouldn't be eating lunch with you today."

Later, after the lawyer left, Janet asked Maxine, "I'm going to ask for another very personal favor from you. I'm somewhat paranoid about Jason finding out about all of this. I'll arrange it with Harriet if you can continue to be my go-between if you'll agree."

"What is it you have in mind, Janet?"

"Nothing much, really; when I have some material to get to her, you deliver it; when she has some for me, you pick it up. We'll use lunch as our exchange point. I'll get a big enough bag to carry those big envelopes, and I'll get one for you; that way, neither of us will be seen carrying any papers."

"That seems harmless. I'll say yes right now. I'll let you know if there's something I'm not aware of that might change it."

That evening, Roscoe is ecstatic over their good fortune.

"We'll be able to load Harriet up with whatever we want!" he tells Maxine. "When she gives you something to give to the lawyer, you bring it here first, and we'll review it. If we have better or supplemental information, we'll replace or add it to hers, and then you take it to the lawyer."

"What if she follows me or has me followed?"

"Good question. Here's how we'll get around that one. I'll be in Martha's parking lot every time you have lunch. Call me when you get something, and I'll follow you to see if anybody else does and call you if there is. If there is, you drive to your place and wait until I can get a make on who's following you."

"Even if there is, how will we get to look at the information she's passing?"

"You're just full of good questions. Make us a drink while I think this one through."

The doorbell rings. Roscoe checks the peephole and sees the pink lady out there, sans the pink. Opening the door, he motions Margie in.

"Hi, Mom," Maxine waves.

Roscoe beckons her to sit and relax for a moment. He enters the locked cabinet and takes out a manila folder and a phone.

"Here's the package. Don't touch the inside of the folder with your hands. Slide the material out, and you keep the folder. At that point, you can fold it up and stick it in your purse. Please don't leave it with the material inside."

"Okay?"

Margie nods in acknowledgment.

"The material is the same as you've already seen; there's no surprises in there."

Margie gets up to go, and Maxine comes over to give her a big hug and wish her good luck. Margie gives Roscoe a wink and leaves.

Roscoe looks at Maxine and says, "We've got a lot to discuss and work out before you meet with Janet again."

Maxine just shakes her head up and down, indicating she's both understanding and ready.

Chapter 22

Margie arrived ahead of time as usual and began her rounds of deliveries that Bea had left for her to do. When she returned to the OR station, Mary leaned against the counter; Bea wasn't to be seen.

"Mary, the other day, you mentioned getting together sometime. Do you still want to do that?"

Margie asks Mary, "Sure, would tonight be too soon for you?"

"Tonight would be fine."

"Great, I get off at one. I'll tell them I don't feel good at eleven and leave when you get off at midnight. That is, unless we get some action. That's something I want to talk to you about. I'll see you at break time."

"Okay," Margie responds.

At break time, Mary slips a piece of paper to Margie.

"That's got my address and phone number on it," Mary tells Margie.

"What about you want to talk about the OR, Mary?"

"Not here, I'll tell you later."

Another nurse joins them, and all conversation about the meeting after work stops. Mary had indicated she would be free at midnight.

Margie thought it funny that Mary had given her the address and phone number when she already had them. She got to the condo at half past the hour and saw Mary's Lexus parked with nobody in it. She figured Mary must be inside already. When she got to the door, Mary was waiting inside.

"Thought this would be easier than finding the name and ring and all that, you look so much more like a person without those pinks on."

"Thanks on both accounts," Margie tells Mary.

Once inside the condo, Mary asks Margie if she wants something to drink as she's mixing one for herself.

"Tangary and tonic if you have it."

"Coming right up. I'm going to change out of this monkey suit," she says as she hands Margie her gin and tonic. Mary returns virtually naked, wearing only skimpy panties.

"I like to be comfortable in my own house."

"It's your house."

Margie manages without choking on her words. Margie hopes she doesn't make any moves on her; she wonders if she can out-muscle her if she has to. Taking a deep breath, Margie says, "So tell me this mysterious OR story."

Mary lounges in an easy chair; she has a young body most men would die for, with round, firm breasts standing straight to attention; she has an allover tan unless there's any white skin under those panties. As if they were chatting in the break room, Mary relays the story about when the OR was all geared up for an incoming, and nothing happened. When she inquired, she was told the incoming had died in the ER of heart failure. Margie almost choked on those words.

"Did you find out more about it?" Margie asked, leading because Mary must be concerned, or she wouldn't have brought it up earlier.

"I checked with ER and was stonewalled; it made me angry. We had to prep up, which comes from our budget if we can't charge it to a patient. So, I checked the records and the ambulance service that delivered the patient to us."

"What did you find out?"

Margie didn't want this to stop on any technicalities.

"Our records just showed it was a Mr. Alfonso P. Stephano of Tampa, and the ambulance said they were routing him to Tampa General when they got a call from dispatch to haul him out to Plant City. They also said the guy was stable from a food disorder. When I asked who ordered the OR, they said they sure didn't."

While Mary relayed this story, Margie slipped the folder from her purse.

Margie asks if more is known: "How could a stomachache turn into heart failure and death?"

"I've never been able to find out; when I asked some people, I got nasty answers, and one told me not to meddle in areas that didn't concern me. My budget was still hit for all the prep work, and I'm told to shut up and let it go. I still get angry when I think about it. I'm sorry I've burdened you with this, but I wanted to tell someone who might understand, and you seem like someone who would."

After all that, Margie is almost feeling guilty about what she's to do, but not quite.

Mary is still in the lounging chair when Margie makes her move.

"Mary, that's quite a story, and I think you have picked the right person to listen to it; I know you have. I have something I want you to look at."

With that, Margie slides the folder contents onto the side table beside her. Mary gets up and walks over, and she halts as soon as she sees the top picture.

"What's going on here?" she says, looking Margie straight in the eye. What Margie can't take her eyes off are Mary's nipples. They got rock hard as soon as she looked at the top picture. Mary picks up the remaining print images and leafs through them. Margie can see the understanding overcome Mary. She takes the pictures over to the couch, spreads them out, sits on the floor, and looks at each one very carefully. Mary finally says after studying the prints.

"If you've been sent to spy on me for the hospital, please leave my house; if not, I think you owe me an explanation."

The phone rings as Mary finishes her statement. She gets up to locate her cell phone, and Margie is sure she won't leave at this point; she has to get to an endpoint before leaving, so she settles in for the duration of the call. Mary sits back in the lounger, pulls the lever that leans back, and brings up the lounger portion. Margie hears her cooing into the phone.

"Sure, honey, I've got a handful of tit."

Which she does. Mary continues to talk and fondle herself, and Margie realizes she's giving someone phone sex.

Mary says, "Yes, Big George, tell me, do you have your big hand on your cock? That sounds so good, lover."

Margie now assumes she's talking to her husband, George, and wishes she could be anywhere but here, but she can't take her eyes off Mary and understand it. Margie watches Mary play with herself and feels something she's never felt.

She hears Mary say, "Yes, Georgie, I'm all wet for you."

Margie notices Mary is indeed wet with her hand massaging her pussy. Without the slightest comprehension or belief, Margie finds herself standing next to Mary's stretched-out body, and she gently removes Mary's panties, sliding them down her long tan legs and pressing them to her face. Mary catches Margie's eye and smiles at her as she's licking the long finger on her free hand, which she plunges into her pussy all the while whispering sweet nothings into the phone. Margie shakes herself into the now and places the panties between Mary's wiggling feet; she gets herself back to the chair she was in and continues to watch the Mary show; Mary starts to moan and arches her back, and then starts panting into the phone and finally screams and sets the phone down. Margie was stunned; she had just witnessed a grown woman masturbate and bring herself to an orgasm, something Margie had done in the privacy of her own home but never in another's company.

She liked it, and she knew it.

Mary returns the chair to its upright position, the panties fall to the floor, and she says matter-of-factly, "Thanks, I like to lounge around with nothing on."

She curls herself up into the chair.

"Did I embarrass you, Margie?"

"I'm not sure; I don't think so; this was a first for me."

"Well, thanks for not running out of here. I had another gal up here once, and I frightened her so much she ran out crying. Let's talk about these pictures. I asked you to leave if you were from the hospital, and you didn't leave, so let's talk. What do these mean?"

Margie is still trying to come to grips with looking at a naked woman lounging so casually within the same room she is in. She takes a deep breath and responds, "Some people I'm associated with are in a consortium to defrock Dr. Jason V. Johnson. He has committed several crimes by the consortium's definition. You described one this evening that would need investigation. You became noticed by this group when Dr. Road drove in your car. The pictures you have were obtained over several weeks."

"Okay, remember I told you the first night we met that I liked to fuck? I wasn't kidding; that's why I have anything to do with Jason. I think he's a liar, and I know he's a cheat. Tonight, you're telling me he might be a murderer; it makes me cold to think about it. We were in bed last night. You see, Margie, my husband George is a wonderful man but a terrible lover, he likes the phone stuff but can't do it live as hard as he tries and wants. I satisfy my needs outside without Big George's knowledge and plan to keep it that way. If he knew about Jason, he'd probably kill him."

"Mary, you don't have to give me any reasons or apologies. Your business is your business."

"But what will I do with this information you've just given me?"

"Well, I'm in the same boat; I don't know what to do with all the sensations you've given me."

"Did you like what you felt?"

"Yes, I didn't understand it, but I did and still do; I find looking at you like this very enjoyable."

Mary gets up from the chair and walks over to Margie's seat. She sits on the floor at her feet. Margie is wearing a pantsuit with a blouse and is all buttoned up. Mary slides a hand up one pant leg, and Margie shudders. Margie says, "I'm old enough to be your grandmother, Mary!"

"This, what I'm doing, has nothing to do with age. Does it feel good or bad?"

"Then forget about the age thing and relax and enjoy it."

Mary snuggles closer, keeping her hand up the pant leg, and lays her head in Margie's lap. With her other hand, she unzips Margie's pants, and Margie lets out a swoon she didn't know she had. Mary says, "Someday I'll show you what I do to that banister there."

Margie responds with, "What's wrong with tonight?"

Mary almost jumps to the challenge and gets up, walks over to the stairs, walks up about halfway, flips her leg over, and gives Margie a show she almost can't believe. Involuntarily, Margie feels herself cum and moans with delight. Mary hears her and rolls back onto the stairs and begins fondling herself to reach an orgasm of her own. Margie gets up and undresses, not feeling the least bit self-conscious. Mary gets up and comes back to Margie, now standing as naked as Mary, and embraces her, takes her hand, and leads her upstairs to the bedroom. Mary gently tells Margie she has never been with another woman in bed, so they will learn as they go. Later, when they've spent each other again and again, Margie comments that she's never been so satisfied in all her life. She also comments that she enjoyed watching Mary as much as touching Mary.

Mary gives her a firm embrace and says, "We don't ever have to give this up if we don't want to, Margie. I'll strip for you, masturbate for you, masturbate you for you, get a dildo, anything we want. This can be our world if we want it to be."

"I want it to be very much."

Margie squeezes Mary's behind. They agree to keep their arrangement private. Margie makes a mental note to ensure Roscoe hasn't put a tracking device on her car. Margie tells Mary she won't return to the hospital as a pink lady; she'll call Nancy Beggs tomorrow and say she is ill. As far as the doctor is concerned, Mary agrees to continue seeing him until Margie tells her otherwise.

"Maybe I can give him a disease or something; I get him in some very compromising situations," she says.

Margie tells her that it might not be a good idea.

Margie retrieves her clothes and prepares to leave; Mary, still as naked as a jaybird, accompanies her to the door. "When will we get together again, my love?"

Mary coos into Margie's ear.

"Soon, very soon, maybe you can come to my place during the day."

"Maybe, we'll see, but let's make it soon, wherever."

Margie leaves feeling happy, sad, and fulfilled. She reminds herself not to mention the good side of Mary to Roscoe and Maxine when she gets there.

Chapter 23

It's almost 5 AM when she knocks on Roscoe's door. He's up and opens the door on the second knock. He motions that Maxine is sleeping and is anxious to hear everything. She tells him it was a tough sell. Mary was angry at first, but came around and will continue to see him until we ask her to stop. Then Margie tells Roscoe the surprise.

"He's killed again, Roscoe."

She gives him the name and date, and she can see the light bulbs going off in his head. He says, ''I'll have to double check, but if I remember, about a million dollars was dispersed across his network of banks about that time."

They both look at each other like the Earth had just been discovered.

"What do you think that means, Roscoe?" Margie asks.

"I can't be sure, but I believe he's in the employ of others besides the hospital. I've encountered patterns in deposits that usually indicate laundering of some sort. It didn't hit me until you said this today that I should correlate deposits to deaths. I just thought he was grossly incompetent! You must be exhausted. Do you want to crash here?"

''No, I'll get to Maxine's before the morning rush begins. I left the pictures with Mary, and here's the folder."

She reached into her purse, saw a note on top of the folder, and was careful not to let it slip. She hugs Roscoe, kisses him on the cheek, and tells him to get some rest. There is a lot to do now; things are falling into place. Margie leaves and, while driving back to Maxine's, can't wait until she can read the note. Just thinking of her evening with Mary sends chills down her body. The note is sweet, it reads.

"Thanks, Margie, let's do it again and again and again. Love you, Mary."

Mary is lying in bed, still thinking about everything that has happened since she left work last night. The news about Jason didn't startle her as much as she would believe if someone told her cold, or if she read it in the paper, or saw it on the news. And Margie, what a wonderful lady, wouldn't have begun to think any of what they did together could have been possible. She makes a mental note to pick up several dildos, including one that straps on. They can take turns being the man; She feels glad for the first time in a very long time. She hopes that Margie can keep up their newfound friendship. Sleep finally takes over, and Mary rests better than she has in several years.

Roscoe can't sleep, not with all the new information to check. It's like he hasn't even started, and he's been at it for several months. Football will begin in a few weeks, so he must remember to talk to Maxine about that. Well, he went to the Jimmy Buffett concert and enjoyed it. Maxine can handle some gridiron action, but he must remember to talk to her about it. This is almost unbelievable; a death also accompanied a deposit, but not the other way around. There were more deaths than deposits. Did he do it for fun or to hide the others? These were terrible thoughts, he felt. If any of this is true, they've uncovered a diabolical, sinister plot to kill people of someone's choosing right under the noses of everybody except M & R. Roscoe feels a chill. Are they biting off more than they can chew, or is he just being paranoid because he's tired? He decides to sleep on it and recheck it all again later.

Jason is sitting in a room in Essex, on the south side of Central Park in New York City. He doesn't like being summoned by these goons, but he knows they own him, and the perks are good. The bottle of Glenlivet is gone, and he ordered another, but that was two hours ago, and it hadn't arrived yet. They had probably left instructions; they always do. All he did was tell them that some people had been asking about his last job, and he didn't like it. They were supposed to insulate him. It was bad enough that he had to move so many times and take menial work to keep them happy. He knows he could have been the best surgeon in the world if they hadn't moved in and taken over. They did it to his Father, and now they're doing it to him. The damn government, they always say it's for the better good. Fuck them and the boat they rode in on. He leaves the room, finds an open liquor store, and buys two bottles of the golden scotch. He doesn't see the shadow men who follow him in every move. He returns to the room and opens one of the bottles, and the world is beginning to sort itself out again as he takes a long drag right from the bottle. Later, these shadows will enter the room, and unknown to Jason, he will report everything he knows, and when he wakes up, he'll think it is just a scotch-induced hangover. These little reporting sessions happen about every six months or so.

The shadows don't like him to get too confident.

Maxine rushed home after work, Mom unplugged the phone, and she didn't want to disturb her. She hollers, "Hello, Roscoe."

As she opens the door, he returns the greeting, "Hello, Maxine. How are you? Get yourself comfortable. You've got a lot to listen to."

"How's mom? She turned the phone off."

"I imagine she's still sleeping, and it was about five this morning when she got here to brief me."

"Well, that answers that, she's not getting any younger, you know."

"Here's what she told me and what I've deduced from it."

Roscoe relates what Margie told him and what he put together with the deposits. Maxine almost falls off the chair, then catches herself, and sits back, trying to disbelieve what's been told. She feels all her fears have come to rest in the here and now, and she's terrified. Roscoe sees the change in her and suggests a drink to steady her nerves or something. He mixes a gin and tonic for her and tells her, "This does change some things, but not many. If there is a force out there that controls Johnson, and I believe there is, I can't for one second believe they've caught onto us, or we wouldn't be here now. You must take comfort in that, Maxine, all my paranoia is paying off right now."

She takes an intense breath and looks at Roscoe, looking for reassurance. He holds her hand and says, "Everything will be alright. Our goals and objectives haven't changed; it's just how we do them. Remember, we're using the lawyer now, which insulates us even deeper. If ever you feel another presence around you, come running home, don't think twice about it, drop whatever and come running, we're safe here, believe me."

Maxine crawls inside herself. Never before has she felt so vulnerable about anything. She curls up in the chair and sets her chin on her knees.

She sits there for about half an hour, and Roscoe gives her all the space she wants without a word.

"What if people are watching him constantly?" she says.

"I would have tripped on them sooner or later, Maxine, and no one, regardless of how powerful they are, can have 24-hour coverage 365 days a year. If he sends a distress signal, then yes, the watchers will probably be here. Believe me, Maxine, we've been careful. I checked and double-checked everything I did. Look how Janet knew she was watched. If you put her on truth serum, she couldn't finger me. You could put me in line up and tell her the watcher was in the lineup, and she couldn't pick me with certainty. That's how careful I've been, and when we became us, I didn't change anything regarding security. You and Margie thought I was nuts with the flying all over the country. You know you did it, but couldn't prove it ever happened. Even the layover you had to make never happened, according to the records, which people rely on for proof. Do you remember how I told both of you to dress plainly and with no bright colors? Even people you talked to would have trouble proving they ever talked to you, even if you coached them. That's the nature of our beast, and it's a darn good one. I would never put you or Margie in harm's way, which you can take to the bank and earn interest. Enough of my lecture."

"How often have you had to bail me out of my dungeons and black alleys?"

"I'm not keeping count. When you love someone, counting should stop."

"That's the first time you said you love me, Roscoe. Is something happening I'm missing?" He looked at her sheepishly and smiled like a little boy. Maxine got up, walked over to him, took his hand, and pulled him to the bedroom.

"You've made me feel better; I'm going to make you feel wonderful," she whispers in his ear as they're lying beside each other, still a little sweaty, and they hear a phone ring. Maxine realizes it's her cell and leaves to get her purse in the other room. Roscoe comments on the lovely site she makes walking around au natural, Maxine wiggles her behind for him. The caller is Janet. Maxine didn't think it could be someone else; she hadn't given the number to anyone else.

"Hello?"

"Maxine, this is Janet. Can we meet for lunch tomorrow?"

"Sure, as long as it's about 2."

"That's fine, see you then."

Maxine walks back to the bed, and he comments on her looks again.

"Man, you just can't get enough of a good thing, can you? It begins tomorrow," she tells Roscoe as she slides back into the bed and gently wraps her hand around Roscoe's manhood.

"We'll talk strategy later; now it's time to see if all this gym work is paying off." Afterwards, he explains his plan.

"Okay, I'll be in the van and be at the restaurant before either of you gets there, so I can observe if there's any strange traffic around. I'll see you when you get there, don't even look for me or at me if you see the van. I'll know where she is because I have a tracking device on her car. I assume there will be a transfer since she's calling the meeting early. When you leave, get in the Jeep and drive out like normal. Your phone will ring before you get to the street, and it will be me. I'll tell you what I can observe and give you the first call on where to go. I'll carry a complete set of the financials I have compiled so far, so we could meet in a parking lot if needed."

"Let's hope we can do it right here at our leisure," Maxine follows.

Janet awaits Maxine in Martha's lounge, thinking about her soon-to-be-ended marriage. She met Jason during her last year at NYU, and he just started at the New York Medical Center Emergency Room. She had taken a nasty fall and was carted off to the ER by the EMTs. Nothing was broken except her pride, and the attending physician asked her out for a date. That was her first meeting with Jason. She wonders what it would have been like if she hadn't fallen that day so long ago. She got pregnant with Angie in New York and has been tied to her baby since then. She didn't mind being married if there was some give and take; she loved to be a mother until he took the fun out. Why was he such a bastard? She knew about the women, but he always came home with some for her, so she kept a blind eye. She still can't be positive why she hired the private eye, but something he did once got her so angry that she did it impulsively. Not until the reports showed him going to the airport and taking a plane to New York did she ever suspect anything like that. She had to use the Christmas fund to pay for the trip, which took him to the Essex for one night. He's done this twice since they established the pattern. She has never found out who he sees in New York. Maybe this divorce will uncover what they are for.

Maxine sees Janet at the bar and joins her.

"Hi, Janet."

"Hello Maxine, so glad you could make this on such short notice. Please take this." Janet hands Maxine a large pocketbook.

"I have one identical to it." Janet goes on, "When I've got some information or you have some for me, we can be as casual as we want to, and no one will be the wiser unless they're hiding in the purse. My first delivery to Harriet is in there."

"Does she know this is coming?"

"I haven't called her, and I don't intend to. You will be my messenger for everything except dropping the proverbial bomb."

Maxine takes the bag and slips hers inside.

Margie has gone to the condo every afternoon since she met Mary on Tuesday evening. She can't remember feeling this good for so long in her entire life. The toys Mary introduced were the most fun she had ever had with her clothes off. She left Mary's before Big George got home and is now headed for the weekly get-together at Roscoe's. She's been wondering how she will explain why she looks so good and is full of vitality. Mary had told her to wear makeup to hide the vitality when she mentioned she was going to see her daughter tonight, but she gave that up as a bad idea. She decides to wait and see if anybody notices and then play it by ear. That Roscoe, though, doesn't miss a thing.

Roscoe has everything ready for the Friday evening cocktail party, and Maxine is resting up in the bedroom when the bell rings. He lets Margie in.

He looks at her and thinks something is different about her, but he can't put his finger on it.

"You look great tonight, Margie," he says as she asks, "Where's Maxine?"

"She's resting," he replies.

"Get her up, I'm not starting without her here, produce her or pay the consequences, sir." She smiles while saying and pouring a glass from the pitcher marked with a T. He returns from the bedroom, saying, "She'll join us in a couple of minutes."

"You know, Roscoe, while I've got you to myself, I'd like to tell you that I've come to thoroughly enjoy these Friday night get-togethers, the cocktails, dinner, company, and the jazz."

"Thanks, Margie, those are nice words."

"What are nice words?" Maxine joins in.

"None of your beeswax, if you can't be here to hear, then tough."

Margie winks while saying, "Who wants to go first with a weekly report?" Roscoe inquires.

Maxine agrees to be first and describes mainly for Margie because Roscoe has heard it all. She recounts her two lunches with Janet and the messenger service she started for Janet. Roscoe had added much information to the scraps Janet had given her to deliver. She further described how the transfer went without a hitch, and she dropped the information at the designated drop location specified by the lawyer. She will pick up the first drop from the lawyer on Monday for the Tuesday meeting with Janet. And Roscoe said he loved me, she finished up with me. Margie complains that she can't top that. She reports that her meeting with Mary is only the business part of the Tuesday meeting anyway.

"How will Mary find happiness in her soon-to-be afterlife?" Maxine asks, remembering almost all the arguments they got into on this topic several weeks ago.

"Funny you should ask," Margie replies. "She told me not to worry about her love life; she would take care of that on her own when I asked her that very question."

"My tum," Roscoe announced, and the two women gave their undivided attention.

"I've heard from all the mail-outs. Three of them thanked us and said no. The rest want a piece of his hide. I cross-checked the payments to the deaths and found each of the respondents who want a piece of his hide to be survivors of payments made for services, and that includes you, Margie. He deposited 1.5 million after your husband died. In my case, there was no payment. I could check the origin of the source of this last payment series. Thanks to computers, it's difficult to hide things if you know how to look for them. The original amount was drawn from the Federal Reserve Bank of Philadelphia from an account, I believe, that belongs to the government, but beyond that, the trail evaporates. I believe they are controlling the bastard Jason V.

Johnson, for some reason, is far out of our current reach. It's obvious to me that he was ordered to kill Mr. Stephano, and the only glitch in the whole operation they planned was that somebody ordered the OR prepped. I got into those records and could not find anything useful. Whoever that was is a friend of ours. Possibly, it was someone in the Stephano clan who knew how to activate the OR room into action. Mr. Stephano had friends in potent places in the Tampa Bay area and Miami. The information Janet was transferring to the lawyer was just the children's names and three bank accounts, which must be the only ones she knows about. We replaced it all with complete bank account information, which includes the children's names and account numbers. That information should keep the lawyer and her staff busy for a while. We will monitor the information Janet gets from the lawyer because there's no direct communication between them, thanks to Janet's paranoia and Maxine's resourcefulness."

Margie had gotten up, refreshed all the glasses, and played hostess, passing around the cheese and crackers.

"Mom and I are out there gathering all the intelligence, and you sit here processing it into something incredible. Roscoe, I, for one, am very impressed," Maxine says.

"Your intuitive powers are great, Roscoe, and I second what Maxine said. And Roscoe, do you need the tracking device on my car?"

Margie snoozes and digs.

"I never have had one in your car, Margie. Do you want one?"

"I don't think I need one, do you?"

"No, I don't, and neither does Maxine's car."

He reassures them both.

"After all those reassuring words, I'm hungry. Is one of you buying tonight?" he throws out the fish line.

"I'll treat," Maxine says.

"Then let's go," Margie urges.

Tonight, the jazz combo is featuring a local boy, Dick Hyman, an old swing era musician.

Chapter 24

Roscoe is busy making a new letterhead for Harriet's law firm, at least one as close as he can. Harriet's note back to Janet said she was very impressed with the data sent and to keep it coming. Roscoe wanted to tone it down somewhat. He stresses the keep part and almost eliminates the impressive stuff. He had to steam open the envelope and iron it so an untrained eye wouldn't notice anything. He sends the lawyer's original note through the shredder just like he did the one from Janet. This arrangement will work just fine. By his best estimates, Jason V. Johnson can lose upwards of 15 million from the divorce alone. He now has to think about how to get the remainder without leaving telltale trails; when the axe falls, he wants the scumbag to wake up totally and broke. He's sure he'll contact his other employer, but if his feelings on this other employer are correct, they're the kind that calls you; you can't call them. Maybe he'll share this with the group at Friday's get-together.

Margie would like to move in with Mary and is very distraught at the thought of moving back to her own house so many miles away. Maybe she'll check out a few things back home before she mentions anything to Mary. Margie rings the bell at the condo and is buzzed in. When she gets to door 12E, it opens, and there stands the au-natural Mary, who grabs Margie by the lapels and pulls her inside. Another afternoon of fun and games begins.

In the study of the late Al Stephano in the stylish neighborhood north of Tampa known as Chagal, two of his former associates are in a conference call with another senior former associate from Miami. Tampa says they've exhausted every possible avenue and come up dry. They told Miami they were with him when he complained of stomach pains. We called his doctor, but he was out of town; we checked, and it was planned for four months. So, we called 911, figuring out we'd take potluck; we followed the ambulance when it left here. We thought it was headed for the Tampa General Hospital, just down the expressway; when it got to 1-4, it swung east and put the pedal to the metal. When it reached the US92 ramp, it went down there and never slowed down. We were right behind him, and then we were pulled over by a county Monty for speeding. By the time that's all over, we find the first hospital in the direction the ambulance was headed, and he was DOA.

That's what the doctor in the ER unit told us; they had his body in one of the curtained rooms. We told the ER doctor, Johnson, that we wanted the body, but he said the Medical Examiner had to look at the body first. So, we just sat there. We had it picked up when they released Al and went to work on the ambulance people. The driver was some bull we found in Ybor City, and she told us they were headed to Tampa General, and dispatch rerouted them to Plant City. We talked with the dispatcher; he told us the first call for that unit was Tampa General, but they reported complete, and the backup is Plant City. We went to Tampa General and nosed around until we found someone who would and could talk with us, and found the opposite of what the dispatcher said. They said they weren't busy that night, so we gave double Cs and asked them to be specific. They came back positive. We went after the dispatcher. Now he's on vacation. We checked the airport, bus, and train, but there was nothing. We called that guy in Kansas City. Al always used to find out if somebody used a credit card. He turned up nothing on the dispatcher's name. We used variations of the names, but still nothing. He's not scheduled to go back until next month. We found the county Monty, who pulled us over, and after his tongue loosened with several beers, he told us he was ordered to that location just minutes before the ambulance, and we came flying through. We got his dispatcher's name and went to talk to him, and he was on vacation. We then checked the doctor's vacation, and he's not due back until about the same time. We're sitting tight, waiting for these three to return with their tans, and we'll have a few heart-to-hearts with them. Miami tells them to get the photos of these three down to Miami; he'll get them passed around the world to see if anybody knows where they are. My guess is they're together, wherever that is. You two don't get too comfortable; you might be traveling soon. The secure connection was broken.

Chapter 25

Maxine gets to the lawyer's office to pick up Harriet's message for Janet. The package is with the receptionist, with a bit of a note attached asking Maxine to see her before leaving. In fact, as soon as Maxine has identified herself, the receptionist buzzes Harriet, and she walks toward Maxine just as she is putting the envelope in her big purse.

"Maxine, how are you?"

Harriet extends her hand towards Maxine. Maxine accepts the gesture, shakes Harriet's hand, and says, "Fine, and you?"

"If you have a minute, I'd like to talk to you. Would you mind stepping into my office?"

Maxine follows Harriet to a plush office with mahogany-paneled walls and a huge Rosewood desk. There are couches and chairs in one corner, like a living room. Maxine thought this décor was masculine. Harriet announces she's inherited this friendly corner office and hasn't had the decorator in it yet. She motions Maxine to the couch and takes a chair facing Maxine.

"I wanted to ask you some very pointed questions. Why are you doing this?"

"I told you the last time we spoke, Janet and I go back a long way."

"In all my considerable experience as a divorce attorney, I've never encountered so complete a messenger as you are, and it sends my antennae up."

"She asked, and I agreed; it's that simple."

"Nothing's that simple."

"That's what you say, I'm telling you that's all there is to it," Maxine declares, her anger beginning to swell, and she wills to control it.

Roscoe had foreseen this and warned me it might happen, she thinks.

"Maxine, it's just that a person like you has never presented themselves so unselfishly for this kind of work."

"She asked, and it didn't seem to interfere with anything I'm doing now, so I was glad to help, an old friend in need."

"I will tell you I've stressed to Janet that she stop this liaison and meet with me."

Maxine remembers Roscoe saying her ego would get in her way sooner or later. Their job was to get information to the lawyer, which was almost completed; one more delivery should do it.

Maxine responds, "You do what you must; I'm committed to my friend; until she says otherwise, I shall continue. Will there be anything else?"

Maxine gets up and starts to go to the door.

"I'm sorry, Maxine. I must have confidence in the people I'm dealing with and my clients. Please accept my apologies, and rest assured that I haven't said anything mean about you to Janet."

Maxine nods and leaves. The woman's gall to suggest I reveal that I know more than I do, she thinks with a smile. Roscoe will have fun with this tonight.

Maxine got to Roscoe's only to find him sound asleep. She mixes herself a gin and tonic, settles into the big easy chair, and turns on the TV with the volume low so Roscoe can sleep. She finds an old B&W Betty Davis film and leaves it on. She wonders what her life will be like once this Johnson thing is finished. Roscoe has said he's going after the next candidate on his list. That means he'll usually be gone, tracking down the next one. She doesn't want it to stop, she realizes. Maybe if she can stay clean with Janet, they can have a relationship. That probably wouldn't work, though. Janet's children would be around, changing their relationship considerably. Who knows if Janet will stay in the area after the divorce? She hears Roscoe stirring and goes into the bedroom.

After a warm greeting between them, Roscoe tells Maxine, "Margie called and said she would visit one of her friends for a couple of days and will see us on Friday."

"Must be nice."

That is all Maxine can respond with. She fills Roscoe in on the Harriet thing and gives him the courier envelope. He takes it and holds it to the light, seeing that all the glue has been moistened. He goes into the kitchen and puts the tea kettle on.

The note to Janet was pretty hot, warning Janet that using Maxine could compromise their situation. Roscoe mentions to Maxine that he only has one more delivery for the lawyer unless Janet comes up with something he hasn't already taken care of.

"If you want, you can break it off; tell her anything you want that would prevent you from continuing."

"No, I want to help Janet. She's innocent of wrongdoing, and I want her to get as much as possible. If I can help her get it, then I will."

"Okay, okay. I didn't want to start WWIII. I just wanted you to know our part can be finished rather soon, is all."

She gives him a hug and whispers, "Everything's okay, Roscoe."

Then starts to laugh.

"What's so funny?"

"It's just that you always tell me that."

They both get a good chuckle from that.

"Have I told you how Janet should determine if this Harriet is worth anything?" Roscoe asks.

"You've hinted at it several times but never all the way."

"The children will be well provided for; their trust funds will be locked for withdrawals by anyone but the court. Janet will receive around 13 million, possibly 15 million. The house will have to be sold, the car is hers, and she keeps it. Custody is the only thing I don't have a handle on, but I doubt he'll want them. I think I've figured out the rest of his money. I need a couple of more pieces to fall into place."

Mary couldn't believe her good luck; she called in sick for a couple of days, hoping Margie would be available. It was almost four full days of fun and mayhem. She had told Big George about her new friend, how she was a nice woman and motherly to her. Big George was happy for her, even happier when she told him she might stay over a couple of nights during the week. The phone rings, and the doorbell rings. Let the games begin; the phone can't be important.

Margie decided to call Mary and break the news about her having to get back north. When she called Mary, she all but ordered her to pack a bag and get over to the condo. I have to break the news to her over the next couple of days; that's all there is to it; I can't stay at Maxine's forever and pay a mortgage on my house. All this she's thinking about as she's riding up the elevator to the 12th floor. The last time she was here, Mary practically raped her when she opened the door; this time, she was going to stand back a little after she rang the bell.

Jason is furious; how can she be sick and not answer the phone? That bitch is as healthy as a horse. We were supposed to meet tonight, he's thinking. I'll barge in on her later, he says to himself.

The Tampa pair of Stephano's clan has been ordered to detain the ER doctor for some questioning. They're waiting outside the staff door when he exits, and each grabs an elbow and manhandles him into their car. Miami is at Stephano's house, where they're taking him.

Chapter 26

Miami was in the kitchen on the phone with the New York clan of Al Stephano's family.

He motioned the Tampa duo with the Dr. into the study.

"I'm telling you these are good fella's here in Tampa; why do you think they had anything to do with Al's death?"

"I'll tell you, it all started with the call. We only have their word that Al was ill with anything. I talked with him that day, and he was fit as a fiddle. I listened to the tape you sent off their report a dozen times, and there's nothing about how he got sick; they eat his food before he does; if it was the food, they should have been sick, too. Al liked his fancy ice cream. Find out as discreetly as you can if they know if he had any that night. If he did, one of them knows more than he's telling us, or both do. How long have they been with us?"

"Al had them with him every time I saw him for six years."

"You find out about the ice cream; if he had it, get rid of them both very quickly and slowly so they know why. For tonight, with that Dr., take him back to his car and have them belt him in the stomach good so he has to admit himself into his own hospital."

Miami goes into the study; they have the Dr. kneeling on the floor, blindfolded with his hands bound behind him. He motioned one over and told him to take him back to his car, and they needed to do the rest.

When the Tampa duo returns from the doctor, Miami is lounging in the study with his feet up and watching TV. They sit in any available chair.

"How'd it go?" he asked.

"Great, we got him good. I think we busted something; he went into his own ER and doubled up like a newborn."

Miami says as if an afterthought, "Al used to like ice cream, didn't he? Is there any of it left?"

One of the duo responds very quickly, "I don't think so."

The other says, "Let me check."

He gets up and goes to the kitchen. He doesn't realize those three words will save his life. The 'I don't think so' excuses himself, makes an emergency phone call, and then leaves the house immediately, never to be seen by a Stephano clan member again for five and a half years.

Roscoe is sitting in the van at Martha's, as has been his practice since Maxine became the messenger. He watched as Maxine's Jeep rolled in, and she went into the restaurant; he's a lucky guy, he thinks to himself. He sees the Mercedes enter the parking lot and then sees something he fears and waits for. Janet has a tail on her, very sly and seemingly unassuming. He calls Maxine and tells her to be very aware and make sure she leaves last to ensure the tail doesn't pick her up. He can't see the license plate and won't reveal himself to try to get it; maybe he'll get lucky when it follows Janet out. One of the shadows gets out and is heading toward the restaurant door.

He calls Maxine, "Get up and go to the ladies' room NOW! Take your purse and stay there until I call you."

After ten minutes, the shadow returns to the following car. He hits the dial again.

"All's clear; remember, leave last, like ten minutes."

Janet is jittery when Maxine returns to the table, "Are you alright? You get a secret phone call saying Okay, and off you go for twenty minutes."

"So sorry, just as the phone rang, I had this attack and needed to be in the powder room. I haven't been feeling the best the last couple of days," she lies. "I'll be alright; nothing, a good lunch with my friend won't cure."

Janet gives her a look just to be sure and says, "Okay, let's switch purses first, get the business out of the way."

Maxine takes the phone out, carefully puts it in her jacket pocket, and they switch purses. Janet tells Maxine, "Jason didn't come home last night, stayed at the hospital, it's true, I called and checked, I wonder if something's wrong with him?"

Maxine relays the conversation with the lawyer.

"That bitch!" Janet says, "The gall to call you that; I've half a mind to cancel everything with her over this."

Maxine tries to console Janet; she doesn't need her to quit now. All Maxine was trying to do was get Janet's reaction out of the way before she saw Harriet's Roscoe watered-down note.

Maxine follows Roscoe's instructions and waits for fifteen minutes after Janet leaves to leave. She sees the van and goes to her Cherokee. The phone starts ringing as soon as she's inside.

"I'll see you at home in a little while, got a few things to check out," Roscoe tells her. She doesn't know what has happened, but she's grown to trust Roscoe completely, so she asks no questions.

"See you later," she tells him.

Roscoe was in luck and got a good look at the plate of the shadow, which dutifully waited and followed Janet. He was tracking her, and so far, she appeared to be heading home. The plate belonged to one of the smaller car rental places at Tampa International. He's been trying to hack his way into their system for twenty minutes without luck so far. He heads for the barn to put the van to bed, being very careful to be sure no tails have grown on him.

He calls Maxine again, "How about meeting me at Floyd's?"

"Okay, see you there."

When he gets to Floyd's, he sees the Jeep. Bill wants to know which way he wants to go.

"It's a good day for Jack," he tells Bill.

He walks up to the smiling Maxine and gives her a serious hug and a light kiss.

"Let's take a cozy booth," he whispers to her.

They take their drinks and mosey to the corner booth they both favor, and Roscoe sits so he can see the bar. Once they're settled, he asks, "Did you get home before I reached you?"

"No, I was just passing here when you rang, sir."

He breathes a sigh of relief. Maxine seems to get a little worried and asks, "What's going on today, Roscoe?"

"Funny you should ask, my dear. Janet acquired a shadow today. Did she say anything about that sixth sense of hers that she suspected a shadow today?"

"Not a word, she wondered where I went for so long, but that was it for the paranoia. She got pissed when I told her about Harriet trying to can me."

"Her tail grew out of New York. I got lucky, hacked into the rental company's friendly system, and found two non-deplumes from NY. I can't believe they were following Janet just for her sake. They were looking for who she met, so I had you get away from her. I saw one of the shadows go into Martha's. I didn't want them eyeballing you."

"Jealous are we?"

"I asked if you had gotten home yet because I got paranoid about them waiting for you out in the street after you left Martha's; if they did, they'll be here soon. I asked Bill to give me the high sign if somebody strange is looking around." No strangers came in looking for anybody tonight. Roscoe and Maxine relaxed and enjoyed a nice meal.

"How do you feel about Football?" Roscoe finally asks Maxine.

"I love it; I've been a Jets fan since Broadway Joe lit up the scoreboards. I have never been able to become a Bucs fan. I have been to many of their games, but the Jets still own me. Why do you ask?"

"I've been a Green Bay Packers fan since number 5 played at Notre Dame. We can enjoy together; my dish is signed up for all the home games everywhere."

When Roscoe reads Janet's note, he realizes there isn't much to say. She tells the lawyer how she feels about her husband's trips and believes he's had mistresses and lovers most of their married life. There is nothing new or newsworthy. He lets this one go as is.

When Maxine delivers the note to the lawyer's office, she's again beckoned into the Mahogany room.

"No slings and arrows this time, Maxine," Harriet says.

"Please call Janet today and tell her I can file as soon as Friday this week if she wants me to."

As soon as Maxine leaves the lawyer's office, she calls Roscoe and gets no answer. Then she remembers that today is Y Day. She'll go to Floyd's and wait. He'll stop if he sees the Cherokee, precisely what he does. After he's settled, she relays the lawyer's verbal message.

"I will suggest that Janet meet with her for lunch on Friday. They can discuss strategy, and I don't even have to be there," Maxine tells him.

"That sounds great. Let's make the call and see where that takes us," he replies.

Maxine calls Janet, "Hello."

"Janet, this is Maxine. I have a message from Harriet."

She tells Janet what the lawyer said and what she feels about the lunch meeting.

"I want you there; I don't feel safe with that woman," Janet pleads.

"Okay, I'll be there," Maxine resigns.

Chapter 27

Roscoe thinks this through very carefully. He's logged into the car rental database to see if that license plate number has been returned. He can't determine if it has or hasn't. He doesn't like this at all; it means the shadow car is most likely still around. He asks Maxine to call the lawyer to confirm the meeting. Maxine tells him all's set. He explains what must happen at the meeting to ensure safety.

As soon as Jason was able to get to a phone the other night after he'd been so brutally attacked, he called the emergency number he had. That was a busy night for emergency calls to the shadows from the Tampa area. After Jason's call, a team was dispatched on the private jet, always waiting. They were in the area before sunrise the next day. They took up vigil at Jason's house and Stephano's house. Having found nothing of value to report, they were scheduled out on Thursday night around midnight and had to collect Jason for a detailed report.

Roscoe drives Maxine to the rendezvous with Janet and Harriet in the Town Car dressed as a chauffeur. He delivers her to the door, and she waits in the car until he can come around and open it like a good chauffeur. He scans the parking lot and sees the two women's cars, but no shadow car, and he's very relieved. As Maxine is sliding her hand in his, he tells her.

"Apologize for being late and listen very well; we don't want to get stonewalled."

"Yes, master, I thought this was supposed to be the other way around."

She wiggles her behind at him as she walks into Martha's.

"I'm so sorry I'm late, car trouble, had to get a limo."

Janet looks at her strangely, and Harriet nods as if it's an everyday occurrence. "Okay, Harriet, you can begin," Janet says.

Maxine is pleased that Janet has shown her this loyalty by making Harriet wait. Harriet begins by reiterating Janet's position.

"I'll file first thing Monday morning. I expect he'll get consul, and there may be war; we're ready. Angie and Jason Jr. will be millionaires by their eighteenth birthdays. You, Janet, will be filthy rich when the judge hands down the degree."

Janet's mouth is hanging open. Maxine knew all this, and Roscoe had foreseen it. Janet gets her lips together again and mumbles.

"How filthy."

"Once I file, I get discovery, and I'll have the final figures, but by the way, we've been able to piece it together from the notes you gave us and some we found on our own; I estimate around ten million." Janet's mouth falls open, practically off. Maxine can't believe what she's just heard. Roscoe has said several times that it should be 12 to 13 on what he gave her, and possibly 15 if the lawyer knew her stuff; that's a long way from 10 when you're counting millions.

Later, when Roscoe drives them home, Maxine is in the back seat just in case. He says, "She's not as good as I thought, or she's got terrible investigators. The information I gave her was a perfect road map to 12 without looking for anything. That's why I thought they could get to 13 with a little legwork and maybe 15 with great legwork. Oh well, if she can't get it, we will," he comments as they get home.

"Margie will be arriving shortly, and nothing is ready." He cries, "Blue-collar work is never over."

Margie has been packed for over an hour; she doesn't want to go; these have been wonderful days with Mary. She knows she has to go; Big George comes in on Friday, and there is no way she wants to run into him. Her talk with Mary left them both tearful, but she could do nothing. Mary comes out of the bedroom, where she is changing the sheets. She calls Margie, "Watch this."

And she slides down the banister, slowly for Margie's enjoyment. Then, she comes to where Margie is sitting on the couch and drapes herself over Margie's lap, looking up at Margie. "You look ten years younger, you know."

Mary says, "I've seen it myself; it feels great."

"Good," Mary says, "What would you like to see before you leave?" She rubs her hands up and down her naked body. Margie says, "If you keep that up, I'll never leave."

'That's the idea," Mary responds, increasing her hand motions. "Please, if you don't stop, I'll have to change and 1'm all packed."

"Tough," Mary says, but does not stop; she knows Big George will be along anytime.

"You call me the minute you can, you hear?"

Mary says getting up and sticking her rear end in Margie's face. A tearful hug at the door, and Margie's in the elevator going down. When she reaches the ground level, she realizes it's the first time since Tuesday. She sees Big George's truck, so they don't have a moment to spare. She's looking forward to seeing the kids and hopes her newfound vitality won't become an issue.

Chapter 28

Roscoe is just finishing the pitchers when Margie rings the doorbell. Maxine pitched in and got the goodies ready for their Friday night get-together. Roscoe opens the door and steps back, "I'm sorry, do we know you?"

He can't believe Margie looks so good and younger by over a couple of years, and he tells her so.

"I've just been feeling better these last couple of days, must have been the fresh air," Margie lies.

Maxine hollers from the other room, "Mom, you look great, do you feel as good as you look?"

"Thanks, Maxine, I feel good."

Roscoe pours for all and proposes a toast.

"To the beginning of the end! We had a lot happen this week."

Margie thinks, I sure have, but we'll never discuss that. Roscoe goes on, "A couple of close calls and some surprises. Maxine, please brief Margie. I'll go last tonight."

Maxine relays the meetings with the lawyer, the lunches with Janet, and the missing money. Margie comments that the lawyer must be all show and no go. Roscoe fills the glasses and passes around the cheese and crackers Maxine had put together. Margie comments that the quality of the Friday treats has diminished since Maxine moved in.

Maxine gives her a nasty look, and Margie smiles at her and says, "Well, they have, and I blame the host, not the hostess."

Roscoe shrugs his shoulders, saying, "There's never enough time to drive the kids, make the lunches."

Margie buts in, "Yea, Yea, Yea. Speaking of driving, I'm driving home tomorrow."

Once they're all settled in, Floyd's Roscoe states, "My report" gets both women's attention.

"The money, there's going to be much more to divvy up than I thought. Here's my plan A. The two children will each get an extra million to grow on. The three survivors will get the amount they received for what they considered services, plus interest. That includes you, Margie; your share will be two and a quarter million. The other two who responded that they wanted a piece of his hide will each get one and a half million. Five million will go to the fund researching degenerative diseases, which can prove they are making positive strides toward arresting at least one of these killers. Plan B. All of Plan A plus 5 million to the joint account of Mrs. and Mr. Maxine Peacock and Roscoe Find, wife and husband, respectively, and if that's not acceptable, 3 to Maxine and 2 for me."

Maxine looks at Roscoe with soft, tearing eyes and says, "I accept. Yes, I'll be Mrs. Peacock Find."

"Well, I'm glad you've found yourselves," Margie says.

Roscoe reaches and gently holds Maxine's hand and continues, "We have the extra in Plan B because of the ineptitude of the lawyer. I plan to drain every one of his accounts down to one dollar as soon as the divorce judge passes down the decree. Nothing I can do about the house or his car. Short of burning the house and stealing the car. Within an hour, all the money will be transferred, and our job with the scumbag will be over."

While Roscoe gave his report, Margie had flagged for another round and toasts.

"To the greatest couple I know, may you have a long and enjoyable life together."

Jason wakes up in Essex and can't remember getting there. His stomach still burns from the vicious blow he took the other night. An unopened bottle of Glenlivet sits on the desk in the room. Unknown to him, he was programmed never to let a bottle of this expensive scotch go unopened for very long in his presence, many years ago. He's fighting the urge to open the bottle because he knows he'll never remember anything after that. The shadows are watching this also. He tries to think back to the first time he was in this room with a bottle of Glenlivet. He was in the final months of his internship when the dark suits showed themselves. He remembered them once around his father. His father hadn't given him a second thought until this very second for all these years. He was a good man, and he was also a doctor of ER medicine. He had fought hard to get him into both the University and the Medical School in Boston. He was always afraid of something, but Jason never knew what that was. What Jason would never know was that the drugs used on him weren't available during his father's time. The shadows used fear on his father, drugs on him, and more than likely drugs on his son in the future. Jason's mind wasn't that cluttered, but he shed an uncontrollable tear. Was it for his dead father or himself? He had no idea. He got up and reached for the bottle. He doesn't know he will give a complete report like always. He will be flown back to Tampa in the shadow plane, put in a taxi, and given a shot as he's getting in the cab. When he arrives home, he'll be wide awake and not remember anything but the sore stomach he still has.

Chapter 29

Mary can't sleep thinking about Margie. They had such a great time together. Neither of them had ever considered being with another woman until that night with the pictures of Jason. They must have talked about that night for days, it seemed. What chemistry caused such different people to unite so totally and unabashedly? She gets tired just thinking about that. She wakes up George, gets him as hard as the rock of Gibraltar, and jumps on. After she tells him she's quitting the hospital. Big George likes that a lot; he never liked her work. Then she tells him she will visit her friend up the coast for a week or two. George thinks that's great, also; he's happy she's happy again and tells her so. She gives him Margie's phone number and tells him to call in the evenings like always, and she assures him she'll get a private room to talk to him in. All the time thinking how much fun Margie will have watching her get Big George off the phone. Big George had an early call, so they stayed up. Five minutes after he left, she was locking the door behind herself. She, too, was happy not to be working at the same place Jason did. She knows she promised Margie she'd keep fucking him until Margie said to stop, but she thinks Margie said to stop the moment she stripped for her. She drives through the early morning mist and arrives at Margie's just as Margie wakes up after her first night in bed for almost a month.

Margie hears a knock at her door and wonders what's going on. She looks out and sees the Lexus and gets a chill. It's Mary! Quickly, she drops her robe and does to Mary what Mary did to her that day at the condo. It's only been a day and a half, and they act like it's been a year. Mary confesses she had sex with George. Margie chides her, "He's your husband, for Christ's sake. You better be fucking him."

Margie has an evil thought: Mary's Lexus has a tracking device, and she knows she must deal with that soon. But today she's going to introduce Mary to the country. But she can't get that tracking device out of her mind, and she doesn't like for a second that Roscoe could know about Mary and her. She tells Mary they must return her car to the condo for security reasons. Margie dresses as fast as possible and urges Mary to do the same.

They each drive their vehicle back to the apartment, and Mary rides to Margie's with Margie. Along the way back, there's no hurry, and they stop for breakfast; they're both famished.

Harriet arrives at the circuit court offices as they open and files the papers concerning Janet Johnson versus Jason V. Johnson. A divorce proceeding. Later that same day, as Jason reports to work, the deputy sheriff waits and serves him. He reads the pleading and calls home,

"Bitch, you'll regret this. I'll see you in hell."

Janet, not afraid to use the phone any longer, calls Harriet, "It's adversarial, I'd say."

Maxine and Roscoe have decided to wait until Johnson is humbled to tie their knot. But that doesn't prevent them from practicing married life together, especially in bed.

Maxine has been pleased with herself for getting Roscoe into such good physical shape. She knows he won't be able to satisfy her the way she's become unless he keeps up the workouts at the Y. She will urge him to keep up that membership year after year.

Janet and Maxine keep their lunch date even though Maxine is no longer the messenger. "Maxine, I don't know if I could have gone through this without you," Janet says.

"I want you to have this as a little memento of my affection and appreciation."

Janet reaches into her purse and gives Maxine a nicely wrapped box. Maxine accepts the box and opens it. Her eyes open wide when she sees its contents.

"I know you are a very functional one all the time, but I just thought there were times when something less functional and a little more feminine would do."

Maxine is most surprised; she is looking at an 18k gold Lady's Rolex with a diamond bezel.

As is Maxine's nature, she protests such extravagance, "I can't accept such a beautiful gift for being your friend."

"Oh yes, you can and will; I'll take no more argument on this."

"Thank you so much," Maxine says as she takes her black ladies' sports model off and replaces it with the Rolex, holding out her hand to admire it.

"No, thank you!" Janet insists. "It looks great on you. May you have everything your heart desires and then some."

Janet declares this a drinking lunch. She tells Maxine that since she will be so wealthy very soon, she's buying lunch from now on.

"Harriet called me and said a hearing judge has been assigned, and he set a date one month from now, with discovery to be completed five days before that, at which time he will not listen to any motions for continuance. Wow, I can't believe I remembered all that. Do you know what discovery is?"

"I think it has to do with both sides telling the other side what they know."

They have a nice leisurely lunch, and Janet lets herself go a little more than Maxine has seen her. Being the good friend she is, Maxine calls a taxi to take Janet home.

As the taxi pulls away, she digs out her phone and calls Roscoe.

"Are you very busy right now, Hun?"

"No, just laying around relaxing," he tells her.

"Good, I've got an errand to run and need another to help me. I'll pick you up in a couple of minutes."

"Nice watch," he says as he gets into the Jeep.

Together, they deliver Janet's car back to her house. A *For Sale* sign is in front of the house. Both of them seem surprised. Roscoe suggests they go slumming, and they stop at Rickey's. Kevin, the bartender, calls out, "Hey, stranger, how are you, Roscoe?"

Maxine looks at Roscoe and says, "Have you been hiding something from me?"

Once seated at the bar, which isn't busy at this time of day, he tells her how he came to this bar and some of the names of the people he met here.

"Did you know me then?"

"Sure, you were just a coach then."

"Got any other spicy tales to tell?"

"Sure, I do, and you'll get to hear them all in time." It's the first time she's seen him drink a Bud.

She says, "When in Rome, you know."

They discuss the For Sale sign for a while and agree that Janet's just anticipating having to and getting a jump-start. Maxine tells Roscoe, "I've got a present for you."

"Oh boy, I love a present," he says. "Can I know what it is, or do I have to guess?"

She slips an envelope into his hand.

"Can I peek?"

"Please do."

He opens it and sees two Packer/Buc tickets inside. He turns and kisses her. "Thanks, who's the other one for?" he says with a wink and a smile.

"Thought you might like these; my company gets them for a song, so I've told them to reserve all the Packer games for me. How's that for seniority!"

He looks at the tickets, "Into December, that'll be fun."

Jason had retained a local divorce specialist, or so he was led to believe. This lawyer had just called and told him about the timing of the divorce. I'll take everything she has, he thinks. She'll get half the house, and he can't stop that. He's sure he can get the car away from her. What he can't figure out is where Mary went. No one has seen her at the hospital, and her car is at the condo, but no one has answered the phone. She probably took off with that big oaf of a husband she's got. He remembers her saying that they did that sometimes. If that's the case, she'll be back.

Mary and Margie are snuggled in for the duration. Margie tells Mary about the divorce and how Mary could be called if somebody knows about them besides Margie and her friends. Mary doesn't think so, and besides, if she stays right here, they won't find her to serve. She'll deny she ever knew Jason if they do find her.

"You can stay here as long as you like," Margie tells her.

"What would you like to do today, Mary?"

Mary responds, "I'm already doing it."

Maxine tells Roscoe she's a little worried about Margie.

"I called her, mentioning we might stop and see her this weekend, and she told me no."

"Don't worry about Margie; she can take care of herself; she did a great job for us and herself, and she'll get a nice payday out of this, too."

"How come Mom gets more than the other folks who lost loved ones?"

"That's easy, he got paid more for your dad than he did for the others. Finding out the way to that wasn't so easy."

"Did you, I mean, find out about Daddy?"

"Yes, I believe I did. It took a lot of patience, that's all. Do you want to hear it?"

"I'm not sure if I do, maybe Mom should be here also."

"It's up to you. I waited until someone asked about it, and you did."

"Okay, let me hear it. I can tell Mom myself later, or you can."

"You know he was a pilot."

"Yes, I did."

"When they got to the States afterward, he took work with the United Nations. He flew dignitaries all over the world. Sometimes into places that weren't what we call stable. Sometimes to the capitals of other sovereigns. He got to see an awful lot of places and faces. It's evident now that one of the three men I have narrowed it down to wanted to cut his losses and burn his bridges. Three of them did, one of them ordered the death of your father as the pilot, and the chauffeurs were also eliminated. I've traced the actions of all three during the period, and all three are still living. One in Spain, one in Miami, and one in Rome."

"That's incredible. Why would they do it?"

"If you want to disappear and you can afford it, you eliminate every and anyone who can point a finger and say, 'That's him,' that's what happened to your father."

"But which one, you must have a pretty good idea."

"Well, we know that the payments to the scumbag were made from the Federal Reserve Bank in Philadelphia. I've traced two of the payments from that bank. That links the government to the payments, leading the path to Miami."

"What's the name?"

"Does Rekosso ring any bells?"

"No, I've never heard it that I know of, maybe Mom will know."

Margie and Mary have traveled to the condo office of one of the new high rises, in the finishing construction phases, on St. Pete Beach on the Gulf side. Margie tells the woman she wants to look at a 2x2 above the 14th floor, the 13th in Florida, facing the Gulf. They're shown a penthouse unit with a wraparound vista. Both Margie and Mary fall instantly in love with it. When Margie inquires about the price and fees, she asks the woman for something slightly lower but still above 14. The unit they settled on is on the 16th floor facing the Gulf. Margie gives the woman a check to hold the unit, and she explains she has a house to sell before the contract can be executed. The woman, also the real estate agent for the building, signs and seals the documents, and Margie and Mary leave. They drive to Mary's condo to check the route and mileage for Mary, who will continue to spend her weekends with George. Mary comments, "We'll spend a lot of evenings saluting the sun as it falls into the water. If we don't look up too much, we won't be reminded there's anything above."

Margie responds, "It will be nice, won't it?"

Privately thinking of the man, so many years ago, to whom she gave all her undying love, who has provided for her all these years later. He was a good man; he didn't deserve to be terminated like he was. She felt good about what M & R would be doing about it. A strange path to this car seat, the future, is something she, in her wildest dreams, would never have envisioned for herself. She looks at her passenger with tenderness and love, reaches out to Mary's hand, and says, "I'm going to be a wealthy lady in a couple of weeks, and I want you to be a part of it."

Mary, being true to her nature, lifts her skirt, exposing her privates; she never wears panties since she's been with Margie, and starts stroking herself with her other hand. Margie sighed, pulled her hand back, and steadied it on the wheel. She didn't need to be arrested or, far worse, get in a crash, but watched out of the corner of her eye. She's never been able to take her eyes off a Mary show since that night with the Jason pictures, which seems like years ago.

Today is the day both lawyers have agreed to meet. They decided not to have the principals at this meeting; these two have met many times before. This time is different; Harriet is equipped with hard information. Her opponent may not know the value of his client. It doesn't take long to get to the assets phase; when viewed by third-party people, most marriages only see the tangible. Harriet notices the smugness in her adversary's demeanor. He slides a sheet of paper listing all the assets Jason has disclosed to him. Harriet scans the document; house, car, and small savings are all listed. She looks at her opponent.

"I'm instructed to inform you that we will contest everything listed on our assets declaration, claiming she has no right to any of it," he says.

Harriet responds, "We have anticipated your reluctance and have prepared our own pro forma assets declaration for your review."

She slides a stapled set of papers across the table. This set includes all the information Roscoe had provided her in a legally prepared order. Jason's lawyer's demeanor changes, and his jaw slackens somewhat.

"I didn't know."

That is all he can say. Harriet tells him, "Review this information, which shows his assets at 24 million plus his house and car. We will not vary from our claim for half of every penny, and if he fights dirty, we'll take it all."

He nods like a subordinate. Harriet says, "How about a drink?"

"Sure," he comments.

The meeting is over. Later, over drinks, Harriet reminds him of her goal and tells him she will fight tooth and nail against a petition for a continuance. Then she says, "Would you like to come to my place for a while?"

"Sure," he comments.

At their next luncheon, Janet tells Maxine what the lawyer has told her about the naivety of Jason's lawyer, and they have their second good laugh of the day. They had always chuckled at the moron who seated them every week. Janet says, "I'm so excited, I can't believe it, it's only a couple of weeks and I'm free. I've got the house up for sale, and I've made arrangements to send the children to private schools in different parts of the country, depending on their ages. They'll all attend Harvard when the time comes; everything before that will be geared to that one goal."

Maxine notices the difference in Janet and realizes this might be one of the last times she sees her.

She mentions this to Roscoe, and he offers no hope.

"Money can change a lot of things. Take Margie, I bet she will have some news for us tonight."

"What makes you say that?"

"Just a feeling, a money feeling. Remember, I made my living around the stuff. Let's stop at that deli over there, and I'm serving rumaki tonight. She will not get away with a cheap shot like last week about cocktail time."

"What's rumaki?"

"Chicken livers wrapped in bacon with a water chestnut and fried. I learned to like them when I was on the convention circuit."

They get the deli package home. Maxine heads into the ladies' room, which is also the men's room, with fewer men. She remembers she has to get rid of her place reasonably soon. Roscoe is preparing the pitchers and placing the rumaki on a preheatable tray. He turns the Jimmy Buffett CD on and lowers the lights. Margie knocks on the door, and he lets her in with a little flourish.

"Welcome to our lounge. May your palette be titillated, and may our libelous liquids please, madam."

"Very well done, keep up the good work."

Margie says as she enters and pats Roscoe's arm. When the three of them are together, Roscoe declares this Friday's meeting to be official and requires all present to agree that these meetings continue. Maxine thinks it will be easy for her; she'll be married to Roscoe. Margie says it will be easy for her; Mary will go home to George every weekend. Roscoe takes the lead and gives the weekly summary.

"The lawyers are living up to our best expectations. The beneficiary survivors have responded to our generous offer and declined. I took the liberty to call each of them and act like I was the agent for the consortium, which contacted them, and tried to make them believe that the monies would be automatically deposited in accounts they specified."

They each declined emphatically and quite firmly. So, I propose: "Since this money has always been earmarked for survivors, it shall remain with survivors."

Both women agree.

"I'm glad to hear you agree with me. Margie, you are the only survivor eligible, so you get it all."

The surprise is evident; neither woman was thinking along those lines. Maxine nods in approval. Margie excuses herself, goes to the bedroom, and closes the door. She calls the realtor and tells the woman to change her choice to the penthouse unit they looked at. She rejoins the others. She has to answer questions about her health from both of them and announces.

"All this money has made me rethink how I want to spend the rest of my days. Earlier in the week, I rented a condo in one of the new places on the beach. I just called the realtor and told her to make it the penthouse."

Both Maxine and Roscoe congratulate her. While Margie was making her phone call, Roscoe had heated the rumaki, which he now served to rave reviews. He makes a general comment, "This place is on a month-to-month basis, and your place will go. Maybe we should get some new digs. It's fun spending money we don't have, isn't it?"

"It certainly is," Margie says. "What's my take now?"

"Should be a little over 5.5 million," Roscoe informs her. "Janet's lawyer never figured out the road map to the fortunes I laid out for them, according to what Maxine reported from lunch with Janet. That means more for the masses, and we're the masses. It should all happen within two weeks."

"Thinking about all this money makes me hungry. Got any of those bacon things left?" Margie says. Roscoe serves the rest of the rumaki and tells Margie there's brandied ice waiting for later. Laughing, Margie says, "I knew if I insulted the chef, he'd come around."

"Sticks and stones and all that," Roscoe slides in. He continues, "I think we'll have one more Friday meeting before the scumbag releases all his millions. I've always been proud that once we became a team, we did it with dignity."

Roscoe said that with a choking in his throat. In a rare instance, Maxine takes the floor.

"I, for one, walked into this blind. I had no hidden agenda, working or closets full of ghosts, but I eventually bought into our endeavor one hundred percent. Our actions were humane, above-board, and, in my opinion, done with dignity. So, I join you, Roscoe, and agree with you."

Margie says, "I'm famished, let's go eat."

Chapter 30

After Margie leaves for home on Sunday morning, Roscoe says to Maxine, "Can you get some time off?"

"I'm sure I can. What's up?"

"I've booked us on a week-long Caribbean cruise while we wait for Janet's divorce. I've also invited my friends from Chipley, FL. Jeff and Janis. I want to show you off."

"I don't know. I've got lunch with Janet on Tuesday."

"Call her and beg off; you'll have one more before it happens."

"Okay, it sounds good. I want to meet some of your friends."

"Great, I'll call them, and we can leave today, I'm sure."

Jeff and Janis were thrilled to hear from Roscoe and agreed to the cruise. Roscoe checked with the travel agent and determined they would travel first class to the western Caribbean. It will be a seven-day cruise, starting on the upcoming Saturday. Jeff and Janis would arrive on the Thursday before the cruise. Roscoe hired a limo to take them to the Port Canaveral ship and return after the cruise.

On two nights of their cruise, they had dinner with the captain and his immediate staff. The weather was good throughout the cruise. When they got home, Roscoe told Maxine.

"Remember to call Margie tomorrow and ask her to contact OR Mary and tell her she may be approached by one or both sides. She could mess up the work. Suggest she take a vacation or something until this is over."

Al Stephano's house has been relatively quiet lately. Miami has stayed on since the disappearance of one of the Tampa duo. Miami, under instructions from New York, tells Tampa, "Both dispatchers and the doctor are due back in Tampa on Friday after this one. Please take a few of the guys, meet them, and convince them to accompany you. Bring them all here; we'll debrief them ourselves."

Margie has been busy. She called the realtor, who convinced her to let her take occupancy while the paperwork on her house goes through. She sold her house to the realtor to earn extra points on the deal. She called the phone company and told them she wanted her existing number to ring at her new place. She did all this while driving down to pick up Mary. She made three more calls before getting to Mary's.

Mary is waiting by her car when Margie pulls in. Together, they stop for breakfast. Margie tells Mary she has secured the condo already; Mary is excited. When they finish, they head for the new condo. Mary presses the 16th button in the elevator, and Margie does nothing. When the door opens on 16, Mary starts to leave, and Margie stays put. She reached forward and pressed the penthouse button. There's also a key entry for the penthouse; she'll get that at closing. Mary gets back in and looks at Margie, "You didn't!"

When they get into the unit, Mary runs to the sliders looking over the Gulf and exclaims, "This wasn't here the other day!"

"Just ordered it. It looks pretty good, don't you think?"

"It's great."

Mary says as she plops into a double-wide chaise lounger with extra puffy cushions. Margie goes to the master bedroom and is pleased. When she went into Roscoe's bedroom last Friday and saw the big bed, she knew she had to have one at least that big.

Margie calls Mary, "Come in here, Mary, I've something to show you."

When Mary arrives, her eyes open wide. Margie is lying on the largest bed she's ever seen. As quick as you can say 1-2-3, Mary disrobes and climbs in with Margie. Later, the phone rings while they're sitting together on the chaise, prepared to watch their first sunset from this vantage point. Margie has to dig it out; it's Maxine.

"Mom, if you can easily get hold of OR Mary, see if you can convince her to lay low for a couple of weeks."

"I'll do it first thing; she still works those crazy hours, you know."

"That'll be great, thanks, Mom. How's everything else?"

"Just fine, just fine. Talk to you later, see you on Friday."

She reaches over and grabs Mary and says, "Maxine said I should get a hold of you."

Together, they watch the sun fall into the water.

The lawyers meet again without the principals. Harriet begins, "Did you get your client to agree, or will we go to the trenches?"

"He's madder than the Mad Hatter. He said he'd rather cut off his arm than give her anything. I told him that if he resists too hard and they dig deeper and find more, they'll take that too. He came right along like a little puppy after that."

Harriet wondered if there was more. She had meticulously followed the data that Janet had given her; it's possible there was more, but if there were, it would mean delays, and she wanted a fast payday. She says, "Want to come to my place?"

"Sure."

Jason is sitting in the doctor's lounge, trying to assemble what's been happening to him recently. He was kicked out of his house and his lover's bed all within the same week. It's been several weeks, and no one has heard from Mary. That blood-sucking lawyer trying to threaten him the other day, the gall of him. If he loses, see how fast I don't pay him. He'd checked with his banker and found all but three had been frozen. That bitch, how did she find the ones she did? He must have left some paperwork at home, but he couldn't remember ever doing that. Maybe tonight he'll go cruising the bars.

The realtor, Janet, had placed the house with a contact; she had an eager buyer. They were coming from Minnesota and wanted a fast close. Janet called Harriet and asked if part of the divorce proceedings could be made. The house was all ready.

Harriett told her. Janet explained, "I mean, can the sale of the house be done then? I have a buyer."

"Let me do some checking," Harriet tells Janet.

Janet had arranged to close on a 12-room apartment condo on Central Park East. She had appointments with private schools for the children. She would find a nanny to pick them up and welcome them home daily. Life was finally becoming what she always thought it would be.

Jeff and Janis were treating Roscoe and Maxine like royalty. Jeff told them he was taking them on a surprise trip on their second day. They ended up at a marina an hour's drive from the Gulf. Jeff was pleased to show off his 30-foot sailing sloop, with only a small outboard for emergencies. They had christened it the 'Lazy J's.' Jeff had enrolled in the Coast Guard course on sailing and safety and could launch and land without problems; his tacking was just about mastered.

"How about a sail for a couple of hours?"

Roscoe, being a landlubber, was cautious, asking how the weather would be in an hour. Maxine was raring to go, giving it to the wimp Roscoe, while Jeff and Janis found it all amusing. Roscoe was outnumbered and didn't want to be the spoilsport, so he grinned and bore it. Sailing on a boat was a significant difference from sailing on a ship.

Four hours later, Jeff landed safely back at the marina. They had sailed west to Panama City, docked, had lunch, and returned. Maxine and Roscoe admitted how peaceful the sailing was, with no noisy motor, which always smelled of diesel. They all stayed at the marina that night after a great meal of freshly caught fish with only four or five 'I hate Allen's toasts.' The next day, during the drive back to Tampa, Roscoe filled Maxine in on what had happened to Jeff and Janis and began planning next week's big day.

The rumaki was such a big hit last time that he decided to have an encore. When all three were together, Friday Roscoe began explaining his plan. He wanted the notebooks he had given them back. Margie said she had never moved it from where he put it in her car. He told them he would also have his from the van, which would give him four. He felt he could do it with four; the big one could handle two banks, the van laptop was strong enough to handle two, and the girl's machines could handle one, which was perfect. He explained to the questioning looks that he was talking about banks. He wanted to be in the banks and log into the accounts with a keystroke. Maxine would call as soon as the judge decreed, and he would get to work and make the transfers that would make Margie rich and give him and Maxine a very comfortable lifestyle. All the accounts where the funds would go have already been opened and are waiting.

He thanked both Maxine and Margie once again.

"I didn't know this would turn out this way; you both did most of the legwork; it's my turn now to do what I do best, move money and balance accounts; within an hour of the judge unfreezing the accounts, Jason V. Johnson, aka the scumbag, will be broke."

He told them dinner was his treat with all the trimmings. This would be the last Johnson meeting. He teased them that he might tell them who the next target could be at dinner.

Margie told them she was going home after dinner. Mary was staying this weekend out of paranoia that Jason or his wife might decide to serve her. All Margie's furniture was on the second day of the Gulf. The penthouse was now home.

This would be the last lunch and probably the last time Maxine would ever see Janet.

Janet was right on time. She looked a little concerned, Maxine thought.

"How are you holding up?" Maxine asks.

Janet responds, "Maybe a mite jittery is all. This is a big step for me. Not only will I be divorced by tomorrow, but I'll have also closed the house and dropped off the car to its new owner."

"Wow, you've been busy. Where will you sleep tomorrow night?"

"At the Essex, he stayed there enough; we can do it for a night. We've been at the Marriott airport for the last two nights; the removers took everything the day before last. Our new place won't be ready until Thursday."

"I'm going to miss you," Maxine says. "Every time I look at my watch, I think of you."

"We don't have to be strangers. When you get to the Big Apple, look me up," Janet gave Maxine a piece of paper with her new address and phone number. They enjoyed a parting lunch. Janet told Maxine she had wanted out of this marriage for almost as long as she had been married, but didn't know it until Maxine happened along and gave her courage.

"I'll never forget what you've done."

Maxine thinks she only knows the surface of it. It's thanks to Roscoe, but Janet will never know it.

Chapter 31

That evening, Roscoe mentions to Maxine that he's talked with his children, and once it's over, he would like to have Maxine meet them.

"If it's okay with you, I'd like to head up to New York for a couple of weeks, then head out to California via Green Bay, and then back home via Las Vegas, where we can be married."

"Sounds great to me; I only have one concern."

"What's that? You said you were quitting today."

"I did; that's not it. Will we be back for the game against the Bucs?"

"Plenty of time, and as luck would have it, your Jets are playing host to my Packers while we're in the Big Apple. I don't know about that game until next week; my contact who owes me is out of town until then."

"I'm looking forward to our life together. Who will be at our wedding?"

"I've talked to Margie, and she said she wouldn't miss it for anything, my two children, you, and me."

"I know I'm going to enjoy it; not getting up to go to work will take me no time to get used to."

"Don't get too used to it too soon, one more; you have to be in the courtroom tomorrow to be our eyes and ears."

"I will be, I don't consider that 'work,' that's a labor of love."

With this turn of events, Maxine thinks she will probably see Janet sooner than either of them thought she would.

Margie and Mary are snuggled together in their new digs. Mary's complaining, "Why can't I go with you to Las Vegas?"

"Both Roscoe and Maxine know what you look like; all we need is for them to see you there and start asking questions we don't want asked."

"I could stay in the room. It's not like I want to interfere with your festivities. I don't want to be left behind, that's all."

"I'll think it over. We've got a month or so before it happens. We'll work it out, love."

Maxine got to the courthouse at half past eight, found the call sheet for divorce proceedings, went to the courtroom, and waited. Harriet was the first of the principals Maxine knew to arrive next.

"What are you doing here?"

"You don't think I invested as much as I did and not be here for the end, do you?" Maxine blasts her. Shortly behind Harriet came another person, who was introduced as a real estate attorney from her office. They were closing the house today. Janet came next, looking business-like and proper, nothing flashy or severe. Harriet gave her approval. Janet looked at Maxine, and the two winked hello without saying a word. Please don't give them anything, Maxine thought; good for you, Janet. Jason's lawyer came in, and Harriet pointed him out to everybody.

Jason came in; Janet told Harriet, "I thought you told me he wouldn't be here."

Harriet responds, "With the house thing, he had to be. We tried, but you both need to sign how the house was purchased. There will be two checks. Once the decree is handed down, you two sign and receive your checks."

"Okay, just have someone run the papers between us. I don't want to look him in the eye or ever talk to him again. I think I'm paying enough for that privilege."

The court is brought to order, and the first case is heard. Maxine slips out and calls Roscoe; she wants him to know about the scumbag being in court. She returns to the courtroom just as the bailiff calls the matter of Johnson vs. Johnson. Harriet and her counterpart approach the bench. Harriet presents her pleading, but he has none. The judge asks if there is any contest or if any witnesses will be called. Both lawyers say no. The judge reviews the Material again: Harriet made sure copies were in the judge's chambers yesterday, with a healthy envelope for the judge. The judge looks serious and asks.

"Are these all the assets under the division of this court?"

The judge looked straight at Jason when the question was asked. Jason's lawyer spoke and said, "They are your honor."

The judge said that Mr. Johnson had to answer that one himself. Jason looked a little confused, took a deep breath, stood up, stared the judge in the eye, and said, "I am."

"That's all the assets there are, your honor."

Only two people in the courtroom knew that to be a lie. Maxine and the scumbag, the rest just guessed. The judge asked because that was the condition of the nice envelope from Harriet. The judge then lightly pounded the gavel and decreed that the divorce of Jason V. Johnson and Janet Johnson be final as put forth in the plaintiffs' pleading. With that being said, the bailiff called the following case.

Harriet's associate consul immediately turned to Janet with a pen in hand and asked her to sign where indicated on several documents. Once done, the associate went to Jason's camp and got the signatures there. She came back to Janet and gave her a check for her half. No one noticed while all this was unfolding that Maxine had pressed the redial button and whispered.

And disconnected.

Jason took his check, which amounted to $101,215.00, his net after taxes, points, and fees. He left immediately without a look back. No one but Maxine noticed. She knew how bad Roscoe was going to feel about the scumbag getting such a nice present. By the time Jason had cleared the threshold of the courthouse, his total net worth was $101,221.00. It's not a bad sum for someone like him. Jason went directly to the closet bank holding one of his accounts and made a deposit, asking for a balance. He couldn't speak when he looked at the balance. He told the teller there was a mistake and reran the balance.

Roscoe was so pleased when Maxine called to tell him the real estate checks would be disbursed right after the divorce. That meant there was an outside chance that the scumbag would deposit it as soon as he left the courthouse. If he did that, Roscoe would take that too. And so, he did; as soon as he saw the amount credited to the Johnson account, he transferred it out.

By the time Jason had gotten the attention of the bank manager, the balance had slipped to $1.00.

Janet hugged Maxine and said goodbye; she had a plane to catch. Maxine told her she'd see her in a couple of weeks. Maxine left and went home. When she got there, Roscoe was as happy as he could be.

"It's done, it's done, I got it!"

"I never doubted you for a minute."

"I mean, I also got his house money!"

"That's great. Does that mean he's broke?"

"He has to go to work. There's nothing even for him to pay his lawyer! I'm so happy I could shout. Let's call Margie and spread the good news!"

When Margie hangs up, she stands over Mary and declares, "I'm now, as of this moment, a wealthy lady!"

Mary says, "That's great. Let's celebrate."

Jason doesn't know what to do or think; what just happened must be a mistake. He called all his other accounts and got the same story: a balance of $1.00. Even the three she didn't find. He sleeps on it, and as soon as the banks open, he calls them all again, only to get the same answer. He's panicking, not sure what has happened. He calls his emergency number. He explains all his troubles to the listening shadow and asks for advice on what to do. He's told to sit tight. Everything will be taken care of. Jason feels better and does as he's told, sitting tight.

The lead headline on the front page of the Tampa Tribune the following day reads, "Local Dr. Linked to Stephano's death."

In the Miami Herald, a smaller front-page headline reads, "Local Tampa Doctor Linked to Death of Al Stephano."

In New York, on page two of the Times, "Tampa doctor to be charged in Stephano's death."

Jason, who has been following orders and lying low, was astonished when two plainclothes policemen took him into custody when he reported for work.

Roscoe and Maxine leave for New York City. Roscoe's children meet them at the airport. This is the first time Maxine has seen Roscoe's children and vice versa. Big hugs go all around.

Margie calls Maxine, wondering where they are. Maxine tells her they are in New York Airport, where she enjoys meeting Roscoe's children. All Margie can say is she'll be there tomorrow. What she fails to mention is that she will bring Mary with her.

Roscoe hires a car to take Maxine and his children to the Waldorf Astoria Hotel in New York. He tells his children that their stay for the wedding is all Daddy's expense. They look at him and wonder why they each have their own money, but Roscoe insists, and that's that. Roscoe picks up a paper once they're all checked in. He finds out why he bought the paper on page two, folds it, and puts it under his arm.

Margie and Mary arrive in New York the next day and check into the Essex Hotel on Central Park South. Once they checked into the Presidential Suite, Margie called Maxine to tell her she was in New York. Maxine tells her to meet them for dinner this evening. Margie begs off, stating she's tired from the long trip. After the call, Mary calls from the bedroom, and their fun begins. When Margie enters the bedroom, Mary is all-natural, playing with herself.

Roscoe informs Maxine that a meeting of M.R. Associates must occur after the football game. Maxine calls her mom and tells her about the meeting. Margie asks where the meeting will take place. Maxine tells Mom that the meeting will be in the lobby of the Waldorf Astoria after the game in New Jersey. Mary promises Margie she'll lay low for her during the entire trip. Margie looks at Mary, still naked, and tells her she is so proud of her for keeping her promise. Then, she asks Mary to do something to make her tingle. Mary puts her hands on her breasts, which are still firm, and then slides one hand down to her hairy bush and sticks two fingers in her pussy. Margie swoons over and over.

Margie took a cab to the Waldorf after the game was over. No one is in the lobby that Margie knows, so she takes a seat and waits. Roscoe and Maxine show up fairly soon, and Roscoe orders drinks. Margie, being the firm's President, calls the meeting to order. Roscoe looks at them and tells them their work has just begun. He tells them of cells in Dallas, Denver, and San Francisco. He tells them that the East Coast operation was the beginning of everything, and each city followed them. He also tells them, for security reasons, they can stay where they are. When Roscoe takes a break, Margie asks the first question. How can we stay where we are, and these drinks need to be refilled?

Roscoe gets the drinks going first and then answers Margie's question. The modus operandi is the same as they use OR DRS. to do the deed. Two items aren't the same. We don't have a loved one at either of these sites, and we don't know who the OR guys are yet. We once said that we would continue wherever it took us. That's what I need to know from both of you if you're willing to proceed.

Maxine goes first. I'm currently very busy with the wedding planner. After that, I would like some time to think about this. Roscoe joins in, saying to take all the time you want. These new adventures are for the money.

Margie chimes in next. Count me in, Roscoe, right now.

Roscoe says that's 2 out of 3. Here we all are in New York City, and I told you we should be able to work from our digs in Florida.

Margie thinks about how good that will be for her and Mary.

Maxine informs the group that the wedding will take place at the Waldorf Astoria, and the reception will follow immediately afterwards, also at the exact location.

Margie asks when this will take place. Maxine states that today is Thursday, and the wedding will occur this Saturday at noon.

When Margie returns to the Essex Hotel, she tells Mary that they have only Friday to find a gown for Margie and have enough time to satisfy each other. Mary tells Margie there will be time for everything. Mary is stroking her pussy as she's telling Margie. Margie strips her clothes off as fast as possible to match Mary.

After Margie and Mary had satisfied each other, Mary brought all the toys with her on this trip. Margie asks Mary what she'll do during the wedding on Saturday. Mary responds that she has been looking at Central

Park and will have plenty of things to do. She also tells Margie that she had better be ready when she returns from the party.

Friday arrives, and Margie and Mary head out to find a gown for Margie to wear. They end up in Quinces, and in no time, they're walking out with a lovely gown for Margie. They head back to the Essex Hotel, and Mary suggests they have a drink in the lounge. They end up having two drinks. They stumble up to their room. Once they're in the room, Mary undresses faster than Margie can watch and enjoy.

Maxine, Roscoe, and his children are getting ready for dinner on Friday, and Margie calls Mom to invite her to join them. Margie feels she should join them on Friday. She tells Maxine she'll be there at 8. She rolls over to Mary and kisses her. I can't keep saying no to her; it's her wedding weekend. Mary squeezes Margie's behind and tells her to eat well and come back to me. I will, I will.

Margie once again takes a cab to the Waldorf Astoria. She goes to the dining room and sees the wedding group. Maxine stands as her Mom approaches and introduces Roscoe's children to Margie. The boy's name is Craig, and the girl's name is Michele. Margie shakes hands with the children and says to Roscoe, "Is there anything to drink in his high-valent place?" Roscoe reaches behind his chair and produces Margie's Tangary and tonic. The rest of the evening is grand.

When Margie returns to the Essex Hotel, Mary, all natural, greets her at the door. During the time Margie was gone, Mary's husband called, and Mary had phone sex with him. As Mary was telling Margie, she was undressing Margie.

The Wedding Day has arrived. Maxine looks marvelous. Her dress is a pale violet, and so is Michele's. The men looked great in their tuxes. It didn't take long for the Lady to make Maxine and Roscoe promise to be faithful to each other till the day they die. They both said, 'I do.' The photographer that Maxine's wedding planner provided took about 100 pictures. Then the wedding planner ushered the party into a swank room for the reception.

Margie had her first hug with Maxine on this day. And sang Saddie, Saddie, married lady, which made Maxine smile and hug her Mom even tighter. They both walked to the bar and ordered their first drink of the day. As they were enjoying their drinks, Margie asked where the new groom was. Maxine nods over her shoulder, and Roscoe is talking with his children. He's telling them he and Maxine will be gone for a month starting Tuesday. They both wish their dad and his new wife a lovely trip and that they come home safely.

Roscoe comes over to the bar area and gives Maxine a big hug and a kiss.

Margie chimes in. They'd better go up to their room. Roscoe winks at Margie and asks if she needs a refill. She says yes, and Roscoe orders drinks for all five of them. Then, they all take their seats at the provided table. Margie strikes up a conversation with Craig and Michele. Salads are served. Roscoe doesn't like rabbit food and doesn't eat it. Filet Mignon is next served with loaded baked potatoes and asparagus. All enjoy the food. The first to leave is Margie.

Margie cabs back to the Essex Hotel. Mary is asleep on the couch, fully clothed, which surprises Margie. Margie undresses herself and gently wakes up Mary. Mary wakes up, hugs Margie, and quickly undresses herself, and their after-party begins.

Margie and Mary are the first to leave and go back to Florida. Craig and Michele also leave for their respective homes. That leaves Roscoe and Maxine; they leave for New Guinea on Tuesday morning.

Margie and Mary get back to the condo on St. Pete's Beach. They both say almost in unison, 'What a view. Margie tells Mary about Roscoe's declaration that they wouldn't be back for a month or maybe two months. Mary, who is undressing herself, says, "That's all the more time we have for each other." Margie wonders if Maxine will even consider M&R Associates during the time she is away.

Two months seem to slip away in an eye blink. Maxine calls her Mom to tell her they are back in Florida. This happens to be Friday. Margie asks Maxine if there is a meeting with the group at Roscoe's. Maxine puts her hand over the mouthpiece and asks Roscoe if there will be a meeting on Friday evening. Roscoe nods, "Yes, and the time is 6 o'clock."

Mary is leaving because Big George is due back this evening. Mary hugs Margie and says she'll see her Sunday evening.

Roscoe leaves to pick up stuff for the cocktail hour. Just after Roscoe finishes the treats, the bell rings. Maxine opens the door and hugs her Mom. Roscoe hands Margie's drink to her and also gives Maxine hers. He pours himself a Gentleman Jack neat.

Margie asks openly, "What's for dinner, and what's the first business we're going on?"

Roscoe responds to Floyd and Dallas. Margie asks why Dallas first? Roscoe replies that it was a matter of luck. Roscoe also mentions that wherever he goes, Maxine will go with him.

Maxine says she's hungry, and they all agree. When they enter Floyd's, Bill says, "Hello, strangers." Roscoe replies, "It's only been a couple of months, and this is my wife, Maxine, and her Mom, Margie."

They slide into their favorite booth in the bar area. The waitress asks if there are any drink orders. Roscoe says yes and tells her Tangary and soda for Mom, Beefeaters and soda for my wife, Maxine, and I'll have a Gentleman Jack Manhattan straight up. The Drinks arrive almost immediately. Bill sends his regards, and they are on the house in honor of your marriage. They all ordered the butt steak with steak fries. For dessert, Roscoe orders Brandie ice. They all devoured them like they had never had them before. The Jazz band begins playing while they're all finishing their dessert. They order another round of drinks and listen to the jazz that they haven't heard in quite a while.

On Sunday morning, Maxine calls her Mom to tell her that she and Roscoe are leaving for Dallas. Margie invites them to see her new place before they leave. Maxine is thrilled to get an invite. Margie called Mary to tell her not to come over too early today and why. Mary says that she understands. When Roscoe and Maxine arrive and ring the bell, Margie lets them in. When Roscoe sees the inside, he says, "I'm not leaving Maxine; we have to get one of these."

Margie says that she'll give them her realty person if they want to. Maxine is holding out her hand.

The successive ringing of the bell is Mary and Margie letting her in. Margie is naked for Mary, and Mary drops what she's wearing, and they go out on the balcony and relax. Margie relays the epiphany that Roscoe had when he saw the place. Mary comments that's good, but they can't see us, or we'll have to leave. Margie promises Mary that she will call the realtor first thing tomorrow and set her straight. Mary, stroking her pussy reaches over and strokes Margie's.

Margie calls the realtor at 9 AM the following day. The realtor says that she knows why Margie is calling.

"My boytoy flies a helicopter for the city and has sometimes taken me up."

Margie says, "That's okay, but please, don't tell him or anybody you know us."

The realtor promises not to make a habit of it.

"I've called you today because my daughter, Maxine, will soon want to buy a penthouse like ours. Please don't show them anything that looks out at our balcony. Yours is the first one built in this area in ten years. They'll have to look down or up the coast. There is nothing old or new in the immediate vicinity."

"That's good to know," Margie says. "And please keep your friend away from us, or ensure you have long-range binoculars."

Margie, in the all-natural state, wakes up Mary as well. Margie asks Mary, "Do you want to eat breakfast here or go out somewhere?"

"Here is everything," Mary says, with her arms open for Margie.

Maxine calls Mom to tell her they took the van because Roscoe doesn't want to be away from his toys. She also told her that she had called the realtor, and it seems we wouldn't be neighbors.

"That's too bad," is all Margie can say.

While Margie is making breakfast, Mary slides up, arms around Margie, and asks, "Shall we eat at the table or on the balcony?"

"Balcony," Margie replies. As they eat the breakfast Margie has made, Margie mentions that they're safe; the realtor told her they will have to go north or south to find a penthouse like this. Mary says that she always felt that Margie had made the best decision when she bought this one.

Roscoe and Maxine are nearing Dallas when they decide to stop. When Roscoe was traveling, he always stayed at the Holiday Inn. So, they took the top room at the first Holiday Inn. Roscoe parked the van in the back so as not to be seen. They ate at the local Steak House and had a good meal. When they returned to the motel, Roscoe told Maxine he wanted to conduct research. Maxine mentioned that she would watch TV in the Van while he was pounding the keys.

Unknown to any of them is that the Dallas operation is more significant than the East Coast operation. The ER doctor, Jesse Jones, has been practicing medicine since graduating from Johns Hopkins in Baltimore. He's 46 years old and has never married.

After Roscoe and Maxine get tired, they lock up the van and head for the hotel. Roscoe tells Maxine that he's confused about who the doctor is in Dallas. He tells Maxine that there are many different hospitals in the greater Dallas area. Maxine tells him there must be an easy way to identify the doctor. Roscoe tells Maxine that she is right, to get some rest, and to find the doctor tomorrow.

After breakfast in the morning, Roscoe and Maxine finished the drive to Dallas. He was surprised that it was over 1,100 miles from Tampa. Roscoe is concerned that the van will need replacement long before their quest ends. They find a recent Holiday Inn check-in and then find a storage place for the van. Roscoe spends several hours searching for the right doctor. Of all the ER doctors in each hospital, Roscoe is convinced that the right one will have several banks to handle all his money. He begins searching for banks in and around the city of Dallas. There are several bank names with branches located throughout the area. He makes a printout of all the bank names and branches.

It's Friday evening; Mary has left to see Big George, and Margie is alone in her penthouse. She is naked as she moves around the place. She has gotten used to being naked while Mary is with her. She feels comfortable in her current state. She pours a large Tanqueray and tonic and sits on the veranda. When she's finished, she heads for bed.

Roscoe feels pleased with himself; he believes he has found the right ER doctor. His name is Dr. Jesse Jones, and he has been employed at the same hospital since graduating. He has Synchrony Bank, Quonyic Bank, Bofk Bank, and Bank of Hope accounts. That's enough work for today. He tells Maxine that they will park the van and go home once he confirms everything tomorrow. No other doctors have accounts in more than two banks. Tomorrow arrives, and Roscoe gently awakens Maxine. She opens her eyes and holds her arms open for her new husband.

After breakfast, Maxine calls Margie to tell her they might be flying home today. Margie is quick to mention that they drove out.

"Why are you flying home?"

Maxine tells her the van is in storage in Dallas.

Roscoe takes the van to the hospital where Dr. Jones works—the Royal Alexandra Hospital. He takes up the long and tedious job of watching. He's early, so he's watching the ER entrance. He parks the Van and goes inside, looking for pictures of the Doctors who work there. He finds Dr. Jesse Jones' image. Pleased with himself, he picks up Maxine and parks the van in storage. He calls a cab, and they head for the airport and take a flight to Tampa.

Margie is pleased to see them and drives them to Roscoe's. Roscoe tells Maxine and Margie they will begin searching for a penthouse atop a building. Margie tells them she is happy for them and hopes they find one soon.

Roscoe mentions that they should have some drinks while they're here. Nobody says no. When they've finished, Roscoe gets up to replenish the drinks. Margie excuses herself, saying she needs to drive home. Maxine says she should stay here, but Margie says, "You don't share my views in the morning." Roscoe mentions to Margie that they have found the ER doctor. He said he can work from here just as quickly as he can work there. Does that mean that the Friday night get-togethers are back on? The answer is yes.

When Margie gets home, Mary is waiting for her with open arms. Margie tells Mary that she's getting the feeling that they should tell Maxine and Roscoe about them. Mary tells Margie she's ok with it whenever Margie wants to. Margie has one request: they stay clothed when the time comes. "Absolutely," says Mary. Mary has a request, too, but only while they're here. Margie nods in agreement.

Margie calls Maxine and invites them over for Sunday Dinner.

"What's for dinner? May we bring something?"

The answer is Porterhouse steaks, baked potatoes, and string beans.

"You can bring dessert."

The answer is, "Yes, we'd be delighted to."

Sunday arrives, and Margie tells Mary that today is the day they will learn about us. They are also coming for dinner and bringing the dessert. What about hoarders? Cocktails and cheese and crackers, how about that? All Mary can say is that she wondered about all the food in the fridge. Mary also wondered why there was a 'T' gin, a 'B' gin, and a bottle of Gentleman Jack. Margie tells Mary that I drink Tanqueray, that's the 'T' gin, and Maxine drinks Beefeaters, and the booze is for Roscoe. What would you like besides water? I'll have some of the booze.

The bell rings, and it's the newlyweds, Mary and Margie. Get dressed. Margie lets Maxine and Roscoe in. Maxine had given Margie a large container and said Put this in the freezer.

Mary walks in, and Margie introduces Mary to Maxine and Roscoe as her live-in mate. Margie also agrees to make drinks. Maxine looks at Mary and tells Margie, "She is so much younger than you, Mom." Mary says it doesn't matter.

With that, Maxine and Roscoe hug Mary and welcome her to our family. Margie tells Maxine and Roscoe that Mary is still married to Big George and goes to her house most every Friday when he drives home. Roscoe says I'm hungry and thirsty, not in that order. Margie gets the drinks, and Mary gets the cheese and crackers.

Margie says, "If you want something fancier, you'll have to bring them." As they all enjoy the drinks, cheese, and crackers, they relax.

Roscoe says, "We must start looking tomorrow; this place is just so perfect."

After the drinks are gone, Margie gets up and replenishes them all. When they're about half, Margie gets up and starts cooking. The Steak dinner with all the trimmings went over with a resounding yum. Maxine tells Mon to bring the container she gave her earlier and get four bowls and spoons. Roscoe takes over when Margie arrives with everything. Brandied ice for everybody, he announces. Mary has never had this treat and asks for more. Maxine takes the floor and says this has been one of her favorite days, thanks to Mom and Mary.

True to his word, Roscoe and Maxine start on the north end first. They check out the available penthouses at the realtor they choose. All of them are 1020 years old, and they want something recent like Margie's. They switch to the south and find what they are looking for. A penthouse built two years ago, and a wraparound. It will be available next month. They leave a healthy deposit to ensure that nobody will overbid them. It's about noon, so they head to Floyd's for lunch. Bill sees them walk in and signals Roscoe up or down. Roscoe signals down. They find a booth they like and slide in. The waitress brings their drinks when she comes to take their order. Roscoe tells Maxine, "You don't get this good service anywhere."

After finishing lunch, Roscoe tells Maxine he must spend some keyboard time. Maxine says she'll find something on the TV. So, they head to their pad, which used to be Roscoe's place. While Roscoe is pounding away, he sees all the banks the ER doctor uses. He's somewhat surprised that the doctor is careless with all his money. Roscoe added up all the deposits that had been made. Roscoe leans back, almost astounded. Each bank has had a balance of over $ 500 million for the last 3 years $500 million. That's over 1,500.000.00 billion dollars tax-free. Roscoe thinks he's missing some banks. There hasn't been a deposit in any of the banks he has found in over three years. Even Plant City did more business. He double-checks all his computations and finds no errors. He shuts down the computer he's been using to avoid any backlash. He gets up from his desk and finds Maxine wrapped up in a blanket, snoozing with the TV on. He gently wakes Maxine and motions for them to go outside momentarily.

Once outside, Roscoe hugs Maxine and relays what he's found out. He also tells her he will clean the hard drive from his used machine and sell it somewhere. He also tells her that there are other banks he is using that he hasn't found and doesn't want to find them. Roscoe asks Maxine to call her mom for an emergency meeting tonight. Tell her to bring Mary if she wants to, and we'll pick them up.

Roscoe is driving the town car, which is big enough for the meeting. When they get to Margie's place, Roscoe rings up to tell them they're here. Both Margie and Mary get into the town car. Margie calls the meeting to order. Roscoe has driven the town car to a secluded park and relays what has happened. He says that the four of them are in two groups. Everybody agrees. Roscoe relates that he's slightly concerned with security. He tells the group that $750 billion should be enough for each group to live the remainder of their lives in relative comfort. Roscoe tells everybody he can get all the money he's talked about cleanly without anyone knowing where it went. He needs the group to vote on his proposal tonight. Maxine says yes, Margie says yes, and Mary has a question: "What about my husband, Big George?"

Roscoe asks Mary if Big George knows anything about your current lifestyle. Mary assured everybody that he didn't know anything. Roscoe says, "Can you keep it that way?"

"Yes," is her answer. This meeting is over. Is anybody hungry? Everybody says yes to that. Roscoe drives to the nearest restaurant he can find.

The following day, the realtor for Roscoe and Maxine called to inform them that the penthouse was available and to ask if they wanted to move in. The answer was yes. They arranged to meet her later today and sign all the papers. Maxine called Mom and told her we'll be about a half hour away any time you want to stop over. Margie was happy for them.

Roscoe and Maxine throw a few things into the car and head to the meeting with the realtor. The realtor lady greets them warmly. She tells Roscoe and Maine that the previous owners left without a hello or a goodbye. She tells them that she was pleased they left a year's payment as a deposit. Some others were interested, but they didn't leave nearly as much as you did. She handed over the deed and the escrow papers for signatures. Next, she gave them the keys and told them no one had the same key code. Tell your visitors to press the penthouse button, which will ring in your unit; you can see who's there.

When they get outside, Roscoe hugs Maxine. He says it was your Mom who got us here. They press the penthouse button; the elevator opens, greeting them as Roscoe and Maxine. They ride up to the penthouse on the twenty-first floor. It is quick and smooth. The view upon arrival is spectacular.

Roscoe tells Maxine they will have to go to Dallas very soon. They bring up a few things from the car.

Mary asks Margie, "Do you think we can live on $750 billion?"

Margie responds, "Do you know how much $750 billion is?"

Mary admits she is a little slow as she fingers her pussy. Margie tells Mary that if she spent $100 a day for ten years, you'd still have $385 billion. Mary tells Margie she's happy and has to get dressed since it's Friday afternoon, and I've got to see Big George.

When Sunday rolls around, Mary returns to the condo. She calls out to Margie, and there is no response. Mary goes to the bedroom, and Margie is in bed. She looks like she is sleeping, but she is cold. Mary sits on the bed, mourning for the best of the time taken from her. After a while, Mary, using Margi's phone, calls Maxine. When Maxine picks up, she hears, "Hi Mom, what's up?"

Mary identifies herself, and Maxine screams, "MOM, where are you?"

Mary gives Maxine some time and explains how she returned from seeing her husband and found Margie dead in the bed. Maxine regains herself and tells Mary she and Roscoe will be over shortly.

Maxine and Roscoe ring the bell in about half an hour, and Mary lets them in. Roscoe takes over. He calls the coroner and asks what they should do. He is told to sit tight, and the men will be over to pick up the body. This process takes about an hour. The men come in dressed in suits and ties, very conservatively. They ask where the body is and follow Roscoe into the Master bedroom. In a few minutes, they wheel Margie's remains out, asking if any among them want to give their last respects. Maxine and Mary step forward. The men pull the covering back to show Margie's face, and Maxine almost crawls in with her. When she finishes, Mary steps up to the gurney and to everybody's amazement, she sticks her finger in her pussy and presses it against Margie's cold lips. With that being the end of the goodbyes, the men cover up Margie again and wheel her out to the elevator.

Roscoe asks Maxine if she knows where Margie should be buried. Maxine says that Margie had gotten her husband John's remains to a cemetery just north of Tampa. They find the graveyard and Roscoe using the same people he used to bury his first wife, and they tell him to be at the cemetery in two days for the final viewing and burial. With Margie taken care of, Roscoe turns to Mary next and asks her what she wants to do. Mary says that she will probably go home to her condo, which Roscoe knows, and chill for a while after Margie's burial.

"And maybe I'll go back to work, I'm still young compared to you both. And I don't need any of your money." Roscoe pleads with Mary to take some of the money, just in case of a rainy day.

Mary, not wanting to argue with Roscoe, says, "Okay," and that's that.

The next time they meet, it's at the cemetery. After the ceremony, Roscoe approaches Mary and slips an envelope into her purse. He tells her that Maxine told him to tell her that she was the best thing in Margie's life during their time together.

Roscoe called the same realtor to tell her the penthouse was up for sale. The realtor informed Roscoe that it was not. There's a clause: if either of them passes away, the other gets the penthouse.

Roscoe calls Mary and asks if she still has the penthouse membership card. Mary tells him she does. Does he want it? No, Mary, I don't need it. Margie took care of everything, and you now own the penthouse lock, stock, and barrel. By the way, Mary, since we got to know you, you've become part of our group. Did you open the envelope I gave you at the cemetery? Mary says no. She goes for her purse, and the envelope is still there. She opened it, and there were $ 100,000.00 in Ben Franklin bills. She picks up the phone and thanks Roscoe and Maxine.

The following day, Mary stopped by the realtor's office and asked if any fees needed to be paid. The realtor said the only payments you must make are real estate taxes. Mary looked at the sky and whispered to Margie, "I love you and always will."

Maxine calls Mary, who tells her she and Roscoe are finishing the money in Dallas.

www.ingramcontent.com/pod-product-compliance
Lightning Source LLC
Chambersburg PA
CBHW041052310726
48978CB00011BA/519